fat
Light & easy

HIGH PRA[ ]
THE EUGENIA [ ]

"There's som[ ] [Eugenia
Potter] as a character." —*The Washington Post*

THE BLUE CORN MURDERS

"Riveting...Delightful plot, colorful surroundings, and
solid prose makes this a winner." —*Library Journal*

"Nancy Pickard deftly mixes culinary treats with tantalizing
bits of Anasazi lore. The real joy in the book lies in a vicar-
ious visit to one of the most magical places on the planet,
those deserted, crumbling sandstone cities that were built
and mysteriously abandoned a century or more before
Columbus set sail for the New World." —*The Denver Post*

"Pickard ably blends Native American history into a modern murder mystery." —*Publishers Weekly*

THE 27-INGREDIENT CHILI CON CARNE MURDERS

"Delightful...Ms. Pickard has given the protagonist a new
lease on life." —*The New York Times*

"Sprightly and action-packed...Be warned: throughout,
you will find yourself getting hungry."
—*Chicago Sun-Times*

"Delightful...Not only do we get a dandy mystery, we get
a budding romance *and* the recipe for 27-ingredient chili
con carne—of the non-lethal variety, of course...."
—*The Washington Times*

THE SECRET INGREDIENT MURDERS

A EUGENIA POTTER MYSTERY
BY NANCY PICKARD

BASED ON THE CHARACTER CREATED BY VIRGINIA RICH

A DELL BOOK

Published by
Dell Publishing
a division of
Random House, Inc.
1540 Broadway
New York, New York 10036

Library of Congress Catalog Card Number: 00-049375

ISBN: 0-440-21768-7

Manufactured in the United States of America
Published simultaneously in Canada

March 2002

10 9 8 7 6 5 4 3 2 1
OPM

For Virginia Rich

Acknowledgments

The entire credit for this mystery series goes to the late, beloved Virginia Rich. But one-half of the credit for this particular book goes to Sally Goldenbaum, cook, writer, and friend extraordinaire.

GENIA'S GINGER CARROT SOUP
SERVES 4 TO 6

This soup is even better the next day, as Genia notes.

1 tablespoon olive oil
2 cloves garlic, chopped
1 onion, chopped
4 cups vegetable or chicken stock
   (or canned chicken
   or vegetable broth)
1 tablespoon fresh ginger, grated
   or finely chopped
½ teaspoon ground cumin
Cayenne pepper
1½ pounds carrots (about 6
   cups), sliced

2 cups butternut squash, peeled,
   seeded, and cubed
1 pear, cubed, core removed
   (drained canned sliced pears
   can be used if pears are out of
   season)
Juice of 1 lemon
Salt and freshly ground pepper
2 cups half-and-half
½ cup plain yogurt or sour
   cream
Zest of 1 lemon

Heat the olive oil in a soup pot. Sauté the garlic and onion until the onion is limp (about 5 minutes). Add 2 cups broth, ginger, cumin, and a dash of cayenne pepper. Add carrots, squash, pear, lemon juice, 1 teaspoon salt, and freshly ground pepper. Bring to a gentle boil, then immediately reduce the heat and simmer until the carrots and squash are tender (about 20 minutes). Stir in the half-and-half. Remove from the heat and puree in batches in a food processor until smooth. Add the remaining broth and yogurt. Stir together and season to taste. Serve warm with a dollop of sour cream or yogurt and lemon zest.

1

GUEST OF HONOR

Stanley Parker slipped his left arm and shoulder through a strap of his backpack, moving cautiously, afraid of pain. When the wary movement didn't hurt him, he felt deeply grateful. The pack was of hand-stitched Italian leather and dated to his honeymoon a half a century ago; the pain was of more recent origin. It was ever increasing, growing as fast as a squalling infant, sensitive as a weather gauge to changes in the temperature, humidity, and the pressure of the atmosphere around him. Tonight, however, the agony was dozing. It was stuffed away inside of him, invisible, like the frosted, squat green bottle of brandy he carried in the weathered old backpack.

The old man alertly stepped onto the gravel of his circular driveway. There was nothing wrong with his hearing; he heard pebbles crunch under his feet, sounding as sharp as pellet shots in the crisp night air. He even heard the hum of the generator that ran the pump that provided fresh well water to his greenhouse, and he heard—or felt—the rhythmic surge of the ocean onto the beach below his home, and the waves drawing back into themselves again.

Tonight, when he moved, no sharp pain stabbed his hip.

Stanley sighed with a depth of gratitude known only to someone who has endured anguish and then finds himself liberated from it for a blessed little while.

"Thank you, Jason, my boy," he murmured.

He owed this freedom to a boy who had taken a risk for him.

The old man lengthened his stride a bit, still suspicious of the price of movement. He was determined to drive his motorbike over to the dinner party at Genia Potter's home this evening. With every step forward he discovered to his relief there was no real pain tonight, only a trace of an ache, and an ache was nothing to him; he might even describe it as "mere."

He had dressed for dinner, but no more formally than was his nightly custom: a starched white shirt, a yellow bow tie, and a light blue summer suit, pinstriped in white, with the old-fashioned wide lapels he had worn in his youth and still preferred. The left lapel sported a cluster of pins that denoted some of the honors he had won over a long, productive civic life: master of this, emeritus of that, honorary such-and-such. Sometimes he forgot which pin signified which honor, and so he made up answers when he was asked about them. *"This pin? Oh, they gave me this at the Culinary Archives and Museum in Providence, for being on their board of directors longer than the dinosaurs roamed the earth."*

A full moon lighted his path, illuminating his features as if he were alone on a stage: He had big ears and white hair that was parted on the right side and which he had earlier pushed flat against his skull with water and a small black comb. His eyebrows were bushy and white and he had combed them, too. Deep runnels had etched themselves into the skin beside his mouth, but the mouth was wide and straight, only slightly turned down by age, obstinacy, and occasional bad temper.

There was unmistakable, formidable wit and intelligence in his faded blue eyes, giving him the appearance of a man who didn't tolerate fools at all, much less gladly.

Through the fragile skin and thin muscles of his back, Stanley sensed his big stone house behind him, looming like a lighthouse but without a warning beacon in its tower. In his imagination its very stones exuded warmth, better than liniment for an aching heart or body. Known locally as Parker's Castle, it had already housed four generations of his family and had become, under his tenure, capable of standing long enough to shelter at least as many more. He hoped none of them would be sired by his daughter Nikki's worthless husband, Randy.

More confidently now the old man continued toward his motorbike, standing propped up and waiting for him on the far side of the drive. At least his handyman, Ed Hennessey, had done that one thing he'd been told to do. Like the backpack—like Stanley Parker himself—the bike was worn, battered, almost all used up.

Glancing skyward Stanley Parker spotted a moon like a wedding mint, all round and creamy. In order to admire it, he had to stop, because he couldn't walk and look up at the same time and still hope to keep his balance.

Moon, he thought, *spoon, prune, honeymoon.*

"Why is my wedding on my mind tonight?" he asked himself.

He'd bought the backpack in a tiny, fragrant leather-goods store on the famous old bridge called the Ponte Vecchio in Florence, Italy, on the day after his marriage. The River Arno had flowed beneath them, polluted, but sparkling all the same. It had felt so odd to the young bridegroom to be shopping with a wife on a bridge over a river in a foreign place. It had all seemed foreign to him in that moment: the country, the shop, the woman, the marriage. Impossible not to buy a souvenir, some object to prove he had really been there, doing that odd thing in that unexpected place. Lillian had pretended to tease him about getting an object so prosaic for himself, instead of a romantic gift for her. Something about the way she'd said it had broken through his usual pragmatic defenses—"*But I need a backpack, Lil*"—and he'd had a feeling that if he didn't rectify this apparent mistake, he'd spoil the rest of his marriage to her. It had been a melodramatic thought, but he had believed it with a kind of urgency.

That night he had filled their suite with roses and champagne, and even hired a fiddler and tenor to serenade them from the street. Lillian had pretended it had done the trick, but Stanley believed it hadn't, not really, and he even understood why: The gesture was born of a desire to appease, rather than of a genuine urge to please her.

Nevertheless, she'd pretended to adore it.

Her pretenses had lasted decades, until they gave out with age, and she divorced him thirty-five years later. Two years after that she met a man who gave her the spontaneous, romantic gestures for which she had never stopped pining, and he did it without even having to be teased into it. Five years ago, Lillian Parker had divorced Stanley Parker, and three years ago she had married David Graham. Now she was dead, leaving behind two husbands in the same small town.

I don't blame you for marrying David, Stanley thought. *I blame myself.*

He still loved his Italian backpack, and he still loved his wife and thought of her as that.

About his backpack he was given to saying, "It's just like me," by which he meant it was softened by a lifetime of heavy use. He suspected that few people grasped he meant that; most thought he meant it was battle-scarred and immortal, which was how he thought he appeared to people.

Who would want to be immortal and live in pain? was his thought now. He felt grateful for this moment's ease, but he knew the suffering would come roaring back eventually.

His motorbike didn't roar, but merely sputtered, and he loved it, too.

I have loved too many things, and too few people, the old man thought, as he tilted the bike toward his body. *Lillian. Our Nikki. All the rest—even protégés like Lew Potter, even Genia—I've merely liked, or used, or moved about my life like furniture.*

The motorbike had a mottled red carcass, reminding him of his own red-veined face, and it had a seat well conformed to his own rear end. He sank onto it like dropping into a favorite chair, with a sigh of appreciation for familiar comforts. Old as they were, both the pack and the bike were young compared to his own seventy-nine years. *Whippersnappers* was how he thought of anything or anybody younger than himself.

And to whom but God am I a mere whippersnapper?

He turned the key in the ignition and brought the motorbike to life. Now the air around him smelled of leather and gasoline. When he gripped the handlebars, it felt like grasping palms as calloused as his own. Cautiously he eased the motorbike off the gravel driveway and onto the dirt path that wound above the ocean between his house and the one which Lew Potter's widow, Genia, had rented for the summer.

Bless her, she'd brought new life into his own.

To his left pine trees blocked a last trace of twilight in the west; to his right and thirty feet down the tide pulled out to sea. Out there was the water of Narragansett Bay in one direction and Block Island Sound in the other, now tugging

.

irresistibly at the shores of his own beloved South County, Rhode Island.

He puttered on down the familiar path, over rocks and summer leaves. As the moon rose higher, the trees cast long, disorienting shadows across his path. The surface of the sea turned white in the moonlight. The air was at the same time soft with salt and sharp with the scent of pine and decaying vegetation.

Once he'd had a real motorcycle, which Lillian had refused to ride. It had frightened her, she'd hated it, and finally he had sold it in yet one more act of appeasement. Years later when he bought this miniature version of the one he'd loved, she hadn't objected. It hadn't appeared so threatening to her.

Or maybe she no longer cared if I fell off, it occurred to him now, as he bumped along on it. *Maybe Lil didn't care anymore if I split my fool head open.*

Lately, everything seemed to remind him of something else.

It's the curse of age, he thought, as the bike nosed between tall trees. *I can't experience anything fresh and new; it's all got to be filtered through a sieve of time.*

As a cookbook collector he thought he could be forgiven for turning life into food and cooking metaphors, seeing the moon as a mint and time as a colander. Genia Potter would certainly understand, if he could remember to tell her. (There was so much else to talk about at her dinner party.) She was an understanding sort of woman—Lew Potter wouldn't have married any other kind—and Stanley had neatly managed to manipulate her into writing a cookbook under his tutelage.

He wasn't entirely ashamed of having done that to her.

It was the cookbook he had long desired for his home

state, full of local recipes and the culinary secrets he had gathered over a lifetime of hobby cooking and collecting. *The Secret Ingredient Cookbook,* they were calling it, which was deeply ironic considering what he had to do and say this evening.

"Secrets and ironies, the ingredients of tragedy," he said aloud.

They had planned this dinner party together, ostensibly to give her a chance to try out some of their recipes. He knew she suspected him of other motives, and she was right, although she didn't know that yet. By the time her niece, Janie Eden, served dessert, they'd all know. It was time to right wrongs, to set things straight in his hometown, and he didn't know how much time there was left for him to accomplish that.

Better not to wait. Best to do it now. For all concerned.

There was a place just ahead of him now where a second path, coming from the paved road beyond the woods, bisected the one he was on. Suddenly a figure emerged from that path, blocking his way. What with the failing light and his own fading eyesight, it took a moment for him to recognize the figure of his own handyman and groundskeeper, whom he had fired that very day.

"Get out of my way, Eddie!" Stanley Parker shouted above the noise of the engine. He let his motorbike slow, then stop, and straddled it while it idled. He was pleased that age had not diminished his voice. Lillian had called it "sand-blasting"—the effect he had when he yelled at people. "What the hell are you doing here, Eddie? I told you, you're fired. You don't do a blasted thing around here that I tell you to do, and if I could prove you steal the way I know you do, I'd have you arrested! I want every damned thing of yours out of the garage by the time I get back from Genia's. Now get out of my way."

But the younger man stood his ground, hands on skinny hips.

Thirty rugged feet below them was a rocky beach, and beyond that the Atlantic Ocean, and beyond that the darkness that the sun had left behind.

In appearance Ed Hennessey reminded his employer of a tough chicken leg, all grease and bone and gristle. Both men had been born and bred in Devon, Rhode Island, on the banks of the Atlantic Ocean, though more than forty years apart. But the stock in which they'd steeped was made of different stuff. One had been rich with the flavor of culture; the other had been a thin gruel, hardly enough to grow a boy into a man, much less into a seasoned man well worth his salt.

He'd hired Hennessey out of pity, to give him a break.

"You think you can fire me, old man?" The voice was deep and hoarse, roughened by cigarettes and booze. There was about it an insinuating, patronizing tone. "I been thinking since this afternoon. You better give me a raise instead. I want another hundred dollars a month. Maybe two hundred. That's what it's going to cost you, unless you want the cops knowing what the kid is doing in your greenhouse."

The kid! Stanley's heart gave a guilty lurch. Genia Potter would never forgive him if he caused any harm to her grandnephew, Jason Eden. Hell, he'd never forgive himself! The humming ache in his hip increased its volume, and he recognized it as a precursor to real pain. "What Jason is doing? What the hell are you talking about?"

That earned him a knowing smirk.

"You're drunk again, Eddie. That's why I fired you, man! When are you going to learn to take advantage of an opportunity when life presents it to you?" Stanley toughened his heart and the tone of his voice. "Go away, and don't pull any stupid tricks on me! I fired you, and you're still fired!"

He tried to make the little engine spit, but it was a puny sound. He turned the throttle, lifted his feet back onto the pedals, and rumbled straight toward the man in his path.

Hennessey jumped out of his way, raising a fist as he passed.

"I ain't leaving here, old man! You'll pay!"

Stanley drove on, determined not to show by even so much as the set of his shoulders how intimidated he felt, how uncharacteristically frightened. Now his hip hurt for real, and his chest felt squeezed.

What have I done? he accused himself.

He tried to shake off the nasty encounter with his hired man.

"No good will ever come of you, Ed Hennessey."

But some good might come of tonight. He was still alive, by God. For a little while he was even out of pain. Or had been until that encounter. Pain or no he knew secrets that ought to be told, and soon, so no one else need suffer from them.

"It is a perfect night to bring justice to the table," he told himself.

If he ever got the chance to meet Lillian in heaven—he should be so lucky—he wanted to see pride and welcome on her face. He wanted to hear her say, *"Stanley, dear, you redeemed yourself there at the end, didn't you?"*

A few yards deeper down the path, he thought he heard his own name called. So lost was he in memories of Lillian that for a heart-lifting moment he thought it was her. He stopped the motorbike again, straddled it, and turned around to see who it was who hailed him on this darkest stretch of path above the sea.

2

GUEST LIST

"Honey?"

From the bathroom where she was putting on her makeup, Lindsay Wright heard her husband call out to her from their bedroom. The endearment he had used sounded as soft and lush as what it labeled, and she closed her eyes for a moment, pleasurably feeling its sweet warmth flow over her.

"Why don't you call Mr. Parker," her husband called in to her, "and see if he needs a ride to Mrs. Potter's?"

Lindsay's finger stopped dead in the middle of the mauve track it was laying down on her eyelid. Her pleasure in his voice and his affection for her felt as if it had ended in a sting. Fearful of smearing her eye shadow, because suddenly her fingers were trembling, she withdrew her hand and picked up a tissue. After wiping her finger clean with it, she grasped the edge of the sink with both hands to steady her voice before she answered him.

"He's so close, he could practically walk there, Harrison!"

She hoped that would end it, but her husband's resonant television weatherman's voice came floating back to her as calmly as if he were predicting sunny skies. "But he's ancient!

And it's going to rain. Wouldn't it be a nice thing for us to do?"

Lindsay tried not to frown, not wanting to crease the foundation and powder on her forehead. Bitterly, and not loud enough for him to hear, she muttered, "Why would I want to do something nice for Stanley Parker?" She abandoned her makeup and walked to the doorway that separated the two rooms. Her blond hair and almost all of her makeup were perfectly in place, but she didn't have a stitch on yet. Not that her husband would notice, she thought with fond exasperation.

Harrison stood at their bedroom window scanning the skies for his beloved stratus and altostratus and nimbostratus. She'd have to be a tornado to get his attention. Sometimes she joked to her friends that she was in serious danger of having her future children named after cloud formations: "*Have you met the twins, Cirrus and Cirrostratus? And this is their older sister, Drizzle.*"

Even in her present state of tension, she couldn't help but admire her own good taste in husbands as she viewed him from the rear: his short cropped hair, his skin as dark as the thunderclouds he loved, his admirable posture, his nice plain suit. She would have loved to get him into something more fashionable, with more color, but he maintained that in conservative old Devon, Rhode Island, his complexion was all the color he dared wear if he wanted to remain a popular local celebrity. He wasn't handsome, even she had to admit that, but there was something so attractive about Harrison that most people were drawn to him instantly, and when they were they were almost always smiling. It made her jealous sometimes, and other times she basked in his glow, sharing it.

"What's this bug you've got about Stanley Parker?" she asked him, trying to keep any hint of agitation out of her voice. Not that he would notice, not when he was absorbed in the weather as he was at this moment. She could have said, *"If you only knew, Stanley's our worst enemy, the one person who can keep us from all we want, and I hate him and I wish he were dead."* And maybe Harrison would hear her, and most likely he would not, not if any clouds were moving. For once, Lindsay thanked God for giving her an obsessive, pre-occupied spouse.

When Harrison still didn't reply, Lindsay felt satisfied that she had managed to hide her true feelings.

What her husband said, instead, and without turning around, was, " 'Odysseus gathered the clouds and troubled the waters of the deep. He roused all storms of all manner of winds, and shrouded in clouds the land and sea.' "

She relaxed slightly. "Okay, I'll bite. Who said that?"

"Homer. I may get to use the other h-word tonight, Lindy."

"Hurricane? You're kidding. Is it safe to go out?"

"Oh, I don't mean tonight, I mean it's building out east and south of us, just a tropical storm right now, but we could see something major by the end of the week."

"What's it called?"

"Phoebe. Tropical storm Phoebe. But she could grow."

"Is that what the National Weather Service says?" Lindsay walked naked to their bed and began to dress in the designer suit she had laid out for herself. Silk, all silk, and not a thread of underwear underneath. Eventually, later, when they were home again and after his last weather forecast from the station, he would notice her. A sharp pang of sexual anticipation pierced her. And then Harrison would turn upon her the same intense attention to detail he paid to high pressure fronts and wind chill indexes. Lindsay shared him with a strange mistress, but at least it was one he couldn't sleep with.

"Yeah, but that's not why I'm saying it."

Enviously, Lindsay watched him smile fondly at the clouds. If she were the weather channel, he'd never take his eyes off her.

"It's what my senses tell me," he continued. "Oh, look, there's a halo around the moon tonight. We might have rain before we leave Mrs. Potter's house."

"How scientific," she teased him, while with nervous fingers she fastened her last button. She heard how brittle and high her voice sounded, and tried to soften and lower it. "A halo."

"I have it on the best authority."

"Who's that?"

"Theophrastus."

"And who's he when he's at home?"

"A student of Aristotle's."

"I knew that," she managed to joke.

He finally turned toward her, smiling. "It is scientific, Lindsay. Sunlight bends when it passes through the ice crystals that are suspended in the upper troposphere, and the crystals act like little prisms that break the light into the colors of the rainbow. Cirrus clouds are made of ice crystals, did you know that? Isn't that wonderful? Theophrastus notwithstanding, a halo around the sun or moon usually indicates a change in the weather, if not always rain."

"You know so much, Harrison."

"About weather?" He habitually scoffed at his own encyclopedic knowledge of his subject. "That only makes me a savant, it doesn't make me a wise man."

"Harrison!" She always objected stoutly to his self-deprecation. It was a duet they played, often reversing their roles. "And what do I know, except clothes and makeup?"

"And art. You know so much about art, Lindsay."

"Yeah, but that's just like a weather anomaly."

Harrison laughed, looking puzzled. "What?"

"It's just this unexpected talent I have, you know? Who'd have ever thought that dumb ol' Lindsay Wright could tell a Matisse from a Monet? It's not even a talent, really. What artists have is talent. What I have is like perfect pitch, only without being able to sing."

"You think you're just a pretty face."

"And even that won't last."

"You're funny, you're sexy, you're a wonderful wife, and you're a lot smarter than you think you are. Do you think I married you only for your looks, Lindsay? What would that say about me? That would make me as shallow as...as..."

"A thin layer of cirrus clouds."

Harrison laughed appreciatively. "Exactly. Thank you."

Lindsay felt warmed and embraced by his laughter and the compliments. "A wonderful wife," he'd said, and the words made her tingle. She tried so hard to be just that; Harrison didn't have any idea how she worked at it sometimes, and she didn't want him to know. Lindsay thought she'd do almost anything to keep him from knowing, because if he knew, he might not think she was so wonderful anymore.

"Harrison, you can't be using the h-word lightly on the East Coast," she teased him, changing the subject to something safer. "It's like screaming wolf when there isn't one. Or screaming tornado, I guess, for you folks from Iowa. Did you know that Mrs. Potter's from Iowa, too, originally?"

She heard herself babbling, and made herself stop.

"So how do I look?" she asked, pirouetting beside their bed.

"Gorgeous. I still think we ought to call Mr. Parker."

Lindsay sat down abruptly on the bed and stared at him. "Why? Did Stanley say something to you?"

"Me? I hardly know him. You're the one who says I ought to cultivate the important people in town." It might have sounded cynical, even harsh, except for the clear, trusting expression in his eyes. Sometimes Lindsay wondered if her very smart husband wasn't also a bit naive; if he didn't trust people—even her—too much for his own good. He wasn't like her; he'd come from middle-class privilege, not from the wrong side of the tracks in a town so small there was only one bus a day to Providence and then another one that returned at night. "I just think it would be a courteous thing to do."

"Stanley wouldn't know polite if you whacked him in the head with it."

Harrison looked startled. "Has he ever been rude to you?"

Lindsay got up again, walked toward him, and pressed her body against him, hoping he wouldn't feel the trembling she felt inside. When he wrapped his arms around her, she tilted her face up to look at him. "Yes, he's been just a beast to me." Teasingly, trying to keep it light so that her husband wouldn't suspect anything was wrong, she added, "What are you going to do about it, Harrison?"

"Well, obviously, I'll have to kill him. No man can be rude to my wife and live."

It was exactly the right thing to say, and she kissed him for it.

David Graham paused while dressing for dinner to gaze at his late wife's portrait. Lillian. Painted only one year before her death, it captured her natural elegance, which had only been enhanced by letting her dyed blond hair go fully white after they married. He had encouraged her to do that, and in fact, to do anything that made her feel completely herself. For Stanley Parker, she'd been the perfect bank president's wife, groomed, dyed, lifted, preserved in wine and sherry. But all that David had ever asked her to be was herself, and in the short time they'd been together, Lillian had relaxed into that most contented of roles.

David smiled wistfully at her portrait.

"I hope I made you happy, Lil."

He held one black sock in his left hand; his right foot was bare.

"You've made my life so easy, it doesn't seem fair."

She'd been wealthy—partly from birth, partly due to her divorce from Stanley—and when he met her he had been looking toward his "golden years" with worried eyes. Now she was gone, which meant she'd left him wealthy, but without her to spend it on. He'd loved giving her gifts, first with his own money, which he couldn't afford to spend, but which he'd lavished on her anyway. And then—with her blessing—with her money. She had loved his taste, and he loved giving things to a woman who appreciated them. Lillian had thrived on romance, and so did he. He loved everything about it—the wooing, the courting—and the more passionate the better. Bless her, she had lapped it up like a starved dog who'd been kept by a mean master.

"Stanley meant well," Lillian had said in faint praise of her ex. "But you *do* well, David."

"My dear," he had responded with a bow, which had made her smile. "A man always enjoys being favorably compared to his wife's first husband."

She'd laughed at that. He missed her sense of humor.

In two years of marriage—and the two months of

courtship prior—they had laughed so much, traveled constantly, made love more often and more imaginatively than Lillian at first thought seemly for a couple their age. But she had savored every moment of it.

To her portrait, he said, "I'm glad you can't see what's happening to Stanley, Lil."

No matter how archly she may have spoken of him, Lillian had kept a soft spot in her heart for her first husband, and David had understood that, without resenting it very much. "I'm too old to be jealous of ex-husbands," he had joked, to reassure her. Lillian and Stanley had parented a child together, after all. They'd slept nearly a half century in the same bed. It was only to be expected that they continued to look out for one another. David suspected Stanley had always loved Lil more than she'd known, but the poor fool just never knew how to express that to her satisfaction.

Stanley was acting more and more like a fool these days, and Lillian wouldn't have liked it if she'd seen it.

"Lil would hate to see it," David had confided to one or two of his friends at the yacht club as recently as that afternoon. "Have you noticed? Any idea what's going on with him? Do you know if he's ill? I don't know what's come over him, but he's been doing odd things, like getting me invited to dinner at Genia Potter's this evening. You know her? The woman from Arizona, who's renting that house up near Stanley's? I know Stanley's behind it. It has to be him, because I barely know the woman to say hello on the street. Don't you think it's odd as hell that Stanley Parker would invite me—of all people—to a dinner where he's acting as host?"

When his friends asked him why he was going if he felt that way, David had laughed and said, "To see what the old bastard's up to, of course!" And then, more seriously, he'd added, "And because I think Lil would want me to make sure he's all right."

They told him he was a good man, a compliment he shrugged off.

Now he asked her portrait, "What do you think he's up to, Lil? Do you think I ought to try to have another word with him before the party?"

He imagined how she would shake her head at the very idea of her two husbands getting together for a little man-to-man chat. Devon was a small town, and he and Stanley were grown-ups, so they had never tried to avoid one another, but even Rhode Island wasn't so small they had to seek each other out for lack of other company. At least David hadn't had to do that, because he had had Lillian.

Now he kept a brave face on, partly to keep the town's single women at bay. Maybe that's why Stanley had maneuvered this invitation for him, his friends at the club had suggested, with grins and raised eyebrows: to matchmake between him and the Widow Potter. If David were to marry again, he wouldn't any longer be known primarily as "Lillian's widower," but as somebody else's husband, and Stanley wouldn't have to hear again that title that grated on his ego. Well, Eugenia Potter was an attractive woman, all right—sixtyish, nice face—but if David ever wed again, it would be he, not Stanley Parker, who chose the time, the place, the woman.

"And I'll ask you first," he promised his late wife.

He raised his right foot and balanced on his left while he drew on his other silk sock. A mailed invitation meant dress for dinner. A pale yellow summer dinner jacket lay on the king-size bed, as did white linen trousers, a crisp white shirt, and a pastel print tie. It looked more Palm Beach than Devon, but David knew that he did, too. All he lacked at the moment was a Florida tan to accompany the clothes. And white shoes, of course. In the mirror on his closet door, he caught an amusing glimpse of himself: half-dressed, one foot aloft, bent over like a stork, a slim, silver-haired man of medium height putting on a sock.

When he had both feet on the floor again, he blew a kiss to the portrait. The telephone began to ring, and David debated whether or not to answer it. He was afraid it would be Celeste Hutchinson asking for a ride to the dinner party. He didn't want to escort her, in effect showing up with her as his date, but he also didn't want to hurt her feelings.

"What should I do?" he implored Lillian.

She gazed down at him serenely, as if she believed him capable of tactfully spurning any adoring woman who came his way.

"You flatter me, Lil," he told her. "I don't deserve it."

David Graham walked over slowly in his stocking feet to answer the phone, hoping the caller would give up. He finally picked it up after the fifth ring.

With shaking fingers Celeste Hutchinson had put down her highball and dialed David Graham's telephone number. *I'm a fifty-seven-year-old woman falling apart over a sixty-year-old man, and I will never, never let anyone know it!* She had to wait through five rings before he picked up. Forcing her own tone to sound bright and carefree, she trilled, "David! What were you doing that it took you so long to answer? Taking a shower? You'd better hurry if you want to make it on time to Genia's! I'm so glad I caught you before you left home!" *My God, can I sound like a bigger fool than this?* She heard the multitude of exclamation points in her little speech, and made herself calm down.

"Listen, darling, don't even think about coming by to pick

me up tonight. Larry Averill just insists that I go with him. We're going to pop in on Stanley Parker to see if he needs a lift, too. I know what you were planning, you thoughtful man, but save yourself the effort, just this once, because I'm all taken care of already."

Stop, she commanded herself. *Enough, for God's sake.* The man on the other end of the line said "Oh," in a puzzled way, but then quickly recovered his manners. "Are you sure I can't pick you up, Celeste? You're right, I was just on my way to the phone to call you to see if you needed a ride."

"You sweetie. I just knew it. See you at Genia's!"

Like hell you were. She slammed down the receiver after she was sure he had hung up. *Damn you, and damn Stanley Parker, and damn the whole damn town.* They'd all let her down, the whole town of Devon. They were supposed to be her lifelong friends, her business clients, nearly her family. *I'll just make new friends,* she thought, with a grim determination that bordered on a feeling of panic. *Starting tonight, starting with Genia Potter, and the rest of you can just go to hell!*

She saw what she looked like in the mirror above the table that held the telephone: a late-middle-aged woman in a floral silk dress, with a puffy face and thirty extra pounds on her body. Where was the attractive woman who used to appear in the mirror when she looked? Celeste stared, as if that other, more acceptable, woman might magically reappear. *No wonder he doesn't want me!* As soon as the vicious thought sneaked into her awareness, she took a drink and chased it away again.

Celeste grabbed a purse, a shawl, and the "ticket" to dinner tonight, which was a recipe with a secret ingredient. They'd all been asked to bring one, and she had decided on her mother's lemon cake, with the ingredient that nobody ever knew, not unless she told them. It was called

"Warmed-over Husband," and it was made with stale cake. That was the secret—dry, hard cake you dipped in cream and then fried lightly in butter and topped with creamy lemon sauce. It wasn't on anybody's list of AMA-approved foods, but it was wonderful—rich and sinful. Just like David Graham. He, too, was rich from having been smart enough to marry Lillian Parker, and sinful because surely nobody that handsome could possibly be good.

Her choice of recipe was deliberate, reached after many drinks the night before: She wanted to make a point—a nasty, not-so-subtle one—to show him what she thought of him for dumping her.

She picked up her highball glass and gulped the rest of the liquor.

But instead of releasing her inhibitions as it usually did, the alcohol spoke with a warning voice: *Careful, you're making too much out of it. This is nutty. You might be losing it.* She was losing it all right, she told herself, with a feeling of fear so acute she nearly screamed, all alone in her house. She was losing everything, it was evaporating as fast as salt off the ocean.

Marrying David could make all the difference.

She was crazy to want him, Lillian's warmed-over husband, when he obviously didn't give a damn about her. The times they'd spent together didn't mean a thing to him, that was clear. And that had to be Stanley Parker's fault, because Stanley was the only person who knew just what to say about her to discourage an eligible suitor.

Damn you, Stanley Parker!

Why else would David have stopped calling her? It had to be because of Stanley, who was always sticking his nose into other people's lives as if he owned them. *As if he owns all of us, like he owns the bank.* He always thought he knew everything about everybody.

Celeste swayed where she stood, thinking of what he knew.

Well, there might be one chance left to untangle any damage that Stanley had done to her life. Maybe she could still shift the picture back to hopeful again. If she managed to do that tonight, she would just slip the insulting recipe back into her purse and pretend she'd forgotten to bring one.

When she set the glass down, it missed the edge and fell to the floor, spilling ice cubes at her feet.

From memory she dialed the telephone number of the mayor of Devon. She'd known Larry Averill almost all of their lives. Over the years he had often escorted her to events to which they were both invited, but this time she'd better make sure he was coming so she wouldn't make a fool of herself by showing up alone in her own car. When she got his answering machine instead of him, it seemed depressingly apropos.

"Larry, where are you?"

In real estate sales, you learned to turn liabilities into assets. If Celeste had to drive over by herself, maybe she could turn it into an opportunity. But she needed another drink first. She kicked the glass on the floor out of the way and hurried to the kitchen for a fresh one.

Larry Averill shifted his weight in his car seat and his SUV into third gear and sped through downtown Devon. For some reason that he had never understood, the good voters of Devon forgave him for speeding, and double parking, and turning right on red without a stop. Hardly anybody ever honked at him. Now and then he got upbraided by an elderly person, but that made him feel good, as if he were being scolded by an exasperated but fond parent. It was almost as if the citizens of Devon knew he was in a hurry for them. A mayor was a busy person, even in a town as small as this one. And then there were the county meetings, and statewide referendums, and the going back and forth to the statehouse. Luckily, Rhode Island was only as big as one of the smaller counties in a state like Texas. Sometimes the mayor felt as if he crisscrossed it twice a day, trying to keep his job and maybe earn a step up on the political ladder.

The state legislature, that's what he had his eye on.

He was late for Mrs. Potter's dinner, darn it.

And he hadn't had time to take the shower he needed, or shave. He'd look like a bum in a cheap suit. Well, the only politician in a good suit was the one on the take, in his opinion. Either that, or one who was a lawyer first and a servant of the people second. But he'd grown up without two dimes to rub together and never yet had found a reason to feel ashamed of it. He still didn't have the dimes, but he never had a wife or children to support, either, so that had worked out all right in its way.

"You'll never get anywhere in politics without a wife," people said.

That's what he'd always heard, but the one woman he would have married any time she said yes was much too good for him. He would have wondered what was wrong with her if she had ever changed her mind and accepted his standing proposal of marriage.

"Will you marry me, Celeste?" he'd asked when they were twenty.

"No," she'd said. "I love you, Lar, just not to marry."

"The offer will stand," he'd said back then, "as long as I do."

"Don't be silly," she'd said, laughing. "You'll find a nice girl, and she'll work the polls for you, and you'll have enough kids to staff your own campaign headquarters."

He'd known then that wasn't the way it was going to be.

This was how it was going to be, and was: him, the mayor, her the town's premier Realtor, him so proud of her and still taking her to dinner any time she needed company. Which seemed to be happening more often than usual lately. It worried him. Celeste was drinking more. Not that he judged or condemned her for it. She was lonely, he figured, and there wasn't a single man around who was fine enough to patch that crack in her life. He'd thought for a while that David Graham might fill that bill, but that liaison seemed to have broken apart before it ever really got started, leaving Celeste looking desperate enough to break Larry's heart. He wondered what had happened there but didn't feel he had a right to ask her.

Odd how life turned out. She'd never married, either.

All this time, they could have been—

"No," he said out loud, wheeling right without stopping, just after a light turned red. "It wasn't meant to be." He slowed down slightly now as he drove along the twisting, narrow roads of the seaside residential neighborhood, marveling as always at the beauty of his town. Lush blue-violet hydrangeas hugged the winding stone walls bordering the large estates. The houses themselves were hidden behind thick stands of oak and elm and sycamore trees, but the mayor had been a guest in many of them and knew firsthand the elegance hidden in many of the "cottages," as their owners called them. There were no sidewalks here, and people walked on the side of the road, lugging folding chairs, coolers, and towels as they made their way to the beach. He pulled to the middle of the road and waved to a group of teenagers with towels thrown around their necks, riding their bikes toward the ocean for a twilight swim. Future voters, he thought with an inward smile of affection for them.

Larry turned west then, away from the ocean drive and toward Celeste's neighborhood, a historic area rich in Federal-style homes and carefully tended gardens. It was a neighborhood that didn't quite suit her, he thought, though he would never have said so to her. It was all roses, elegant, old-world, restrained; she was extroverted and her beauty was as lush as blue hydrangeas. Larry felt a pang of guilt at the word "lush," even to apply it to her appearance. By right of family, Celeste belonged in this neighborhood, even if the town gossips now prattled more about her drinking than her lineage.

He parked in front of Celeste's house and trotted to the door.

Trim could use some fresh paint. Maybe I can get to that this week.

The idea reminded him unpleasantly of Stanley Parker. Just last week the old man had made it clear that he didn't approve of certain assistance the mayor had quietly directed toward Celeste, without her even knowing it. Darn it, what was wrong with the old guy? Since when was kindness illegal? Stanley must be getting senile. He was old enough for it. And cranky as heck sometimes. And self-righteous as a preacher with an ax in his hands.

There was only one way to deal with people like that.

Surprised when Celeste didn't answer after three rings, the mayor looked at his watch and found he was running even later than he'd thought. Celeste must have given up on him and driven off to the party by herself. *That sure makes me look good,* he thought in disgust at himself. *I ought to get myself one of those alarm watches and set it every fifteen minutes to get myself going where I ought to be.*

On the other hand, maybe this would give him time to make a stop.

He trotted back to his car and hurried off toward the road that led both to Mrs. Potter's house and to Stanley Parker's Castle, too.

In the house at the end of the cul-de-sac, Genia Potter smiled at the sight of her grandniece "slaving away" over a hot stove. It was an improbable sight: a seventeen-year-old girl, five foot ten, in clunky black shoes with three-inch heels, black tights, a short black pleated skirt, a black sleeveless T-shirt, a golden scarf around her neck, and three golden earrings in each earlobe. Topping it off was henna-red hair that was caught up at the back of her head with a huge green plastic clip. In New York City, Jane Eden might have passed unnoticed on any street, but here in Devon, Rhode Island, she looked as conspicuous as her great-aunt Genia suspected she wished to be.

Genia felt her heart swell with affection for the girl.

Janie had been such a companionable help all summer long, just as her twin brother, Jason, had been up at Stanley Parker's greenhouse. Working part-time for Genia was Janie's summer job; working up at the Castle was Jason's, though he also helped out here in the little herb garden. Their mother might wring her hands over them, but to their great-aunt they were perfect teenagers. Gazing fondly at Janie, Genia was reminded of a time long ago when she had picked up her own little son at his grandparents' house where he had behaved like the little angel he never was at home with his parents. "Why," his mother had asked him, "don't you ever misbehave at Grandma and Grandpa's house?" In his little-boy voice, Benjie had replied, "Because I want them to think well of me." Genia and Lew had laughed till they cried over that one, at his precocious grammar, at the refreshing candor of what he'd said. Now, all these years later, she suspected that might be the reason Janie and Jason never gave her a moment's trouble.

"Ready to stuff the apples, Janie?"

"Sure, but is this gravy supposed to boil like this?"

Genia hurried over to examine what was actually a creamy base for lobster bisque. It was to be the entrée of the tasting party that she and Stanley were hosting this evening for six, maybe seven people, if Janie and Jason's father showed up. Flecks of bright green tarragon—its secret ingredient—floated on top. She was relieved to see that the mixture wasn't actually boiling: One tiny bubble worked its way up but gave up the struggle before bursting and dissolving back into the sauce.

"No, you don't ever want to boil a cream sauce, love, or the milk will curdle. Turn it way down to the lowest setting for now, and then we'll add the lobster just before we serve it."

Earlier that day, grandniece and great-aunt had cored Rhode Island greening apples and then prepared a filling of cloves, nuts, and raisins that Janie had soaked in a fine brandy that Jason had brought over from Stanley Parker's exemplary cellar. Genia had shown Janie how to make a light pastry in which to wrap the stuffed apples and from which they also cut tiny starfish to put on top.

As the two settled at the center island to work, Genia said, "We need to give this dessert a name for the cookbook. What should we call it?"

"It doesn't have a name?"

"Well, I call them yummy."

Janie grinned over at her, and Genia's heart lifted again. It was so nice to see her smile. When she wasn't helping Genia, the girl often went around looking glum or outright crying over a million different things ranging from her mother's

failings to a slight from one of her friends, to the plight of the
rain forest in South America. Genia didn't mean to disparage
Janie's concerns by thinking of them like that; she just knew
that for Janie there were no small upsets. Everything from
curdled cream sauce to war elicited a deeply felt response.

"How about 'Apples in Jackets'?"

"Perfect!" Genia cried. "They're a kind of dress-up dessert."

Typically, Janie's idea was quick and clever.

The girl was smart as a whip, her great-aunt thought, and
despite her appearance made the kind of grades in school that
used to be associated only with girls who wore glasses. And
the child was sensitive, too, to her brother's greater struggle
with academics. "It's not Jason's fault he had dyslexia," Janie
often said. "It's just because he's the boy, and they get it a lot
more often than girls do. I'm just lucky, that's all." Genia
thought that if Janie could have done so, she would have
"split" her grade point average with her twin, evening life
out between them.

"I'll credit you in the back of the book," Genia told her.

"I'll get my name in a book?"

"You bet."

"Wow. My name in a book! Can you put in Jason's, too?"

"I'll find a way." Genia refrained from saying, "It's just a
cookbook." The truth was, it wasn't "just" a cookbook to
Genia, either, and it certainly wasn't to Stanley Parker. She
had a feeling he had been lying in wait for someone like
her to come along and help him produce it. He brought to
the project his collection of cookbooks and his publishing
connections; she had a modest talent for thinking up original recipes; they were both good cooks. Voilà: a perfect
team. They'd devoted many full and satisfying days to their
project.

Genia glanced up at the kitchen clock and felt a shock.

"Janie, it's nearly six-thirty! Where's Mr. Parker?"

"I thought your guests weren't coming until seven-thirty."

"But he promised to get here early. Hand me the phone, will you?"

She took the portable telephone that her niece gave her and punched in the familiar number at the Castle. After three rings, she heard Stanley's familiar gruff voice saying, "Parker here. If you're calling with good news, leave a message. If it's bad news, call somebody else."

Genia smiled as she hung up. That was a brand-new message. And it was so like him! Stanley thought he could say anything he liked to anybody, and they just had to take it. Never famous for his tact, in his old age he was becoming infamous for his blunt, barbed observations.

"I guess he's on his way," she said to Janie.

The girl nodded, but Genia didn't feel so sanguine. He should have arrived a half hour ago, and he hadn't called to say he'd be late. Besides, he was an old man, and he'd been acting lately as if he didn't feel very well. What if he'd had a fall, or even a stroke? There was nobody at the Castle to help him except for that worthless Ed Hennessey, and Stanley had told Genia he was going to fire the man this very day. Genia felt a twinge of alarm. What if Eddie had taken the news badly? What if he had gotten angry and harmed the old man? When another five minutes passed and Stanley still hadn't arrived, Genia put down the apple she was working on.

"Janie, do me a favor. I want you to take my car and drive up to the Castle, and make sure he's okay—"

"Mr. Parker won't like that."

"Pretend you've come to ask him if he needs a ride."

"He'll say no."

"I know he will, but then you can drive back and tell me that everything's all right."

After Janie left Genia found she couldn't concentrate on her cooking. Having made sure that nothing was going to burn, she walked out onto the deck of the house and looked in the direction of the path that meandered through the woods from Stanley's house. She told herself she was being a worrywart. Surely he would arrive at any moment, possibly even sputtering up on that old motorbike of his. On second thought, that was another cause for concern. Maybe she should have sent Janie through the woods to look for him there.

Genia tried to tell herself she was being foolish, that there was no reason for her to stand there fretting over him as if he were a little boy who couldn't find his way home.

Raindrops started to fall, spotting the wooden floor of the deck and the railing. She'd heard Harrison Wright predict this very change in the weather on the last news program she had watched. A few light drops fell on her hair and shoulders, but Genia didn't move. A few sprinkles wouldn't hurt her. She continued staring off into the woods, oblivious to the spectacular ocean view to her left, and thinking instead about Stanley and about her other guests. She wasn't worried about the rest of them getting there; certainly not the mayor of Devon, Lawrence Averill, or the Realtor who had found this house for her to rent, Celeste Hutchinson. Nor Harrison Wright and his pretty wife, Lindsay, who was president of the local arts council. Or David Graham, or her own niece, the twins' mom, Donna Eden. Nor their artist dad, Kevin, from whom their mother was divorced. Kevin, perhaps true to his artist's nature, had failed to RSVP, though Genia hoped he'd show up anyway.

Genia shivered as a cool breeze brushed her shoulders.

She had a sudden eerie feeling of being snagged by a particular moment of time and fate. Here she was in this unlikely place: a rented house on the southern coast of Rhode Island, far from her real home. Last May she hadn't even heard of any of these people, except for her relatives, of course, and for Stanley Parker. And at that time, oddly enough, she had also been worrying about someone she loved. It was amazing, really, how the disparate threads had woven together to catch them all up and bring them together for this one night.

3

An Invitation

In early May of the same year, Eugenia Potter had stood beside the swimming pool of her cattle ranch in the Sonoran Desert south of Tucson with a printed e-mail in her hand. Its message seemed to beg between its lines, "Aunt Genia, help us."

A puff of dry desert breeze ruffled the limp page in her hand. She grasped it tighter. The wind carried a tantalizing smell of barbecue, blending the aromas of mesquite logs and succulent, juicy pork ribs with the lime, vinegar, cilantro, and tomato base of her secret sauce. She had lately come to the conclusion that in another life she might become a vegetarian, but while she earned her living from cattle, she would continue to eat meat, rather than be a hypocrite.

Her stomach growled, and her mouth watered in anticipation, but she held firmly to her resolve to decide before supper what to do about this crisis in Rhode Island. The message was from Lew's niece, Donna Eden, about Donna's son—and Genia's grandnephew—Jason.

Aunt Genia, the frantic message began. *Jason's been arrested for possession of marijuana! He's home now, and they didn't put him in jail, or anything like that, but he*

*won't talk to me, and I don't know what I'm going to do.
They stopped him last night for a traffic violation—the dumb
kid was speeding down Main Street, showing off for his
friends, no doubt—and the police made him get out of the car,
and a joint fell out of his shirt pocket when he bent over! Can
you believe that? How could he be so dumb?!! First of all, to
smoke pot to begin with, and second of all to get caught like
that. They took him into the police station and let him call
me, and I went and got him. But now he's got to appear in
front of a juvenile board, and I've got to find a lawyer, and I
can't afford one, and Kevin doesn't have any money. Thank
God, Jason's still seventeen! In one more month, they could
try him as an adult! Aunt Genia, he could go to prison if he
ever does anything like this again. I don't know what I'm
going to do about my kids! I guess I should count myself lucky
that they didn't catch Janie, too. . . .*

Genia read it as a cry for help of every sort imaginable: financial, advisory, emotional. The teenage son wasn't the
only member of the Eden family who needed help. His
mother needed love and attention at this moment, too. And
no doubt with their family in an uproar over this, Jason's
twin sister Janie could use support, as well. Their dad, Kevin,
was a sweet and talented man who meant well, but he lived
way out on an island and wasn't much use in a pinch.

"Aunt Genia, please come to Rhode Island. . . ."

The e-mail didn't actually say that, but Genia got the message.

She heard a familiar haunting cry, and raised her head to
listen.

It was a coyote calling in the distance, from the mountains
that sloped toward Mexico. Even before the first cry died
out, a second one arose from the southwest, and then a third

from still another direction. It was an eerie chorus and one of her favorite sounds in all the world. It made her imagine a family signaling their vulnerable positions, crying out for the reassuring company of one another.

Genia felt a surge of loneliness.

She lived by herself in a large ranch house surrounded by thousands and thousands of flat acres populated by nothing much more than cactus, cattle, rattlesnakes, and rabbits. Her nearest neighbors were a truck ride away. Her children lived far enough away to make their visits very special. Her husband had died more than a decade ago. On Las Palomas Ranch, there was only Genia, and her new ranch manager's family in a separate house, and nobody else.

Rhode Island was only a plane ride away from her.

She stood beside her pool wearing huarche sandals, a blue denim skirt to mid-calf, a hammered silver belt, a light blue denim shirt, simple silver earrings, and an old straw hat to shield her face. In New England she'd look like somebody pretending to be a cowgirl. Here, she looked like what she was, the owner of a cattle ranch that spread over ten thousand acres.

Rhode Island was only a little over twelve hundred square miles, total.

Genia knew ranchers who could fit it between their fence lines.

It seemed to Genia as if the Edens lived a whole culture away from her, and not just a mere continent away. Here she was deep in the Sonoran Desert, where the moon rose over sagebrush, and the natives drawled their vowels, where men added hot peppers to their food, and cowboy boots peeked out from under the hems of women's dresses. Devon, Rhode Island, couldn't have been more different if it were planted on Mars. It would take more than a change of wardrobe to shift her focus there.

And yet . . .

She loved New England, and now that she had an invitation—practically an imperative—to go there, she felt a familiar longing for it. She'd gone to college there, fallen in love, married, given birth to three children there. She hadn't been back East in a long time. Spring was her favorite season here, though, and this promised to be a spectacular one, with the succulents expected to bloom so profusely they would transform the desert floor into a Berber carpet of color, pattern, and texture. But spring was lovely in New England, too.

And cooler . . .

Under the buttoned cuff of her denim blouse, even though the air was dry, her wrists were perspiring. Her waist, under the silver belt, felt as damp as if she'd been swimming with all of her clothes on.

Much cooler, by the ocean . . .

If Lew Potter were alive, he would drop everything to help his young relatives. Donna's sole source of income was a small gallery where she sold Kevin's unique folk art, a business arrangement which they had somehow managed to maintain in spite of their divorce. And Kevin, like most artists, didn't earn much. Genia loved the whole family, even the ex-husband, but she was especially fond of Jason, whom she knew better than the rest. The boy had spent the summer before last, his fifteenth, on her ranch, working alongside the cowboys, getting strong and brown, and he'd seemed to like it.

She hadn't seen any of them since then.

As she stood by the swimming pool, her mind already half

made up, the other half fell into line. If she traveled to Devon, Rhode Island, she could renew her acquaintance with Lew's old mentor, Stanley Parker. That, alone, would make it worth the trip, even without the excuse of a family emergency. Not to mention the chance to see her good friend Jed White, who lived in nearby Boston.

And...as good as the pork smelled, the thought of a fresh cold crab remoulade salad sounded even more delicious at the moment.

"Good grief," she chided herself, "does your stomach rule you?"

She hoped she would be as willing to fly off to help her family—if they lived someplace where she didn't care for the food!

Genia intended to stay for only a few days in Devon, Rhode Island, certainly no more than a week. She stood with the family through the pain of Jason's hearing on the misdemeanor charge of possession of marijuana. The five-person juvenile board placed him in a diversion program that was intended literally to divert him into healthier—and legal—activities like a job or community service. It was contingent on his staying away from drugs and alcohol. It made his great-aunt feel queasy to think that had Jason been only one month older, he would have received a sentence of adult probation that would have appeared on his permanent record.

"We can add random drug tests," the chairman said to Donna. On this difficult morning Genia's forty-two-year-old niece by marriage looked near tears and barely able to cope with what was happening to her son. Kevin Eden wasn't there, having expressed his fury at a judicial system that would "arrest a kid for doing what every kid does," as he had put it. Genia thought he ought to have been there anyway to help his ex-wife and to support his son. Donna needed help, sitting up there with Jason and the lawyer; this was too much for one parent to bear alone. Meanwhile, the board chairman continued: "But that's up to you, Mrs. Eden. In this state, we leave that up to the parents. Do you want us to?"

"What would that entail?" she asked him, her voice quaking.

Genia knew that the attorney she had hired for the Edens had already gone over all of this with them, but Donna was obviously so distraught she had forgotten almost everything he had told them.

"It means urine tests," the chairman said bluntly. "It means we can test Jason at any time, without any warning, for drugs or alcohol in his system. What's your decision?"

"Yes," said Donna, quickly. "Please do that."

Genia drew back in surprise. She thought Donna had promised Kevin not to do that; she thought it had been agreed by the parents that a child ought not to be punished overmuch for his first mistake, and that it was humiliating enough to be put on diversion, without also having to submit to the mortification of urine sampling.

At that moment Jason turned and stared at his mother as if she had betrayed him beyond forgiving. In the row of seats behind them, his twin sister gasped, and seated beside her, Genia felt an awful sinking sensation. This was a terrible mistake, she sensed, and one which Donna might one day live to regret.

"Mom, how could you?" Janie demanded afterward.

Jason refused to talk to anyone at all.

Donna looked helpless and stubborn, all at the same time. "I just don't want Jason to ruin his life."

"You've just ruined it!" the boy burst out.

"But Jason, if you don't use drugs or alcohol, you won't have anything to worry about—"

"You don't trust me," he shot back.

"I do trust you," his mother protested. "But I don't know if you can trust yourself, and I want to protect you from getting into serious trouble—"

"You just don't understand," his sister accused her.

Genia felt as if she were watching the little family split apart.

If only Donna hadn't promised one thing, and then done the opposite. To a teenager that kind of thing was the worst sort of betrayal. And Jason and Janie were far too young to see their mother as Genia did: as a young woman herself, inexperienced at such things, and grasping for any kind of help for her children.

Genia decided she'd better stay on for a few days more.

After the hearing the twins ran off angrily to find their friends. Genia walked out of the courthouse with her arm around their mother.

"Kevin's going to kill me," Donna told her.

"If Kevin has anything to say, he should have said it in the hearing this morning," was her aunt's tart reply. "It's not your fault he wasn't here."

"Everything's my fault," her niece said miserably.

Genia wasn't going to tolerate that kind of self-pity, not for long, and so she made a point of taking Donna out for a nice lunch at a cheerful restaurant. Before their desserts arrived, Donna was smiling again and saying that Jason could probably live through six months of random drug testing without it killing him.

It struck Genia again that just one month into the diversion program, the boy would be eighteen. Old enough to be tried as an adult if any other drug charge were brought against him. Under the white tablecloth, his great-aunt crossed her fingers and hoped for the best for all of them.

Things seemed to calm down. She could have gone home. But Devon, Rhode Island, worked its charm on her.

Genia was surprised by how at home she felt in the little town, where there wasn't any crime to speak of, and the most controversial thing happening was whether or not to start a citywide art festival like the ones in other towns in South County. It was all so peaceful, so pleasantly civilized. Sometimes she felt almost like a "Swamp Yankee," which was the affectionate nickname given lifelong residents of South County—people like Lew's old mentor, Stanley Parker, and her own relatives-by-marriage. There was something about being in the smallest state in the union that also charmed her. But even more compelling was the fact that Devon brought a sweet renewal of memories of her late husband, who had summered there with his grandparents when he was a boy. Genia suspected that was the real reason she lingered, even when spring changed into summer, and she wasn't even thinking of packing her bags.

Her late husband's mentor, Stanley Parker, worked his wiles on her, too. He was seventy-nine years old, retired from the presidency of the local bank he owned, though not retired from trying to run the town of Devon. Upon her arrival, the old man had invited her immediately to dinner at his "Castle" on the highest cliff overlooking his town.

"I've taken a liking to you," he informed her.

To Genia's amusement and pleasure, she discovered that

meant being swept into Stanley Parker's confidence, his privileged social circle, and his ever-evolving plans.

Afterward she thought that it was all Stanley Parker's fault
when her two weeks turned into three, and then into a
month, and then three. It was all his fault when a Realtor
friend of his located a perfect house for Genia to rent: a
story-and-a-half Cape Cod, weathered clapboard with white
trim, and a wonderful wide deck overlooking the ocean.
And it was Stanley Parker's fault, too, that suddenly she was
busy as a short-order cook in a room full of gluttons.

"Genia Potter," he said with an air of dramatic pro-
nouncement, after only one month, "let's do a cookbook
together. You and I. Rhode Island recipes. We'll get it published by an editor I know who owes me money." When she
laughed in surprise and didn't answer right away, he threw in
the kicker: "Lew would approve."

And so there she was, ensconced in a pretty little house
on the ocean on the northeast tip of the southern edge of
Rhode Island, writing a cookbook, and deeply involved in
her late husband's family's life, and feeling as happy as a clam
that hadn't been caught and steamed yet.

In August Stanley Parker suggested that she host a sit-
down dinner party, whose purpose was to test recipes for
their cookbook. "Whom shall I invite?" she asked her new
mentor.

As if he had a list in his pocket, he reeled off seven names:
"I want you to ask your niece and that artist ex-husband of
hers, even though Kevin probably won't come if Donna's
here, but ask him anyway. And send an invitation to Lindsay
and Harrison Wright—he's that black TV weatherman you
like so much, and she's the president of my arts council—and
to Celeste Hutchinson..."

She was the Realtor who had found Genia the house to rent.

"And to David Graham—"

"David Graham? That's generous of you, Stanley."

"Why, just because he married my ex-wife? That only proves that he and I have something in common, namely excellent taste in women."

"All right." Genia smiled at him. "Anybody else?"

"Yes, the mayor, Larry Averill. Get your niece and nephew to help out in the kitchen, and I'll come over early, to boss everybody around."

She smiled at him again. "Your best talent."

He nodded, looking sage. "And one I have nurtured over a lifetime."

"Why those particular people, Stanley?"

"You don't like them, Genia?"

"I like them fine, Stanley, although I can hardly say I know them well, except for Donna and Kevin."

"Well, I know them very well." From underneath his thick white eyebrows he gave her a look she couldn't decipher. "Better than they think I do."

"Are you up to something, Stanley?"

"Who, me?" He'd pulled back in a patently false show of wounded innocence. "Why Eugenia Potter, what a thing to say to a poor, feeble old man."

"If you're feeble, I'm Betty Grable," she'd retorted.

"Much prettier," said the old man, gallantly.

Genia blew him a kiss. "For that, you get your guest list."

"You won't be sorry, my dear."

The old man started to get up from the chair where he was sitting in her kitchen, but then he sank back down again, after a wince crossed his face.

"Stanley, forgive my asking, but are you feeling all right?"

"I'm fine," he snapped. "Why wouldn't I be?"

"All right, if you say so."

"And who better?"

"You'd tell me if you weren't?"

"Probably not. Why should I tell anybody but my doctor?"

"*Is* there something wrong, Stanley?"

He glared at her like an old buffalo. "There's a saying that's popular with the younger generation these days, Genia Potter, and it goes like this: 'What is there about the word "no" that you don't understand?' "

She held her tongue and reserved her opinion.

That same day, she wrote out and mailed six invitations to seven people: *Donna Eden, Kevin Eden, Celeste Hutchinson, David Graham, Lawrence Averill, Lindsay and Harrison Wright.*

4

THE MAIN COURSE

One after another her guests came, bearing hostess gifts and the secret ingredient recipes she had asked them to bring. And still no Stanley, and even Janie had not returned yet with Genia's car and a report on him.

She took off her apron and forced a smile to her face.

"David, how lovely!"

Genia accepted a bouquet of coral roses from David Graham and held them carefully in front of her. Behind him, raindrops still lightly sprinkled the driveway, and the sky looked darker than mere twilight should have made it. She hoped her other guests would beat the storm.

"It is you who looks lovely," was her guest's gallant reply.

Her smile felt suddenly less forced. He was a handsome, courtly man with an expression of sadness in his gray eyes and an air of brave bonhomie about him. She knew from her niece Donna that the women in town were already after this man, even though his wife had been dead less than a year. Genia smiled kindly at him and hoped he realized he had nothing to fear from her in that regard. She already had a beau, and not all that far away, either, in Boston.

David Graham wore a boutonniere, a coral rose to match

those he had given her. It was an affectation Genia had rarely seen in Arizona; it amused her to think of any of her cowboys appearing for dinner with a rose in his lapel. Here it seemed appropriate, however. She appreciated the obvious care with which David had prepared himself for her dinner. It was almost a lost art, Genia thought nostalgically, the business of making oneself an ornament whom a hostess could display with pride at her dinner table.

"All this and a secret ingredient, too?" she asked him.

He swept a typed card from the pocket of his beautiful dinner jacket and stuffed it down among the roses.

"This was a favorite of Lillian's."

"I will treasure it, David."

A quick glance showed her it was for a dish called, "Pepper Cheese Soufflé." The secret ingredient was listed as "ground white pepper." In his own handwriting, apparently, David had noted, "Secret, because it disappears into the cheese."

"Would you be so kind as to man the bar for me?"

"I'd be happy to have something to do, Genia."

It was a gracious way to say yes, she thought. David Graham had the exquisite manners of a gentleman of another era, and she found it pleasant to be the object of them. And then he surprised her by turning back to say, "It's really kind of you to include me, Genia. I get lonely, don't you, living alone for so long? Or will I just get used to it after a while?"

Her heart went out to him, this sad-eyed man who had buried so recently the woman everyone said he had adored. Gently, she told him, "It's hard at first. But one does adjust, David. It even becomes possible to be happy."

"Difficult to believe."

"I know it is."

He smiled briefly, painfully, and went into her living room.

Thoughtfully, remembering her own slow healing after Lew died, Genia carried the roses back to the kitchen to trim their stems under water and place them in a vase. She got back to the front door just in time to greet Harrison and Lindsay Wright, who arrived bearing "Eye of the Storm" wine and a recipe for "Blue Suede Soup."

"Suede certainly is a secret ingredient," Genia joked with them. They looked young and prosperous and wrapped up in each other, she thought. Lindsay was tall and thin as a model, with long straight blond hair; Harrison was shorter, not conventionally handsome, but attractive in a nice, ordinary kind of way that inspired trust. With Lindsay so light of complexion, and he so much darker, they made a striking couple. They greeted her with light embraces.

"It's really creamed blueberry soup," Lindsay confided to her. "We used to have to go out and pick blueberries till our fingers bled. My mom fixed them every which way, from pancakes to jam. The only way she could get us to eat them like this was to tell us that Elvis Presley invented it and named it after the song 'Blue Suede Shoes.' "

"You had a very wise and funny mother," Genia observed.

Lindsay looked surprised. "I guess so."

Upon reading the label on the bottle they had handed her Genia inquired, "Eye of the Storm?"

"It's from the Sakonnet Vineyards over near Little Compton," Harrison told her. She thought his voice could melt snow. "Some red and white grapes got accidentally mixed up during a hurricane, and they produced this blush wine. That's how it got its name."

"What a wonderful story, and perfect for a weatherman!" She glanced over his shoulder. "Did you order this rain?"

"Everybody blames me," he replied, with good humor. "If you think this is something, wait until later this week."

"Are you saying I should batten down my hatches?"

"What *are* hatches, anyway?" his wife asked.

"In nautical terms, it's the cover over a deck opening," her husband explained, as promptly as if he had opened a dictionary and read the definition there. "That's where we get the saying, 'batten down the hatches.'"

Lindsay beamed at her hostess. "Isn't he something? Can't you just see him on the *Today* show, saying things like that?"

Genia smiled. "Is that where you'd like to be, Harrison, on national television?"

"That's where Lindsay thinks I should go," he said, "but I kind of like living right here where I can look out a window and actually see the weather. In New York, how would I know which way the wind was blowing?"

Lindsay gave him an affectionate shove. "Oh, you. Who needs weather, when you've got all those instruments?"

Harrison burst out laughing. "Who needs me, if we don't have weather?"

Lindsay grabbed his arm and leaned into him lovingly, while looking at Genia. "Isn't he sweet? I'm telling you, he's bound for big things."

Harrison only smiled and rolled his eyes up to indicate forbearance.

"Is Stanley here yet?" Lindsay asked casually.

Genia told her, "No. I am hoping somebody has seen him. You didn't?"

They told her they had not seen Stanley Parker all that day.

They were followed by Celeste Hutchinson, looking glamorous in a floral silk dress and matching shoes. Genia had seen the outfit on her before. She thought it was wonderful when a woman found a style and a particular dress that looked so good on her that she could confidently wear it as often as she liked. Thank goodness the days were gone when a woman could not be seen twice wearing the same dress at social functions with the same people. Those old-fashioned dictums were hard on pocketbooks, though they had once kept legions of seamstresses in jobs.

"Listen, Genia, I'm no cook," the Realtor said, in a confiding tone that implied they were old friends by now. "I stole one of my mother's old recipes for you." She accompanied the recipe card with a quick hug of greeting. "It's not much, but it's the best I could do. I've just been swamped with open houses and new customers. Forgive me?"

"Of course, Celeste. I'm glad that business is so good."

"You ought to buy *this* house, Genia."

"I didn't know the owners even wanted to sell it."

"Well, if they don't, I know a dozen other houses you'd love."

"I'm sure I would, but the last thing I need is another house to take care of."

"Oh, bosh. Do think about it, Genia. You fit in here like a native. We'll do a house tour one day soon, and I'll show you some gorgeous places. Is David Graham here yet?"

Told he was at the bar, she made a beeline in that direction. Genia had smelled liquor quite strongly on Celeste's breath. She made a mental note to make sure that when the Realtor left that evening she was sober enough to drive herself home.

Genia was next caught in a bear hug by the mayor.

"I've brought you something," Larry Averill said, placing a white box in her hands.

She drew off the lid and exclaimed in delight at what she saw inside.

"It's a key to our fine city," the mayor announced.

The key, six inches long and made of brass, had inscribed on it "Devon, Rhode Island."

"Should I give a speech?" Genia smiled at him, delighted with the gift. "Nobody's ever given me a key to a city before, Mayor. I'll hang it in a place of honor."

He beamed down at her like a proud, portly father.

"Celeste here yet?"

"She's in the family room with the others."

While putting the key on the hall table for safekeeping, Genia couldn't help but think of the mayor's rumpled, rather sweaty appearance as compared to that of the well-groomed men who had preceded him into the house. And yet, she thought there was something innately *nice* about Lawrence Averill. She had a feeling he was always running late, not quite put together because he was too busy doing favors for other people to stop and think about himself. She was willing to bet that he kept a box full of brass keys in his car to pass out like candy, but that didn't dilute at all the sweetness of the gesture, nor her pleasure in accepting it.

As guests arrived, she asked if they had passed Stanley on the way. Each time she was told no. None of them appeared to be as fretful as she about his absence. That comforted her, because several of them had known Stanley longer and better than she knew him. If they weren't concerned about him, she would try not to be, either.

Genia glanced in the hall mirror to undo the damage all the hugging had done. A dab of gray eye shadow and a light brush of lipstick were all she ever wore as makeup, and she saw immediately that the lipstick needed replenishing. That, plus a nice silk blouse and long skirt, a pair of earrings, a hint of good perfume, and a polished pair of shoes were what she generally called "dressing up for dinner" these days. She smoothed back a stray strand of her silver-blond hair, which she wore pulled into a bun at the base of her neck. Only then did she notice a dark smudge on her silky white blouse. Where had that come from? From the roses?

Oh, dear, she thought. *I've greeted my guests looking like I've been up to my shoulders in gardening!*

She brushed the spot with the flat of her hand and winced when a slender pine needle, hidden in the smudge of dirt, pricked her palm.

"How in heaven's name did that get there?" she asked aloud.

She hadn't been out of the house since changing into her dinner clothes. This blouse had come right from the dry cleaner's bag. She brushed more vigorously, and discovered too late that the prick was bleeding, and now she had a spot of blood on her blouse! Darn it, now she would have to change clothes or pin on a brooch to cover it.

Before going upstairs to do that, Genia glanced into the family room to see how her guests were managing on their own. Janie wasn't there yet to start the hors d'oeuvres going around, but all appeared normal. David Graham was pouring drinks at the bar, with Celeste Hutchinson at his elbow, putting napkins under wet glasses.

To Genia's eyes it all presented a pretty sight of people and setting. She loved the decorating taste of the owners of this house, especially the living/dining room with its oversized white couches and chairs, its floor-to-ceiling stone fireplace, and windows everywhere, framing the sea beyond. The owners had positioned an oval dining table right in front of the fireplace, near the wide French doors. Someone had ingeniously transformed the antique wooden table at one end of the room by painting it white and stenciling starfish around its edge. Matching small starfish appliqués added a fanciful touch to cream-colored slipcovers on tall dining chairs. Altogether, it was an informal setting, but elegant just the same.

Jason had earlier filled the fireplace with pine logs—so different in fragrance from her Arizona mesquite—in case the evening turned cool, as it was now doing. Genia saw that Janie had done a lovely job of setting the table, and she herself had added simple garden flowers in pottery bowls. They matched the delicate yellow color of the table linens she had found in a chest of drawers. As the Realtor, Celeste had assured her that the owners meant her to make herself literally at home, and anything they didn't want her to use, they had locked up.

Conversation seemed to be humming along nicely.

"Lindsay! Beautiful suit. Is that a Chanel?"

"Hey, Larry, I've been thinking that if you can get the art festival going, it might attract enough regional attention to get you elected to the state house. Your problem is, you've always been too local. Nobody outside of Devon knows you as well as we do. But a big project like that, bringing more jobs than Devon can handle on our own, that could get you grateful voters from far and wide. You ever think of that?"

"Stanley says—"

"Oh, don't mention that man's name to me!"

"Not mention his name? He's going to be here, you know."

"That doesn't mean I have to speak to him."

"Did you bring a recipe with a secret ingredient?"

"We don't need more rain, Harrison. Can you please stop it?"

These people were old friends and acquaintances, most of

them, and they didn't need Genia to break any ice for them. As she walked upstairs to the bedroom she had selected for her own use, she thought, *It's strange, about that pine needle. I wonder where it came from?*

When she glanced out her bedroom windows at Block Island Sound, she saw how fast the clouds were moving now. Rain was beginning to thump against the screens. Suddenly, there was no hiding from herself anymore how concerned she felt. Maybe nobody else was worried about Stanley Parker, but she was. He should have arrived long before this. Nobody had seen him. He didn't answer the phone at his house. He was seventy-nine years old and probably not in the best of health, and he rode a motorbike with his mind on other things.

"He could have fallen," she fretted out loud, "or had an accident, even a heart attack."

From the jewelry she had brought with her from Arizona, Genia picked out her grandmother Andrews' pearl and diamond brooch. Even it reminded her of Stanley because it was big and old-fashioned, emblematic of a wealthy, privileged era: a three-inch starburst of diamonds emerging from a cluster of pearls at the center. Genia loved it, not because it was beautiful—it wasn't, particularly—or valuable, but because her grandfather had given it to her grandmother, who had given it to her mother, who had passed it on to her. Everytime she pinned it onto her own clothing, she felt as if she were reattaching herself to her family. She was thinking of having the brooch dismantled and its stones and pearls mounted in smaller pieces, so that each of her children could have part of it. Now she pinned it to her silk blouse, figuring the blouse was already ruined by the blood.

"There," she said, patting it and checking it in a mirror.

She hurried around the upper floor, closing windows.

Then she went back downstairs to launch a more serious search for the old man. *Lew will kill me*, she thought, *if I've let anything happen to you, Stanley.*

Leaving her guests to fend for themselves, Genia returned to the kitchen and found nearly the whole Eden family there. Janie was filling an ice bucket; her brother had his nose in a fistful of fresh mint, which Genia assumed he had picked up at Stanley's greenhouse, and their mother was washing blueberries at the sink.

Genia immediately asked her grandniece, "Did you find him?"

"No!" It sounded blunt, almost surly.

All three of them stopped what they were doing and stared at the girl, and even Jason looked a little shocked. He was six feet tall, two inches more than Janie, and slim, like her. Both twins had expressive faces; at the moment, hers looked angry, his looked surprised. He was "dressed up" for the occasion in clean blue jeans, with a belt, a white summer shirt, and even a tie. There was dirt on the knees of his denims, suggesting he had knelt to pick the mint.

Genia was momentarily too surprised to speak.

When Janie looked up and caught them staring at her, she blurted out, "I rang the bell for five minutes, at least, and nobody answered, and I hope he doesn't come at all!"

"Mr. Parker?" Jason asked her, sounding puzzled.

"Yes!"

"Janie!" her mother remonstrated.

"But why, honey?" Genia asked the girl.

"Because he's awful, and I hate him."

Suddenly her smart, sophisticated, seventeen-year-old niece looked and sounded like a hurt and angry young girl, and Genia couldn't for the life of her imagine why.

"Janie, dear, was Mr. Parker rude to you?"

"I told you, I didn't find him, and I don't want to talk about it." Janie cast an unreadable look at her brother, who looked at her as if she'd suddenly gone crazy. With uncharacteristic spitefulness, his sister said in a taunting voice, "Do I, Jason?"

"How do I know? What's the matter with you, anyway?"

"Young lady—" their mother started to say in a lecturing tone. But Genia waved a warning hand at her and interrupted.

"Whatever it is, Janie, I'm sorry you feel this way, but we've got a dinner party to put on now. Jason, will you please go down the path and look again for—"

"Yeah," the boy agreed, and in a moment he was gone.

Behind her daughter's back Donna made an apologetic face.

The way her dinner party was going, Genia wasn't entirely surprised when thunder rumbled so close to the house that it shook the kitchen windowpanes. Frighteningly soon after that lightning hit somewhere close enough to raise the hair on her arms and make Janie exclaim out loud in startled fear. The rain began to pour in buckets—or lobster pots, as one might say around here—and all she could think of was *Stanley's out in this*. She wanted to hand out yellow slickers to all of her guests and make them go search for him, but she knew she had to serve them lobster bisque, instead.

Genia barely heard the conversation as it tilted around the table, lurching around the empty chair where Stanley was to sit, and another one where a place was set for Kevin Eden. The storm continued noisily, until it seemed to Genia's distracted imagination like a living thing that was trying to get their attention by pinging at the windows and blowing at the doors. But except for Genia—and for Harrison Wright, who kept staring out at the rain with a pleased smile on his face—the rest of the guests were all talking—arguing was more like it—about the proposed art festival for their town, as if that's all anybody had to worry about at the moment.

"We're all for it," Donna said, emphasizing the plural pronoun.

Genia tried to pay attention and did focus long enough to realize that her niece looked sweet tonight. She was short and plump, with a round face and curly short light brown hair, a complete physical opposite to her tall, thin children who favored their father. Donna's wardrobe consisted mainly of sailor-suit jumpers in red, white, and blue; Genia thought that the one she wore this evening looked as crisp and colorful as a brand-new flag. For a woman who spent most of her days feeling upset about her children, her ex-husband, or money, Donna had an irrepressibly cheerful look about her.

"Well, who isn't for it?" Celeste asked, in a derisive tone. Her voice had a rich, throaty quality that held people's attention. Genia thought the Realtor had the high coloring, the buxom figure, and the dramatic flair of an actress or an opera singer. She knew how forceful Celeste had been during the process of renting this summer home, and she could easily imagine her sweeping young homebuyers along in her wake. Celeste repeated, "Who isn't? Except for your ex-husband and a few backward businesspeople."

"Aren't you forgetting someone?" Lindsay said with a pointed edge to her voice. When Celeste look puzzled, the younger woman pointed to her own well-groomed chest. "The president of the arts council. Me. Surely I have some say in this, since it's our council's money that's supposed to fund this thing."

"What's your objection to it, Lindsay?" Genia asked, making an effort to be an attentive hostess.

"Crafts," was the reply, sounding more like a retort. "We're an arts council, may I repeat: arts. Not arts and crafts. I don't think our town wants to be known for all those ticky-tacky doodads."

"Like Kevin's work, you mean?" Donna inquired acidly. He might be her ex-husband but she was still his sales agent. Kevin Eden created witty seascape "pictures" of wood and paint and bits of this and that. They might not be fine art, but they were charming, and Genia had recently bought four of them and shipped them home to Arizona. She planned to hang one in her guest room and wrap the others as Christmas gifts for her children.

"Oh, she doesn't mean Kevin's," Celeste assured her, with a blithe wave of the same hand that held her glass of wine. Genia held her breath for the tablecloth. "Kevin's pieces may be craft, but they're very . . . *artistic* . . . craft." If it was meant to smooth Donna's feelings, it didn't succeed very well, Genia thought, observing her niece's face.

Good-naturedly, the mayor said, "You can't really blame Kevin and the business owners, Celeste."

"Why can't I?" she asked, and everybody but Genia laughed. Stanley claimed that Rhode Islanders were argumentative by nature. She wanted him to be here to enjoy this. "Kevin just doesn't want to be disturbed out on that island that doesn't even belong to him, right, Donna?"

Genia's niece nodded her head vigorously and briefly wagged her soup spoon at them as if she were lecturing her artist husband. "I've told him, 'You ought to be grateful, Kevin Eden, that Stanley lets you live and work out there at all. So you'll have to lock up your studio for a little while, so what? It's such a small thing to ask for the good of the community.' "

David Graham twinkled at her from across the table. "I'm sure he loves it when you explain it to him like that, Donna."

She looked surprised, then blushed and laughed.

"Kevin and the business owners are just being selfish and shortsighted, Larry," Celeste continued, punctuating her thoughts with sips of wine. "All we're asking for is one measly weekend out of an entire year, and they act as if we're going to take every parking place downtown for the whole tourist season. And who do they think is going to be coming, anyway, if not tourists? We'll make money for them, not take it away."

Larry Averill smiled at her. "I'm on your side, Celeste. But there's more to it than that, and I have to try to understand the viewpoints of all my constituents. The store owners downtown say that all the tourists will be out on the island, looking at art and buying things out there, and all they'll be doing downtown is parking. The downtown restaurant owners aren't happy about it, either, especially since we want to sell food at the festival. You can see their point."

But his old friend shook her head. "No, I can't." She grinned wickedly. "Think of all of those future homebuyers who will be coming to the festival." Then she lifted her glass in a toast. "I say, here's to progress."

"Second that." David raised his own glass and tapped it against hers. "Luckily, it is Stanley's island to do with as he pleases, and it appears that what pleases him is to hold an art festival on it. Your ex-husband can object all he wants to, Donna, but I doubt that's going to sway Stanley. I predict this town will have its art festival out on Parker Island—"

"Over Kevin's dead body," Donna muttered, and they

laughed again when she added, "which I might be happy to provide at no cost to the town!" Belatedly, she realized that her daughter had just entered from the kitchen, bearing a tray for picking up appetizer plates, and had overheard that last remark. "No offense to your father, Janie."

Janie said nothing, but when the time came to pick up her mother's plate she snatched it away and barely missed Donna's nose with it. Her mother looked half-angry, half-amused. To the others she commented, "It's a good thing she makes good grades, although you'd never guess it from looking at her. And if she had to support herself on tips, she'd starve. I don't know what my son's going to do; he doesn't even make the grades!"

Celeste laughed and held out her glass for more wine.

Genia understood that Donna felt embarrassed by her daughter's appearance, and that made her tongue sharp, but there was no excuse for humiliating the child. She felt like kicking Donna under the table. David Graham was frowning, too. He personally handed his own empty plate to Janie, saying as he did so, "Well, I'd tip her generously, Donna. I think she's doing a lovely job. She deserves a lot of credit for helping out her aunt tonight." As Janie removed his plate, he said courteously, "Thank you, child." Her great-aunt Genia's heart warmed in gratitude to him for salving the cut of her mother's hurtful words.

"I heard Kevin changed his mind about the festival," Harrison suddenly inserted, hearkening back to earlier comments.

His wife stared at him. "Where'd you hear that?"

"At the TV station, I think."

"When?" she pressed him.

"Maybe yesterday." He frowned in thought. "Or, maybe not."

"I can't believe it," the mayor said. "Who'd you hear that from, Harrison?"

"Somebody," the weatherman answered, with the expression of a man who sincerely wishes to be helpful. "Might have been the reporter who's assigned to the city council. Or to the arts council. I'm not sure. Anyway, I know I heard it."

"And you didn't tell me?" Lindsay asked, half-laughing.

"Sorry, honey." He smiled beatifically at her and then turned to stare out the window again. "Isn't this a great storm? There must be a gigantic cumulonimbus cloud up there, or we wouldn't get this much of a downpour. It's so exciting when a cold front comes up under a warm front and forces it to rise. That's when we get turbulence like this." He looked riveted to the drama of nature playing outside the warm, well-lighted house. "There's real drama playing up there. Clashing and flashing, banging and clanging. I could watch it twenty-four hours a day. It's better than theater, better than TV or the movies."

His wife grinned and shook her head so that everyone but her husband saw her. "Sometimes I think that if he weren't nailed down, he'd blow away with the first wind."

"I'd love to," Genia heard the weatherman murmur.

"That's what a wedding ring is for," David Graham joked, "to nail a man down. Isn't that right, Larry?"

"Wouldn't know about that," the mayor said jovially.

Genia felt so impatient with them for chattering on about the weather and their art festival when Stanley was missing. But everytime she said anything like "I can't imagine what's keeping him," one of the others would dismiss her worry, saying, "If anybody can take care of himself, it's Stanley." And, "Oh, he just wants to make a grand entrance." And, "Don't worry so much, Genia, you don't know Stanley like we do. He probably stopped along the way to start a committee or launch a museum."

While they laughed and carried on, she seriously considered leaving the table to call the police. *Five more minutes,* she told herself, *if he's not here in five minutes, I'll do that.* It was only because Jason hadn't returned that she didn't hop to the phone immediately; the boy's continued absence reassured her, causing her to imagine that maybe he had helped the old man out of the heavy rain and was even now waiting for Stanley to change into dry clothes, and then would drive them both over in Stanley's car. Although, why the boy hadn't called to tell her. . .

Maybe the storm had knocked the telephones out. . . .

She felt a warm touch, and looked up to find that Harrison Wright was gazing at her with concern in his nice hazel eyes. Quietly, under the hum of the other conversations, he said, "I'll take any excuse to go out in a storm. Would you like for me to drive up to the Castle and look for him?"

She grasped his hand thankfully and was just about to say "Oh, yes, would you please, Harrison?" when the answer arrived in a shocking gust of wind and rain.

The French doors blew open with a crash that startled everyone into silence. For a moment Genia thought the storm had done it. But the open doors admitted not only a torrent of cold rain, but also the figure of a man who stood before them soaked and dripping. A burst of lightning flashed behind him, as if Frankenstein's monster had suddenly materialized there. He had wild hair that stuck out in every direction from his scalp, and he wore brown boat shoes, blue jeans, and a Hawaiian shirt of so many colors it looked as if he had wiped his paintbrushes on it.

"Dad!" Janie, who was serving coffee, set the pot precariously on the table and ran to her father. He reached for her and hugged her close. Kevin Eden stood with his legs spread wide, panting for breath as if he'd run a long way.

"My God, Kevin." Donna looked at her ex-husband's muddy brown boat shoes with disgust. "Look what you're tracking in!"

"It's Stanley," Kevin Eden said, ignoring her. "I found him down on the beach. He's dead. Stanley's dead. Somebody call the police."

At that moment, if Genia had been asked to swear in a court of law how the other people in her house reacted to the news, she would have said *with relief*. If anybody else felt the shock and grief that she did, she didn't sense it. Soon they were all claiming to feel terrible, and maybe they did, she thought, giving them the benefit of the doubt. But in that first instant, the feeling that traveled round the table from one guest to another was . . . relief.

She suddenly remembered Jason and asked his father if he'd seen the boy.

"He's down there," Kevin told her. "I left him with Stanley."

"You did *what?*" Donna exclaimed, looking horrified.

"He can handle it, Donna," he snapped at her. "I couldn't just leave the body there. But I have to get back." He released his daughter, whose skin looked pale as pudding beneath her dyed red hair. Kevin Eden ran back outside into the storm. The mayor hurried to the telephone to call the police. At the dinner table, Genia was the only one to shed tears for Stanley Parker.

5

LEFTOVERS

An endless hour later Kevin Eden returned to Genia's rented house, to her kitchen, trailing his silent, wet, bedraggled son behind him. Everyone else had gone home, taking their speculations and excitement with them, leaving her alone to await some final word. Even Donna had departed with Janie. The girl had wanted to run out into the rain after her father; it took the combined efforts of the grown-ups to persuade her not to go.

"Kevin, Jason," Genia said anxiously to them as she led them in from the rain. "I'm so glad you came back here. I'll fix you something warm to drink. Would you like something to eat?" In a crisis, she felt a need to feed people. "Sit down, and tell me everything, won't you?"

The men looked exhausted as they took chairs at the kitchen table and slumped there, dripping onto the floor.

"We're making a mess," Jason mumbled.

"Don't worry about it." Genia bustled about, pulling coffee and hot chocolate mix out of a cupboard, and then putting a kettle of water on to boil and getting the coffeepot started, too. "You must be cold, and I don't have any men's clothing here to give you. Hold on a minute and I'll be right back."

She hurried to switch on the furnace and then to snatch blankets out of the linen closet. To the absent owners of the house she murmured, "Forgive me for getting your blankets muddy. I promise I'll get them cleaned, or replace them."

Back in the kitchen as the smell of burning dust began to waft from the heating vents, she draped the blankets over the shoulders of the men. Jason, who was shivering, huddled deep in his, but his father shrugged his off his Hawaiian shirt, and it fell over the back of the chair. "Thanks, Genia," he said, "but I'm fine."

"Tell me everything, from the start, Kevin."

She pulled leftovers from the refrigerator, arranging them on two plates and then warming the plates one at a time in the microwave.

"I was coming in to your dinner," he said.

She was pleased to hear it. Donna would have said this proved he was ill-mannered, to appear at a dinner for which he had not called in his RSVP. Genia chose not to judge his manners, but she did reflect upon how little she really knew this man, in spite of the fact that he had fathered her grand-niece and nephew.

"Well, now you're getting it after all," she said equably.

"Yeah, thanks. So, I was coming over from the island in my boat, and I tied up my boat to a tree, and I was starting to climb up to get to your house, and I saw somebody lying in the rocks. I thought—I don't know what I thought—but I went running over, and there was Stanley. He was limp, and his head looked all bashed in from the rocks, and his eyes were wide open. I knew he was dead."

Genia felt a last bit of resistance inside her give way as she finally realized she must accept this news as true: Stanley

Parker *was* dead, and there was no mistake about it. She realized she had been holding out a hope that Kevin would come running back to say he'd been wrong, that it wasn't Stanley, it was some other poor soul. Or that Stanley was injured, but not dead.

She forced herself to speak calmly and to listen carefully.

"You think he fell over the cliff?"

"Yeah. Must have lost control of his motorbike."

"Where was it?"

"The bike? Kinda halfway down the hillside."

"No, I mean where . . . where did it happen, Kevin?"

"Oh, well, I'd say about a hundred yards from here, I guess. On that little strip of beach down there between this property and Stanley's. You know the one I mean?"

"Yes, I frequently swim there." *So close,* she thought with helpless dismay, *he was so close to safety.* "You found him, and then you came running back here?"

"Yeah."

"Jason, where were you all this time?"

The boy started to tell her, but his father jumped in, speaking in a loud, firm voice that overrode his son's. "Jason showed up right when I was getting back up to the path. He was coming from the direction of Stanley's house where he'd been looking for him, isn't that right, son?"

Jason looked down at the cup of hot chocolate that she gave him.

"Yeah. Thanks, Aunt Genia."

"And then the police came?"

"Right," Kevin said.

"What did they do, Kevin?"

He hesitated. "A lot. More than you'd think they would for an accident like that. They measured and took pictures, and called out the medical examiner. They wouldn't even move Stanley's body, or take it away, until the medical examiner said they could. I guess that's standard procedure." Suddenly his voice became heated. 'I'll tell you what isn't standard procedure, though! It isn't normal to interrogate innocent people who just happen to come across a dead body. The way they asked us questions, you'd think they thought we murdered Stanley. It made me so mad, especially the way they treated Jason. Just because they know about his drug arrest, they acted like he's some kind of hardened criminal. I told them to back off. Hell, I went to school with some of those guys. They know better than to treat my son like that. And I told them so, too."

Genia glanced over at Jason as she got out the silverware.

The boy caught her glance. Out of his father's eyesight, Jason gave Genia a disgusted look, as if he weren't as grateful for his father's defense as Kevin might have thought he should be.

"You'll just get me in more trouble with them, Dad."

Kevin looked hurt. "I'm trying to keep you *out* of trouble, son."

"Well, just don't, okay? You'll make them more suspicious."

"Suspicious of what? You haven't done anything."

"You make them think I have!"

"I did not, Jason."

Genia slid their plates in front of them. "Who needs water? Salt and pepper? Kevin, Donna claims you eat Tabasco sauce with everything. Is that true? Should I see if I can find some for you?"

The distraction of food did the trick she had hoped it would.

The father grinned at Genia and said, "That was only because her cooking is so bad, right, Jason? No offense to your mother, but if we hadn't got divorced, I would have grown an ulcer from all that Tabasco I had to eat. But this looks great, Genia, even without hot sauce."

"What will happen now, Kevin? Do you know?"

"I guess they'll take his body to a funeral home."

"I wonder if they've notified his daughter."

Kevin sat up straighter, looking startled, as if he'd only just realized there would be other people who had loved Stanley who had to be told. "My God, Nikki and Randy! She'll be so upset about her dad." A small, wry smile moved his lips. "Randy will have to pretend to be upset."

There was a time when Genia might have felt compelled to remonstrate with Kevin for saying such a thing, when she might have chided him. But she had lived long enough and seen and experienced enough things to feel that it was far better to voice an uncomfortable truth than to speak comfortable lies. She took note of the implied cynicism about Stanley Parker's son-in-law and let it pass. It wasn't as if Stanley himself had ever had a good word to say about Randy Dixon. Why should she be surprised if the bad feelings were mutual?

"Aunt Genia, may I have more of this lobster stuff?"

"You like it, Jason? Your sister helped make it."

Kevin pulled his mouth down into a funny grimace. "It's a good thing you didn't tell us that before we tried it. It's really good. Are you sure Janie had anything to do with it?"

"Stop it, Dad." Jason's eyebrows drew together in the scowl that appeared so often on his face. "Janie's not Mom." Before bending to his food again, he muttered, "And I'm not you."

His dad's face flushed, and he looked hurt again.

When Genia went over to pour extra coffee in Kevin's cup, she placed her hand on his shoulder for a moment,

wanting both to comfort him and to pull him back from saying any more of the wrong things. Gently, she said to both
of them, "I love the way you and your sister support each
other, Jason. I wish my own children had been so nice to
each other when they were growing up. It's good to see."

"Janie is his best friend," his father said.

"No, she's not," his son countered. "My best friend's
dead."

And suddenly, the boy began to cry. He put his elbows on
the kitchen table and bent his face into his knuckles and
sobbed until his whole body shook. His dad looked surprised
and helpless. Genia placed her hands on his shoulders and
leaned over until she could place her cheek against the top of
his head.

"I'm so sorry, Jason," she said. "I'm so sorry."

When she straightened up and caught a glimpse of the
father's face, she was surprised to see that he didn't look
sympathetic, he looked angry again. Was Kevin jealous of
his son's relationship with Stanley? she wondered. *If so,* she
thought a bit angrily herself, *he need never worry about that
competition again!* She couldn't stay mad though; it was unkind to resent a father for loving his son so much. *But maybe
that's why Janie was so hateful about Stanley earlier this evening,*
Genia suddenly realized. *If she wasn't her brother's best friend
anymore, she might understandably feel left out and jealous.* But
why would that anger crop up so suddenly, when the girl
hadn't previously expressed any hostility toward her twin's
employer?

Genia shook off the questions. They no longer mattered.

As soon as Jason and Kevin finished eating, Jason took the
car that he shared with Janie and said he was going home to
his mother's. Genia gave Kevin a ride in the opposite direc-

tion, to a friend's house where he said he could spend the night.

"Weather's too bad right now to get back out to the island," he commented. "I'd have to be crazy to take my boat back out tonight."

"You're more than welcome to stay here, Kevin."

"Thanks, Genia, but my friend will have clothes I can change into. I wouldn't look too good in one of your dresses."

She had to laugh at that, in spite of the burden in her heart. And she felt secretly glad to be able to return to her cozy rented home to collapse into bed, without having to worry about an overnight guest. On the way to his friend's house, and just to make conversation, she said, "I hear you've changed your mind about the art festival, Kevin."

"Me? Changed my mind about what?"

"About holding it on the island. I know you were really opposed to that idea, but I heard tonight that you think it's all right now."

"No offense, but you heard wrong, Genia. I mean, no way. I don't want all those people out there tromping around my studio. Who said that, anyway?"

"I must have heard wrong," she fudged. "So you're still opposed to it?"

"Absolutely. Look, if they want to hold their stupid festival in town, let them. But Stanley rented me that island for my own private use. I've got my little house. I've got my studio in the barn. I've got my dock and my boat, and just enough room for my kids to come out and visit me. Do you know that island's even got a well on it I can use? I'm completely self-sufficient and solitary out there and that's the way I like it. If Stanley wants to invite thousands of tourists to look at arts and crafts, let him hold the damn festival up at his own house."

Genia didn't say anything in reply, because she couldn't speak.

"Oh, God," Kevin said quietly. "I'm really sorry I said that."

They rode in silence, until Kevin broke it.

"I didn't know the old man meant that much to Jason, did you?"

"Well," Genia said, "I know Stanley thought the world of him."

Kevin glanced at her. "He said that?"

"Yes, in many ways."

Kevin turned toward the window. "Somebody ought to tell his mother that, because she thinks he's going straight to hell. I tell her this is normal teenage stuff, and Jason just got unlucky and got caught, but she's determined that if he doesn't straighten up we've got to send him to military school."

"Kevin, no, not really?"

He nodded. "One more slip, Donna says."

Stanley would have hated to hear it, she thought sadly. He'd been sent to military school himself, when he was a boy, and he had hated it, and he had resented his parents deeply for making him go there. "I was only a boy," he'd groused to Genia, "and I should have got to stay a boy until I was ready to become a man. They forced the sprout to grow and that's not natural." She recalled the anger in his eyes as he spoke of it. "Turn a boy into a man too soon, turn him out into the company only of other males, and you'll make him disciplined and hard, and ruin him for living with women." His smile had been wry and bitter. "You could ask Lillian, if I hadn't sent her to an early grave."

"Stanley!" she objected. "It's not your fault she died!"

"Yes, it is," he'd argued stubbornly. "If I'd been a better husband, she wouldn't have left me, and then she wouldn't have remarried, and then she wouldn't have fallen in love with sailing, and then she wouldn't have gone out in that damn boat of hers alone, and then it wouldn't have capsized, and she wouldn't have drowned out there." He looked determined to hold on to self-recrimination. "If I'd been a better man."

"It's not your fault," she had repeated firmly.

Genia resolved to discourage Donna from sending the boy off to military school. It made her feel better, to think of doing something positive for Jason, in Stanley's honor.

While undressing for bed, Genia discovered that her grandmother's diamond and pearl brooch had fallen off her blouse, exposing the bloody spot. She wasn't particularly worried about the brooch at first, because she thought it had to be either in the house or in her car.

Exhausted though she was, she felt she ought to look for it now.

It was large and should be easy to spot.

But after going downstairs and carefully checking every room, she found it wasn't so easy after all. Despite the rain, she even went back out to check her car. Front seat, backseat, in between, under the seats and even on the floor of the garage—no brooch.

Suddenly she was too weary to search for it any longer.

"It's fallen under a cushion," she said to herself. "I'll see it better in daylight."

Her futile search for the brooch left her feeling bereft and discouraged, however. A brooch, even one of diamond and pearls, was a small thing to lose compared to the life of a human being. But it had been her grandmother's and had great sentimental value.

What would Grandmother Andrews have said tonight?

Genia put imaginary words in her grandmother's mouth: "*A person must always be prepared to say good-bye.*" To things, or to people. And the older you got, the more ready you'd better be.

As she slowly climbed the stairs to her bedroom again, a terrible thought crept in: Had Stanley died instantly? Or had he lain helplessly on the beach, hoping vainly that somebody might come along to help him? And when they didn't, did he realize he was going to die? She felt very sad to think of him dying alone and aware of what was happening to him, as the rain pelted down on his face.

6

REGRETS ONLY

Genia slept uneasily that night, waking up several times. Each awakening was, at first, a relief and an escape from bad dreams—until she remembered what had happened to Stanley. Finally she opened her eyes and saw a little light seeping in between the edge of the curtains and the windowsill. It was the quiet that had awakened her this time, she realized: the rain had finally stopped. Looking at the bedclothes, she saw that she had twisted her sheets into braids of damp cotton percale.

"I give up."

Genia slipped out of bed and into her robe and took her worries to the kitchen table until there was enough daylight to allow her to act on them.

She made a cup of tea and waited for the sun to rise.

At six o'clock, as pale streaks of sunlight fell across the kitchen floor, she rose and dressed in waterproof boots, slacks, and a sweater, and carried the weight of her sadness into the day. She didn't know what she would find or see, but gut instinct propelled her out of the house and into movement, toward the scene of Stanley's death. She told herself that she needed to see where it had happened, to convince herself that he was really gone.

The morning air was cool and moist against Genia's skin. In her boots, she didn't have to avoid the puddles.

The adjoining properties meandered in oddly shaped ways, creating a longer walking route than one would have expected from looking at a map. There were two ways to go, one along the dirt path that bordered the ocean, and the other along a paved road that curved through the cul-de-sac, and by which her guests had come and gone last night. The only way to get from one route to the other was to break through the woods or to climb the steep hill from the beach. She took the ocean path, which would have been Stanley's way.

Genia entered the coolness of the woods, where droplets fell like crystals from the leaves of the trees, and the path was muddy. *Difficult to navigate on a motorbike,* she thought.

Did he die before the rain began, or after?

It was a bumpy route, rutted with pine tree branches and tangled roots of ancient oaks that lifted the earth in spots as if underground gnomes had hunched their backs. Stanley had driven his motorbike so often along here that it should have been second nature to him to avoid the worst spots with neat little twists of his handlebars, controlling his speed and direction. To hear him tell it, he was agile as a motorcross rider. It had made her smile to hear his boasts. Genia walked the trail frequently herself, and only today did the tapestry at her feet take on a sinister feel. She could easily imagine a motorbike thrown off balance, tumbling down the rocky incline toward the ocean. They were lucky the tide hadn't swept his body out to sea.

Stanley was always so careful on that bike, or claimed to be.

In all the time he'd owned that bike, *not once,* he'd boasted, had he had an accident. It had a battered appearance, but that was only because he had tended to forget to prop its kick-stand up well enough, so that it was constantly falling over and banging into things.

What was different last night? she wondered.

Was it just the weather? Had that made all the difference? Or was he preoccupied, not paying attention to where he was going, taking his skill ill-advisedly for granted? Or was he ill? Was he in a hurry, because he was late?

She hoped it wasn't that.

From what Kevin said, it happened along here. . . .

She had walked several hundred yards along the path by now. At her feet she saw a maze of footprints and trampled signs of last night's fatal accident and the recovery of the body. The police had marked the spot with plastic strips left tied to trees, and the ends of the strips now flapped lightly in the breeze. She was glad she'd put a sweater on. The air still felt unseasonably cold, and the humidity made it feel even cooler. Branches from small trees and bushes looked snapped off, smashed into the mud by large feet. The interweave of urgent footprints crisscrossed the path and led down the rocky incline to the little beach where she was accustomed to go swimming, and where it was so pebbly she always wore rubber swimming shoes to protect her feet.

Because of the yellow plastic police tape, she had to push her way into the woods and work her way around the perimeter of the scene they had marked off. "You'd think it was a crime scene," she remarked to herself, "instead of the scene of an accident." On the far side of the police barrier, she came back around again to the path, and stood at the edge of it, staring down.

The beach was postcard-scenic, with large boulders.

His fall must have ended at the boulders.

She half expected to see his old red motorbike, but it wasn't there.

The police must have carted it off, too, she thought.

Genia stared at the footprints inside the plastic barrier, footprints that were pressed firmly into the muddy terrain. Some stood out clearly, because nobody else had stepped over them. There was one distinctive grooved tread which went in both directions along the path, although the ones heading back to her house were pressed in at the toes, as if that person had been running. *Kevin's*, she thought those might be, made when he hurried to announce the news.

She looked down at the beach again, where the tide was coming in, and suddenly she was awash in her own high tide of memories. *Thank you for being such an important person in my husband's life, Stanley. Thank you for becoming a good friend to me. There hadn't been enough time. Not nearly enough.*

This moment was what had pulled her here, she realized, this deep need to see for herself where it happened and to try to determine how and why. She still didn't know how, except to guess that his wheel hit a root or a rut, and she would probably never know why.

God, grant me the serenity, she began to pray, *to accept what I cannot change. . . .*

After a few moments there, she walked on toward Stanley's house. When the muddy mix of footprints petered out, she found she was following one set alone and they went back and forth at least once.

Jason's, she surmised, made when she had sent him— twice—to search.

The second time she had told him to drive over, but it looked as if he had come down this way again, probably just double-checking. *And he had come upon his father, down by Stanley's body on the beach. What a terrible shock for the boy!*

Around a final bend the woods fell back, and she spotted Stanley's familiar property in the distance. She quickened her pace and slipped into the clearing. The property looked especially imposing this morning, she thought, and then realized that she had never before seen it this early in the day. It was the light rising over it that seemed to magnify and illuminate it. What a sight it must have looked to sailors coming over the horizon in the previous century!

She felt lonely, being here without Stanley.

If there was a heaven, she hoped he was already in it, reunited with Lillian, telling St. Peter how to run things and riding his celestial motorbike from cloud to cloud. He had probably already started a committee or two. No. Genia had to smile. Not a committee. Toward the end of his life, they became Stanley's idea of hell. A crow cut into her fantasy with a raucous, scolding cry, seeming to say this was his property now and would be until Stanley's daughter, Nikki, arrived to take over with her husband, Randy. Oh, how Stanley hated the notion of his son-in-law living in this house!

A large stone garage was close to the pathway, its two stories housing vehicles below and a caretaker's apartment above. That apartment should be empty, Genia knew; Stanley had planned to terminate Edward Hennessey's employment yesterday. "And not a day too soon," she had retorted when he told her that. Stanley had been generous to give Hennessey a chance; unfortunately the groundskeeper had proved himself unlikable and unreliable in record time. A little guiltily Genia recalled her own concern last night that Ed Hennessey might have retaliated against Stanley when the old man fired him.

The garage sat at the edge of a circular drive that swung around past Stanley's gardens and his home. Behind the house on the ocean side there were more gardens and terraces. A little farther to the south, and separated from the house by a fish pond, was his beloved greenhouse, where her own nephew had been hired to work for the summer.

Genia wandered down the brick path that wound around the house and back toward the ocean view. She walked over to a knee-high stone wall that stood between her and a steep drop to the private pier below. At the moment there was one small motorboat tied to the pier, and she wondered whose it was. Stanley hadn't believed in spending money on boats, which of course had made it all the more painfully ironic when Lillian died on one—

"This is private property."

She jumped at the sound of a harsh voice behind her.

Turning around, she found that Stanley's fired caretaker was standing only a few feet away from her, with a shotgun held loosely under his left arm and a cigarette in his other hand. Although he had the gun pointed to the ground, she felt unnerved by the sight of it and of him.

"What are you doing here?" he demanded of her.

"I could ask you the same thing, Ed Hennessey."

She spoke sharply, unwilling to allow him to intimidate her. "You know perfectly well that I'm a friend of Mr. Parker's," she added for good measure. "He would be glad for me to be here."

He was a wiry, rumpled figure, a man she didn't know well, or care to, but about whose work habits she had heard plenty of complaints. He'd been in and out of prison several times. Stanley had frequently hired ex-convicts, considering

THE SECRET INGREDIENT MURDERS 77

it to be a civic duty in his small state to try to turn its trou-
blesome citizens into better ones. Some of his attempts had
been more successful than others; this one had been doomed.

"What do you mean?" he challenged her.

"Mr. Parker told me he was going to fire you yesterday."

"Was-going-to ain't the same as did." A sly look came
over his face, and it was only the stone wall behind her that
kept Genia from stepping back a pace. "Anyway, that's what
you say."

"That's what he told me, Eddie."

"Yeah, well, let's see it in writing."

"Do you think you can just keep on living here?"

It would be no wonder if he tried; the garage apartment
must be comfortable. And since he never worked hard anyway, this was a cushy place to try to hang on.

"It's my job." He smirked at her and took a drag on his
cigarette. "Gotta do it."

"Mr. Parker's family will have something to say about
that."

"What family?" He said it in a scoffing tone, as if he knew
the only person he had to deal with was Nikki, Stanley's
thirty-four-year-old daughter, who was hardly an intimidat-
ing force. Her exasperated father had often described Nikki
as a pushover for any man with a sad story. "They got to
have somebody staying on to look after this place now the
old man's gone. Who knows more about looking after it
than me?"

After swallowing the lump in her throat, Genia said,
"How do you know he's gone, Eddie?"

"I got ways to find things out."

It sounded like braggadocio, but Genia assumed a more
pedestrian explanation: The police must have told him of his
employer's death.

"You'd better pack up your things and leave, Eddie."

He shifted the shotgun under his arm, so that the nose of it pointed ever so slightly higher, toward her. "I think you're the one who'd better leave." He said it mockingly, aping her words and her tone.

Genia suddenly sensed Stanley whispering in her ear: *"Don't mess with this man. Get out of here now."* She realized that was excellent advice. Eddie was an ex-convict, he was a man with something valuable to lose, and—overriding everything else—he was the one with the gun.

Genia swallowed her pride, put her hands into the pockets of her sweater, and began to walk with as much dignity as she could muster back in the direction by which she had come.

Behind her she heard a chuckle, and although it sounded forced, she knew he was making fun of her. She didn't care about that; she only cared about getting back onto the path and away from him, so that his shotgun was no longer turned toward her back. Should she take the more public road, instead? That was a good idea, she decided, and she altered her direction a bit. She didn't really fear that Eddie was going to shoot her; she sensed that he merely wanted to flex his temporary power and force her off "his" property. But she didn't want to take the chance of underestimating his bad intentions.

Soon enough, either Nikki or her attorneys would fix his wagon, as Genia's father used to say about people with broken attitudes. She made up her mind to call Nikki Parker Dixon the minute she got back home. The Dixons needed to know that a man Nikki's father had intended to fire was now alone on their property, probably with access to house keys.

Her alteration in course took her around the front of the

garage. As soon as it stood between her and the man at her back, she felt her muscles relax a little. Suddenly, she felt a little silly for having let him scare her like that. Surely, there was nothing to be afraid of here.

Off to her right, and hidden a bit by trees, was the greenhouse where Stanley had put Jason to work all summer. She glanced through the leaves hoping for a glimpse of it, and when she did she heard a distinct rattling noise coming from that direction. After first making sure that Eddie wasn't following her, Genia moved a branch aside to try to see what was making the noise. It didn't sound as if it was coming from anything natural. She couldn't see what it was, but it continued in an on-again, off-again way, so she stepped quietly among the trees to go see for herself. A few hidden yards later, she came up to the backdoor of the greenhouse, and there she discovered the source of the rattling.

It was Kevin Eden, trying the doorknob of the greenhouse.

"Kevin?"

Genia kept her voice down, not wanting to startle him, not wanting to be overheard by Ed Hennessey. But Janie and Jason's dad spun around at the sound of her voice anyway, looking as guilty as if he'd just murdered somebody.

"Genia! What are you doing here? I'm looking for... for Jason. But it's..." He turned and looked at the greenhouse, then turned back toward her. "... locked."

"Are you sure he'll come here today, Kevin?"

"Oh. Well, I don't know, I just need to... find him."

"Have you tried his mother's house?"

"No. I didn't have any way to get into town."

"Oh, that's right. Well, Jason's probably still in bed anyway."

"Sure. You're right. I don't know why I thought he'd be here."

"I hope you slept all right at your friend's house?" When he nodded, she pointed down toward the ocean. "Is that your boat down at the pier, Kevin?"

"My boat? Oh, yeah. That's where I left it last night."

"I thought you landed on the beach where Stanley—"

"No, I docked it here."

"I could have sworn you said—well, never mind, I just misunderstood."

"Yeah, you must have, 'cause my boat was here all this time."

He shifted his weight and flashed an awkward grin at her. Her former nephew-in-law was still wearing the loud Hawaiian shirt, and now Genia could see that some of the splotches of color really were paint. Oil paint, she thought, or surely it would have run in the rain.

"Nice to see you this morning, Genia," he said, "but I guess I'd better be getting back to the island."

"Without seeing Jason?"

"Oh, I'll see him later, I expect."

"I'd be happy to give you a ride to Donna's."

"No, no, you don't have to do that."

"Have you had breakfast...?"

Already he was moving away from her, in the direction of the hill that led down to the sea. Genia raised her hand in a farewell wave, feeling confused by their odd exchange. She hadn't misunderstood him the night before, she felt positive: Kevin had said in her kitchen that he pulled his boat up onto the same beach where he found Stanley's body. Why would he change that story now? And why in the world would he come looking for Jason here, at seven o'clock in the morning on the first day after Stanley's death?

Genia cupped her hands at a pane of glass in the green-house and tried to peer in. The glass was frosted over with age, making it difficult to see much more than vague rows of greenery and splotches of color. Whatever Kevin Eden was after here, surely it couldn't have been his son, and if it was, why meet him here, at this time? The only reason that Genia could think of was the possibility that Kevin wanted to see Jason where he wouldn't run into Donna, too.

"I'm making too much out of nothing," she chided her-self.

When she turned to go, she nearly gasped out loud: Ed Hennessey stood not ten yards away, leaning against a corner of the garage, smoking a cigarette and staring at her.

She waited for a moment, to see what he would say.

When he only stood there, but didn't speak, she quickly left. This time she went directly toward the public road and walked home along the gravel shoulder in full view of every passing car. She felt resentful that Eddie had prevented her from satisfying her need to spend some time alone at the Castle with her memories of Stanley. She didn't like being forced to leave somewhere she had a right to be, or of being made to feel so anxious that her heart still hadn't quite set-tled back down to its regular beat. All she had wanted to do this morning was commune with her sadness about Stanley, and instead she felt all worked up. She trudged on unhappily until she pulled up in surprise at the entrance to her own rented property.

What's a car doing parked in my driveway?

It was Donna's, she realized. Her family was up early today!

The minute her front doorway came into view, she saw Donna standing there, and as soon as her niece saw her she came running, yelling, "Aunt Genia! Aunt Genia!"

Genia called out to her, hurrying to meet her halfway.

"What is it, Donna? Is something wrong with the children?"

"No, no, it's about Stanley, Aunt Genia! He didn't just fall off his motorbike! You'll never believe this, it's just awful! The police are saying that Stanley was murdered!"

7

MISSING INGREDIENTS

Genia put an arm around her niece's shoulders as they walked together up the stairs that led to the deck in back of the house.

Donna talked fast, explaining her terrible news.

"They say there were big bits of wood in the wound on Stanley's head, and they think somebody clobbered him with a tree branch, or a baseball bat, or something awful like that."

She paused, breathlessly, to negotiate the steps.

Genia grabbed the railing because her own knees had gone weak. *Stanley, murdered?* It was horrible to imagine.

Aunt and niece sat down side by side on a wicker couch that faced out to sea, and held hands. A temporary clearing in the weather, which Harrison Wright had accurately predicted for this morning, had come. At dinner the night before, he had forecast sunny skies for this day and the next, but had warned them there was "something major" building hundreds of miles offshore.

Genia felt herself rebelling against the implications of Donna's news. She didn't want it to be true, not for Stanley's sake, or for their own. If it was true, then the murderer might be somebody they knew. Or it might be a homicidal stranger. Both were terrifying possibilities.

"Just down the path!" Donna said, looking frightened.

"Who in the world . . . ?" Genia murmured in dismay.

"If they know, they're not saying."

"Do you think they have a suspect?"

"I don't know, but I don't think so."

"Have they found the murder weapon, Donna?"

Her niece stared at her. "Aunt Genia! You sound so cool, as if you've been through this a hundred times before."

In reply, she merely patted Donna's hand, but she thought, *Not a hundred times, but enough to know.* Aloud, she said, "I guess it's all the mysteries I've read and movies I've seen."

"Well, I don't know about a murder weapon, either."

"How did you learn this, Donna?"

"From Kevin. He dropped by real early this morning, if you can believe that, for coffee and to tell me the news."

"Kevin?" Genia stared at her, uncomprehending.

"Yeah, is something wrong with that? I thought you'd be pleased that he would think to tell me first. Maybe there's some hope for him, after all. He wanted to wake up Jason and tell him, too, but I didn't see any sense in that, not after last night. I wouldn't let him go upstairs. I said to him, 'Jason feels bad enough, you don't have to make him feel worse by waking him up to tell him that Stanley was murdered.'"

Genia was relieved to hear that Donna had been sensitive to her son's feelings. "Dearest, I am glad that Kevin thought of you. I'm just in shock from this news about Stanley. Don't mind me if I don't make much sense for a little while. But how did Kevin hear about it?"

Donna shrugged. "I don't know."

"Did Kevin know any other details?"

"I don't think so, and he didn't stay long. He didn't like it very well when I wouldn't let him go upstairs, and he left right after that. I guess he went on back to the island."

But Genia knew that Kevin hadn't gone right back to his island. He had gone, instead, to Parker's Castle, to try to get into the greenhouse, supposedly to talk to Jason. But Jason, according to what Donna said, was back home in bed, and Kevin knew that. There must be a good explanation, she thought, but at the moment, Kevin's words and actions didn't make any sense to her. And he hadn't even told her about this awful news!

"I think you ought to move back in with us, Aunt Genia," Donna said.

Genia was startled out of her own thoughts. "What?"

"Look, Stanley got killed right on this property, or close to it. There could be some crazy person out there in the woods right now." Donna shivered, and looked ready to bolt off the deck and drag her aunt with her. "I won't feel safe until they find out who did it and catch him. You'd better not stay out here all by yourself."

"That's very kind of you, dear, but I think I'll be fine."

"Don't be stubborn, Aunt Genia."

Genia had to laugh. "Who, me? I guess I can be. But I don't think I'm being obstinate, Donna. I just want to wait and hear more about it before I do anything as dramatic as that. I loved staying with you, but it would be quite a bit of trouble to get all packed up again, and it wouldn't be easy for you, either. I promise you, I won't be foolish. If the police say I'm not safe here, I'll be over with my suitcase for dinner."

"Well, all right, if you mean it."

"I do. Donna, why would anybody want to kill Stanley?"

To her surprise, her niece laughed bitterly in response. "Who *wouldn't* want to kill Stanley?"

Over coffee and muffins, Donna told Genia what she meant.

"He made enemies right and left, Aunt Genia. I know you thought he was great, and I guess he was, mostly, but he was pretty domineering, you have to admit. He tried to run everything and everybody. If you were doing something that Stanley didn't like, he told you to stop, and if you weren't doing something he thought you ought to do, he told you to do it. Not everybody takes that kind of thing as well as I do."

Genia was a bit amused to see her niece look so smug.

"I mean, I could take Stanley, or leave him. But he riled up a lot of people, and there was almost always somebody who hated his guts for some reason or other. Just look at the people who were here in this very house last night, Aunt Genia! Lindsay Wright is mad at Stanley for pushing the arts festival, and Harrison automatically hates anybody that Lindsay doesn't like. And Celeste just blew steam out her ears if anybody mentioned his name, and poor Larry is so devoted to Celeste that he'd probably kill anybody who crossed her, and David Graham can't have been too fond of him, because how many second husbands like their wife's first husbands, and . . ."

She had been ticking guests off on her fingers.

"And that was just last night at one dinner party. Multiply that by everybody in town, at one time or another, and that'll give you some idea of who'd want to murder Stanley Parker. Oh! And I haven't even mentioned his son-in-law, who Stanley treated like a muddy doormat, or his daughter, who will inherit all that money."

Genia felt a little overwhelmed by the litany.

"And yet he could be so generous," she protested.

"Yeah," Donna admitted. "I'll have to give him that, but there were always strings, if you know what I mean."

Unfortunately, her aunt knew exactly what she meant. Even in her short acquaintance with Stanley Parker, she had discovered that no good deed of his went unrewarded. He had done a wonderful thing for her by getting her to write a cookbook, but she had sensed from the beginning that she was being manipulated to please him. Not that she'd minded, but still, Donna was right: When Stanley gave, he took. His own best interests were never far from his mind. Even when it came to giving employment to ex-convicts, it meant cheap labor for him. At least, it did unless the ex-con was somebody named Ed Hennessey. But now somebody had taken everything away from Stanley. Was it somebody from whom he had asked too much?

"This is going to upset Jason," Genia warned Donna.

"What doesn't?" his mother asked, and sighed.

And suddenly Genia found herself wondering: *What did Stanley ask of Jason, in return for the favor of employment at the greenhouse?*

Police detectives arrived while Donna Eden was still at Genia's house. They asked questions from every apparent angle, but neither woman was able to provide them with much information, although the police paid close attention when Genia told them about her run-in with Ed Hennessey that morning. Other than that, no, Donna hadn't seen anybody unfamiliar on the road between the houses last night. No, they hadn't seen or heard anything unusual until Kevin Eden burst in with his news of Stanley's death. And neither woman had any specific reason to think that someone might have wanted to kill the old man.

"He made enemies," Donna conceded, though her tone was nowhere near as dramatic as it had been only a little while earlier with her aunt. "But not enemies like *that*." When pressed to say who those harmless enemies might be, she named everybody from the groundskeeper to the mayor, though she did it with every show of reluctance. After the detectives took their courteous leave—having jotted down copious notes—Donna turned to her aunt with a guilty expression, and said, "Gee, I hope I haven't gotten anybody in trouble."

After Donna left Genia tried to reach Stanley's daughter to offer her sympathy and to warn Nikki about the continued presence of Ed Hennessey on her father's property.

Randy Dixon answered on the first ring.

Stanley's daughter and her husband lived in Wickford, only about fifteen miles away, just far enough to separate Nikki's husband from his father-in-law. South County, Rhode Island, was a collection of several towns, closely linked, but individual in their own ways, too.

"Sorry, Mrs. Potter. Nikki just left for her dad's house to start making funeral arrangements. I'll be headed that way myself soon. We're going to stay there for a while, maybe even go ahead and sell this place, and move in there."

His tone, though friendly enough, was flat and matter-of-fact. Both Randy and Nikki were in their early thirties, married six years, with no offspring so far. Randy was a carpenter by trade, dependent on local builders for work, which meant he labored hard for three seasons, but not much at all over Rhode Island's long winters. As for Nikki, she had never held a "real job," according to her father, and now she wouldn't ever have to. The trust fund her mother had set up for her already supported her and her husband. Now with the big inheritance from her father, they were set for life. Genia thought it spoke well of Randy Dixon that he had continued to take carpentry jobs even when he didn't have to, after his mother-in-law died. Stanley had not agreed with her: "He does it to impress me," the old man had scoffed. "He's afraid if he acts like the lazy bum he really is, I'll fix my will so he can't get to any of the money I'm leaving Nikki."

"Would you do that, Stanley?" Genia had asked him.

"You bet I would. I could write it so she doesn't get a dime as long as she's still married to him."

"You wouldn't really do that," she had insisted.

"I might. Damn good-for-nothing."

It wouldn't have changed anything, in Genia's opinion, unless Nikki was a good deal greedier than she seemed. Stanley could have cut her off entirely, and she would still have had the trust fund from Lillian, and when David Graham died, Nikki would inherit the remainder of her mom's estate, too. For now, David had only the use of the income for the rest of his life; the principal would always belong to Nikki.

Now Genia asked the object of Stanley's scorn: "Do you think the police will release her father's body this soon, Randy?"

"Not for a while, I guess, but Nikki doesn't want to wait for that, she wants to hold a memorial service this week. She says she'd rather have just the family for the cremation, anyway."

"I can understand why she might feel that way." Genia well knew that grief didn't wait for clearance from the police. "I'm sure that people here in Devon will be needing to express their admiration for her father in some kind of official way. I think a memorial service sounds just right, Randy."

"Some of it might not be admiration," he said in a wry tone.

"Well, nobody's a saint," she replied evenly.

"My father-in-law less than most," he said.

She could hardly blame the young man for sounding so bitter, given how Stanley had treated him. As far as Genia knew, Randy had never been anything but polite to his father-in-law, but mere courtesy hadn't satisfied Stanley. The problem with Randy Dixon was simply that he wasn't the son-in-law Stanley Parker wanted for his daughter. "Fathers don't get to pick their daughters' husbands anymore, Stanley," Genia had once pointed out to him. To which his tart reply had been, "It's a damned shame we don't."

Before getting off the phone she told his son-in-law, "I need to tell you Stanley was planning to fire his handyman yesterday, Randy. But I went to the Castle this morning, and Hennessey was still there, and he was trying to pretend that he hadn't been fired. He had a shotgun, and he made me leave the property. He acted as if he owned the place. You may have to ask the police to escort Mr. Hennessey off the grounds."

"He forced you to leave at gunpoint?"

Randy Dixon sounded astonished, appalled.

"No, no, he was just carrying the thing around with him."

"Oh, I get it." His tone flattened out again. "I'll let Nikki handle this, but thanks, Mrs. Potter." He didn't sound particularly concerned; she hoped he would remember to inform his wife.

"The police were just here at my house, Randy, to ask my niece and me if we had noticed anything suspicious last night," she told him, and then she emphasized, "I told them the only suspicious behavior I've seen was the way Ed Hennessey behaved toward me this morning."

"Like I say, I'll pass that along to Nikki."

She had to be satisfied with that, though in truth, she wasn't.

Her phone conversation with Randy Dixon was yet another reminder that not everybody shared her high opinion of Stanley Parker. Even if she had never had the chance to get to know him well, she still would have loved him for the sake of his kindnesses to her late husband when Lew was a boy, such as hiring him for summer work and lending him money for college. But as Donna and now Randy had made clear, not everyone in Rhode Island felt as positive about the old man; she needed to remember not to idealize her friend or to assume that other people felt as she did about him.

The information Randy had passed along told Genia exactly what she might do to help the young couple. If Nikki and Randy were staying at the Castle, they would need food, and they wouldn't have the time or energy to shop or cook.

The thought of being able to help them eased her feeling of helplessness in the face of tragedy. People would be paying condolence calls as soon as word got out that Stanley's daughter was in Devon. A table needed to be set, drinks put out, and Nikki didn't have any mom, or aunts, or cousins to help her do that. She would need coffee, desserts, bread and cheese, pies and cakes, various things for her guests to nibble on. Not to mention actual meals for Randy and Nikki and for any out of towners who might come to stay with them. Of course, the women of the town would leap in to assist; it wasn't as if Genia, a newcomer, should feel a compulsion to take charge. Nevertheless, there were many things she could do to help.

She hurried off to shower and change clothes, thinking, with bittersweet pleasure, *What good things would you like me to fix for your friends and relatives to eat, Stanley?*

Before Genia could step into the shower, the phone rang.

"Mrs. Potter?" asked a male voice on the other end. "Ma'am, I'm Ted Massey, one of the police officers who was just out to see you."

"Oh, yes, Officer Massey, what can I do for you?"

"Well, you can tell me again what time—to the best of your knowledge—each of your guests arrived at your house last night. I'm sorry to have to ask you to go through this again, but we need to double-check these times."

Genia's heart began a rapid pounding as she took in the implications of the question, even as she began to try to answer it. "All right. Well, I think I can tell you almost exactly, because I had been watching the clock—because of Stanley." She repeated for him—within a few minutes of possible error, she believed—when and in what order David Graham, Harrison and Lindsay Wright, Celeste Hutchinson, and Larry Averill had come knocking at her door.

"Weren't there other people at your house last night, too?"

Was it her imagination, or did the way he said that make it sound as if he thought she had "forgotten" some names on purpose?

"Oh, well, my niece, Donna Eden, I forget to think of her as a guest. And..." Reluctantly, Genia repeated how her grandniece and -nephew had also been on the premises, helping her out with the dinner party. Patiently, the police officer led her again through her memories of the number of times, and the length of those times, that the teenagers had come and gone from the house. And then he made her guess again at the time at which their father had flung open the French doors so dramatically.

"I suppose you have to ask these questions," she said tentatively, trying to keep resentment and worry out of her voice.

"I'm afraid I do, Mrs. Potter, this being a murder and all."

"Do you know exactly what time Stanley . . . was killed?"

"We're working on that now, ma'am. It might help if you could tell me the last time you saw or talked to Mr. Parker."

This was a new question, and she tried to answer it accurately.

"About two hours before the party," she informed him, and she also told him about calling the Castle and getting the answering machine. "Is there anything else I can tell you?"

"Not at this time," he said formally.

He was the first to hang up. Genia felt terribly unhappy as she clicked the receiver down upon its base again. This house and Parker's Castle lay on a cul-de-sac, with only one way in and the same way out. There were only five other houses in the neighborhood, and at least two of them were currently empty, their owners off on summer vacations. Because of the timing and the location, it seemed possible to Genia—as surely it must also look to the Devon police—that whoever killed Stanley might be somebody who came into the cul-de-sac around the time of her dinner party.

That put her guests under a deep shadow of suspicion.

The memory of a sharp pine needle came unbidden to her. She hadn't noticed it until after she had greeted all of them. All of them had hugged her, or handed her objects which she had clasped to her breast. From which one of them had she picked up that pine needle, and had it come from the woods where Stanley died?

She was horror-stricken to think that she might have

cordially greeted his killer at her front door almost immediately after the terrible deed. She might have embraced that
person, smiled at him or her, welcomed him, fed her, entertained him.

"No!" For the time being she would cling to the hope
that no killer had dined at her table. She would pay attention
to evidence of her guests' innocence, as well as of their guilt.
"It could have come from anywhere, it could have blown in
with the rain." But pine needles didn't ordinarily just blow in
with the rain and attach themselves to one's white silk blouse.

Genia sank down into a nearby chair, and hung her head.

"Oh, Stanley," she whispered. "Who hated you so much?"

8

Food for Thought

Jason fumbled with the lock on the greenhouse door. The key slipped between his fingers as if he'd greased his hands. It was only perspiration, but even when the door swung open, he could hardly get a good grip on the knob.

He was scared and in a hurry.

He had to get in now, as his dad had instructed him, before the cops came here, before his mom knew he was gone.

It was either now, or it might be never.

Once he was in, brilliant color greeted him: the rich purple and lavender of orchids, the sharp reds and blues of cardinal flowers, the sunny yellows and orange of marigolds, and all other manner of bloom and hue. Row after row of beauty. God, he loved this place.

Would he ever get to come back here again?

He was so scared he felt as if he were moving in slow motion. Once, the first time he had ever ridden a really high roller coaster, he'd felt like this when he was standing in line waiting his turn to get on. It was as if he got lethargic all of a sudden, the way those science shows said that a predator's prey did when it got grabbed. Feeling more like a sleepwalker instead of a focused man with a mission, Jason began to move between the neatly planted tables of plants, herbs, vegetables. Home. That's what this place felt like, more than his real home did, even more than the island did. It was how Mr. Parker had encouraged him to feel about this place.

Mr. Parker...

No, he commanded himself, don't start thinking. *Just do what you came to do, Eden. Do it, and get out, like Dad said.* But he couldn't stand it: There was morning watering to do, and nobody to do it if he didn't. Ed Hennessey would never think of it or care enough to do the job. Besides the daily watering, there were dead leaves to pick off, and stuff that needed thinning and harvesting, like the tomatoes in the outside garden where the sun shone all day long on good days. He knew his mom and his Aunt Genia would like it if he took them some fresh tomatoes.

Jason turned on a hose in the center of the room and picked up a watering wand, staring at it for an instant as if it were something strange that he'd never seen before. Then he walked up and down the raised rows, spraying bedded plants with one hand and with the other plucking off dead leaves and spindly stems.

"Why don't you get one of those automatic watering gizmos?"

He'd asked the old man that question, early on, and gotten the sharp, offended retort he'd deserved.

"The world's altogether too automatic, already! Automatic this, automatic that," the old man had fumed, "and nobody ever has to do things personally the way they ought to be done. You'll never get to know your plants if you let some machine take care of them for you. These people who let machines milk their cows! Or cram chickens all together in a chicken concentration camp! No wonder things don't look or taste as good as they used to. We don't do it that way here.

You water each plant, you take a close look, you look for bugs, you look for wilt, you look to see if it's a happy damn plant, you get acquainted with every one of them. Then maybe you'll be a gardener, but not before."

Over time, doing it that way, Jason had come to know the plants in the spacious greenhouse and the garden as individuals with distinct needs, appearances, and even personalities. And he reacted to them like that. Not that he would ever in a million years admit this, but he liked to spend time with the pansies, for instance, who were sophisticated and elegant, and he didn't like the petunias, who were brassy and thought entirely too much of themselves. He enjoyed the company of the sugar snap peas—and liked to eat them raw with ranch dip—but didn't much care for any of the beans, who seemed like a lot of trouble for not much taste, unless you added a lot of stuff for flavor. Beets were interesting, but they smelled like dirt, and who could eat that? Garlic was cool as hell; it amazed him, the way it looked like a big fat papery flower with bulbs for petals. If it were *his* nursery, he knew exactly what he'd grow, which flowers, which fruits and vegetables.

Mist soon hung in the trapped space, until he felt he was in a fog that covered him and made him invisible. It was only him and the plants now, just the way he liked it, although it had been nice when Mr. Parker worked with him. Droplets of water fell onto his hair, his face, his clothes. It felt good, proof that he was alive and not dead the way he felt inside.

Mr. Parker. Murdered.

His dad had told him that, warned him in a phone call that had shot him out of bed, into his clothes, and then into his car to come here.

"I know what you've been doing out there, Jason," his dad had said, making his heart jump into his throat. "I tried to get in there this morning and destroy the evidence of it, but I couldn't get in. You've got to do it. Get out there now. I ran into a cop I know when I went to breakfast at the diner this morning, and he told me they wouldn't be searching Stanley's place until late this morning, so you've got a little time. Don't get caught, son. Be careful. If somebody shows up and asks you what you're doing there, tell them you're just there to water the plants. And if that doesn't work, blame me. You got that? You tell them I sent you out there to do your job."

And then his dad had said, "How could you be so—"

Stupid. That was the word that had hung in the air like the mist that now hung in the greenhouse. His dad hadn't said it, wasn't the kind of dad who ever would say something like that, but he'd come close this time. *"How could you be so stupid, Jason?"*

He had wanted to tell his dad the truth, but he couldn't.

So he'd just muttered "Okay," and hurried to the greenhouse.

Mr. Parker, murdered...

Who would do such a thing?

He couldn't stop himself from thinking about it.

The old man had scared the bejesus out of him one day right after his hearing when he got put on diversion. Parker had come out of nowhere, charging into the local pizza joint known as "RIPPP's." Its real name, "Rhode Island and Providence Plantation Pizzeria," was based on the official name of the state. The kids all boasted that Rhode Island pizza, a thick-crusted kind without cheese, was unlike any other pizza on earth. Everybody knew that the secret to its appeal was its tangy, oily sauce. One of the kids had said that noon, "Let's go get Ripped," and so Jason was hanging out there with his sister and some of their friends, sharing a large pie and dribbling vinegar over fries, another favorite culinary habit of their state.

"Are you Jason Eden?" the old man had growled.

Janie and their friends had stared at the old man, then at Jason, and then they'd all edged away, except for his sister, who never backed down when he needed her for anything. But his friends had cringed back until it was just him, and Janie, and the old man at the table.

Parker had looked a little crazy, with thin hair that shot out in all directions like he was some kind of Einstein, and eyebrows that looked like caterpillars stuck on his forehead. He may not have known for sure who Jason was, but Jason knew who he was. Everybody did. Old Man Parker. From the Castle. He practically ran Devon, even though he was older than God. Jason's own dad lived on some of Parker's land, one of the islands. Jason hadn't even been able to imagine owning your own island, but this old guy did, and more than one of them, too.

For a moment, they'd sized each other up.

Jason had felt the silence in the restaurant and he'd known what everybody else was thinking: *Eden must be in trouble again. What did he do this time? Steal something from Old Man Parker? Is it drugs? Pot again? Maybe coke. Who knows what either of those twins will do?*

In the greenhouse, Jason felt like crying.

Yeah, who knew? Who knew the old coot would become his best friend, even better than his sister. It was because of Aunt Genia that Parker had come after him. Aunt Genia had talked to the old man about Jason's trouble with the cops, about the marijuana, because Parker knew about that, too.

Oh, yeah, he knew *all* about *that.*

Great-aunt Genia also told Mr. Parker about how Jason had worked on her ranch two summers ago, and she must have said he did an okay job down there, or else why would the old man have hired him? Jason thought that working on the ranch was the best thing he had ever done, until this summer when he got introduced to growing plants instead of cows.

So what did the old man do that first day but haul Jason out of the pizza place—under the hostile stare of his twin sister—and feed him a bowl of the best chili Jason had ever tasted. "Your aunt's recipe," the old man had told him. "Twenty-seven damn ingredients, believe it or not." And then he had offered Jason humongous bucks for daily help in the greenhouse and outside gardens. And all he had to do was tend the plants and care for the herb garden, and Mr. Parker would show him how. Well, there were a few more delicate details about the job that would have to be explained, the old man said that day. And then Jason would have to decide...

Midway through the watering, Jason half smiled at the way Mr. Parker had presented his real proposition: completely businesslike, in that great deep voice of his that Jason had grown to find as comforting as a big warm blanket on a cold New England night. Hell, Jason had thought that day, he'd be rich by the end of the summer with pay like that, plus Aunt Genia's hefty checks for helping her out when he wasn't at the Castle. So he'd signed up, "lock, stock, and a barrel of water," as Mr. Parker had called it. He'd done what the old man asked, *everything* he'd asked, even kept the old man's secret locked up inside of him.

His mom said he didn't have any loyalty in him. She said because he used drugs and got caught that meant he was disloyal to her and his dad, to their whole family, and that he didn't care about anything or anybody except himself.

She said the only welfare he cared about was his own.

But that wasn't true, and he'd already proved it, and if he had to, he'd keep on proving it, whatever the cost to himself.

He hadn't even tried to defend himself to his dad. He couldn't. He'd sworn to Old Man Parker that he'd never tell anybody, ever.

At first, he hadn't liked it when Mr. Parker came around the greenhouse and watched him work, asked questions, eased himself into his life. A job was one thing. Being subjected to the Great Inquisitor was another. But almost before he realized it had happened, he began to look forward to the company of his scary employer. The old guy was a hoot. He cussed around Jason, and didn't mind if Jason did, too, and he said hilarious, sarcastic things about grown-ups Jason had known all his life, people who hadn't necessarily been very nice to him or his sister when he got into trouble. Man, what Jason knew now about this town that he'd never ever suspected before! He could write a book.

Jason found he missed Parker's company when there was a meeting of the arts council, or the bank, or when Parker went to work on the cookbook he was doing with Aunt Genia. She was somebody Mr. Parker never said anything bad about. Of course, Jason would have had to knock his block off if he had, 'cause his aunt was the greatest, a real relief after living with his mom. Aunt Genia and Mr. Parker actually seemed to *like* kids. Incredible. Jason found he could talk to the old guy, maybe because Parker had his own pain, and he understood Jason's because of that. He never seemed to judge Jason, although he could lecture like a teacher when he got going on something. And if he thought Jason was making a stupid decision, he'd say so in no uncertain terms.

Mostly, though, he just listened, nodding that big white head of his, and accepted whatever the hell came out of Jason's mouth. Except for Aunt Genia, and except for his dad sometimes, he'd never met an adult who acted that way around kids. Sometimes the two of them—old man and boy—just sat on tall greenhouse stools in total silence. "Watch these plants grow," Parker had instructed him. "Smell 'em, taste them, listen to them. You might surprise yourself and actually learn something. And then when you've got a real feel for plants, then we'll get started on cooking. You don't want to depend on women all your life to do the things for you that a man ought to be able to enjoy for himself."

Jason had been surprised, all right, at what he'd learned.

But he had felt safe here, anyway, and accepted for whatever he was, whatever he was worth. Parker sometimes talked with him about things like college, about business. "You've got a green thumb," he'd said a lot of times. Even told Jason he could see him running "a whole damn string of greenhouses" someday. That made sense in Rhode Island where nurseries were a major industry. The dream had stuck, and they kept it between themselves, a dream hung out there to think about and stretch himself toward each day.

Jason turned off the hose and hung it up.

He wandered into the tiny supply area tucked into a corner of the greenhouse. They kept a small refrigerator there, filled with soft drinks for Jason and bottled water, wine, and beer for Mr. Parker. That's one thing the old man never let him do—drink alcohol or smoke. "Cussing won't kill you, unless you cuss out the wrong man," Parker had claimed, "but drinking and smoking will do you in."

In the refrigerator, there was always food.

Peering inside, Jason realized he hadn't eaten for a long time.

He pulled out a thick hunk of pale cheese and a loaf of Mill Hollow bread that Mr. Parker had baked just a day ago—a lifetime ago—and placed them on a high pine table where the two of them had sat to eat, and to argue about baseball.

They had a running argument about the longest game ever played in professional baseball history. It happened right there in Rhode Island, when the Pawtucket Red Sox—the Boston Red Sox's farm team—beat the Rochester Red Wings 3–2 after thirty-three innings played over three days. The game had begun on April 18, 1981, and been temporarily called at four A.M. the next morning when the score was 2–2. It didn't get finished until two months later, on July 23, on a Marty Barrett single with the bases loaded. Wade Boggs had been there, playing for the Pawsox.

Stanley Parker had watched the second half from the stands, but he was a purist who claimed that the feats of farm clubs didn't belong in the Baseball Hall of Fame in Cooperstown, N.Y. Jason had just as vehemently argued that they did, because they were also professionals, after all.

Guess I win, Jason thought disconsolately.

The old man had promised to take him to a game sometime.

He rubbed a thumb absently along the rough edge of the table which was worn from long use, and thought of the hours he'd spent here watching the old man get red in the face about the designated hitter rule, and also learning about Mr. Parker's early life as a banker, about his wife and his daughter, his devotion to the arts, his respect for the work of Jason's own father.

That had felt good, to hear the old man say that.

But the last week their conversation had turned strange.

Mr. Parker had seemed troubled, distracted, and people kept coming and going up at the Castle, always somebody new coming over for lunch, a different one every day, and always just one of them at a time. Jason had recognized all of them. Ms. Hutchinson. Mr. Graham. Randy Dixon, alone. Then Nikki on another day. Mrs. Wright, without her husband. Even the mayor. Even his own mom, and then later in the week, Jason's dad. Old Man Parker had been busy entertaining all those people, and so he hadn't come out to the greenhouse as much as he usually did. When he did come by, Jason had listened for once, instead of doing so much of the talking. The old man had said weird things then, about how people weren't always as nice as they seemed, that they could be phonies and fakes, and they could do terrible things, and nobody would know it was them.

Jason felt sure he, himself, would know.

He'd just *know* who was good, and who was bad.

Mr. Parker was one of the good ones. So was Aunt Genia.

He finished off the cheese and two thick pieces of Mr. Parker's bread, and then put the leftovers back in the refrigerator, thinking, *I'll never have any of his homemade bread again.* He grabbed the plastic container where the old man usually kept cookies and found three double-chocolate ones inside, and wolfed them down, one after the other.

Mr. Parker also made great cookies.

As he gobbled the cookies, he wandered up and down the rows, saying good-bye to the plants, while cookie crumbs fell to the floor.

He wondered what would happen to this place now.

Nobody else cared about it like him and Mr. Parker.

Well, he'd better get it over with, what he'd really come to do.

It didn't take ten minutes, but he hated every hypocritical moment of the job. *Stupid drug laws.* When he was done, he came back inside the greenhouse. He fingered a new leaf on a coleus plant, unfurling in a multitude of dark colors. In Hawaii, Mr. Parker had told him, this same plant might grow as big as a bush. He'd like to see that. They seemed kind of puny and dull here. But plants were so cool. Jason squeezed his eyes shut and tried to stop the painful sting behind his lids.

The damp air, the smells of growth and earth and young flowers folded around him. He didn't think he could stand it that the old man was gone. It was like losing a grandfather, only worse, because he'd had him for such a short time.

For the first time in his life, he'd felt needed.

"I need you, kid. To tend my plants."

That's how it all began. His job was so simple. To water the plants . . . and . . . and . . .

"Oh, and, kid, there's this other part of the job, but you'll have to think about it long and hard before you say yes. I'm probably a wicked old man to ask this, but I'm a powerful old codger, too, and if we get into trouble, I'll buy us out of it. May not be the best lesson in the world to teach a young man, but at this point, I don't have a choice."

Jason had agreed to do it. Done it willingly, proudly.

"This may be the worst mistake I ever made," the old man had said. "I hope you don't live to regret what I'm asking of you. I may be a selfish old bastard, and maybe you ought to tell me to go to hell."

Jason hadn't done any such thing.

He slumped to the floor, wrapped his arms around his knees, and bent his head, and cried. He'd do it all again, even if his father found out all over again. And how the hell *did* his dad find out? Even if it pissed off his dad, and got him in trouble, and nobody understood why he'd done it, he'd still do it all over again. And he'd never tell the truth about it. Never. He'd show his mom, he'd show everybody. He could be as loyal as a goddamned dog. He could be committed to something and somebody, all the way to death and past. Let them think what they wanted, he didn't care. Screw 'em. He'd made a promise to Parker, and he'd keep it, or die trying.

9

SHOPPING LIST

Genia had fallen in love with downtown Devon the first time she laid eyes on it. On this lovely, sunny afternoon, only hours after she'd learned that Stanley had been murdered, the colorful, cheerful bustle of its quaint streets and the sight of its neat little harbor felt immensely comforting to her.

She had come to shop for Randy and Nikki Dixon.

As she parked her leased car, she felt glad to have a purpose for the next few hours to distract her from the reason for this shopping trip. But everywhere she turned she found yet another memory of Stanley Parker.

Genia had learned that during Larry Averill's long tenure in civic offices Larry had cajoled, bargained, and twisted Devon's collective arm to get it to clean itself up from its early fishing port days. Now it was quite the tourist attraction and as quaint as a New England seacoast village ought to be.

"If it were any cuter," Stanley had once grumbled to her, "I couldn't stand it."

It seemed as if his forceful presence was abroad in town on this first morning after his death . . . his murder. Everywhere she went, people were excitedly talking about it, about him, and about who might have killed him and why.

"I knew it was no accident, I'll tell you that much."

The owner of Stella's Bakery looked knowing as she handed over to Genia a white paper bag full of plain cake donuts and a box of gingerbread. Genia had learned that Rhode Islanders loved donuts, preferring them crisp on the outside, dense on the inside, and more cakelike than airy in texture. Instantly upon eating one, she had become a devotee.

The air inside the shop was warm and moist, redolent of sugar and dough.

Beneath Genia's feet, old wooden planks creaked when she moved down the counter to the cash register to pay.

As good as the donuts were, and the malassadas (fried sweet bread dough), the real specialty at Stella's was the gingerbread, made from a famous old Rhode Island recipe. In Devon, they called it "Stella's Gingerbread," even though every order of it came with a little printed card that gave all the credit to one Stephen Green, baker of Little Rest, circa 1826. The only ingredients were milk, molasses, butter, ginger, salt, and "saleratus," the old-fashioned word for baking soda. Mixed all together by Stella's deft hand, it was nothing short of ambrosia, and with a little homemade whipped cream on top, it rivaled anything heaven had to offer, in Genia's opinion.

Stanley, she thought as she counted out her money and listened to other people talk about him, *I hope you find something in paradise that's even better than this gingerbread, though I doubt that's possible.*

Of course, they had planned to put it in their cookbook.

"Now, I'm not saying a word against the mayor," the shop's owner continued in a confiding air that all seven customers in the shop could easily hear, "but I know for a fact that he and Mr. Parker hated one another like vinegar hates oil. If one of them came in a room, the other one left, and that's the God's honest truth. I've seen it happen."

"Where was that, Stella?" a man in back asked her.

"Town council meetings," she replied without a moment's hesitation. "I was there the night Stanley brought up that idea for the art festival, and the mayor latched on to it like a bee on a trash can. He said this was something the town council ought to take up, not the arts council, and I thought Stanley Parker was going to have a conniption fit. Got up out of his chair and left the room, plain as you please."

I'll bet Stanley was just going to the men's room, Genia thought. She didn't think it her place, as an outsider, to say it out loud, but it did bother her to hear Stanley's relationship with Larry Averill so terribly misrepresented. Stanley had never described Larry as the brightest bulb in the political spotlight, but he had seemed to like the mayor personally.

With donuts and gingerbread in hand, she moved down the sidewalk toward the Red Rooster Deli, which advertised itself with a painted wood carving of a Rhode Island Red rooster. The distinctive sign, which hung from a black wrought-iron arrow, reminded her that Stanley had only recently called Larry Averill "dumb as a rooster." But still, to say the two men hated each other?

Genia didn't believe that for one minute.

She couldn't quite remember why Stanley had referred to the mayor in that insulting way, but she thought it had something to do with Celeste, and how it had appeared to Stanley as if Larry had pined his life away for her. *But Larry hasn't wasted his life, Stanley,* Genia argued in her mind with his spirit. *No man has wasted his life who has accomplished so much for his hometown. Larry's just a devoted kind of man, that's all.* She could almost hear Stanley's retort: "Yeah, like a dog."

Even preoccupied as she was, she couldn't help but enjoy Devon's quaint downtown and credit the mayor for its fine state of preservation. Along the west side of Main Street where she walked, the architecture was all of a kind: red brick attached buildings in Federal style, with glassed-in display cases bowing out toward the street, showing off regional ware such as Peter Pots pottery with its distinctive blue or brown glazes, and Stone Bridge dishes. The east side of the street looked charmingly eclectic, architecturally speaking: There were Victorians, next to Georgian revivals, abutting colonials with white picket fences, and even Gothic revivals. Four centuries of architecture were represented. The centuries before the Europeans came were also represented in a small museum that housed artifacts of native tribes: Narragansett, Patuxet, Wampanoag, and a dozen others.

On the way to the deli she passed The Independent Man, which she knew was not an expression of male chauvinism, but rather a bookstore named for one of the founders of Rhode Island, Roger Williams. This was a state whose early history gave it a right to pride itself on tolerance, civil dissent, and independent thinking. Stanley had seemed to Genia the very model of a Rhode Island "independent man," even if tolerance might not have been one of his stronger traits.

She walked past a New York System Wiener Stand, where the grillman was lining up little spicy-hot red wieners in their buns along his forearm, in the approved Rhode Island way. He had three customers waiting for their wieners to grill. Genia's niece had told her that the mayor pushed through the idea that when their town gussied itself up for tourists they should concentrate heavily on the favorite foods and famous history of their locality.

It had proved to be a commercial windfall for many people.

Larry Averill was predicting that the Devon art festival could be a local windfall, too, not only for artists, but also for all who might profit from an annual tourist attraction.

As Genia entered the Red Rooster, she made up her mind that quahog chowder would be just right to take up to Nikki and Randy at the Castle, along with the baked goods and a few other things. "Quahog"—pronounced co-hog— was the local word for the hard-shell clams that were devoured every which way, from steamed to fried to boiled, and even stuffed, with their own special appellation: "stuffies."

"I'd bet money it was that awful Ed Hennessey who did it," one customer whispered to another, right in front of Genia at the fish and seafood counter in the Red Rooster. "I told Stanley he was a fool to hire that man, and him just out of prison. I happen to know that Ed's father was just like him, no-good from the get-go. I'll bet you a ham sandwich that the police arrest Ed before this day is out."

"You think so?" her companion whispered back.

"I hope so," the first woman said with feeling.

"Why?"

"Because if it wasn't Ed, who was it?"

The two stared at each other, and then glanced back at Genia behind them. "You hear about the murder?"

She nodded her head, but didn't say anything.

"Just awful," one of them said.

"Scares me," the second one echoed. "I know for a fact that Ed Hennessey stole tools from my sister when he mowed her lawn. And he scared her half to death. He was a Peeping Tom, she told me. Always sneaking around, and staring in her windows."

"Stanley should have known better," her friend said ominously.

"Well, I guess he knows better now," was the smug reply.

Genia bought a sackful of fresh clams, and then carried her purchases back out to her car. Then she set out for more shopping. As she stepped off the cobblestone street onto the sidewalk, she ran into Lindsay Wright, who also seemed to be shopping this morning.

"How pretty you look," Genia told her.

In a lemony sundress the young woman looked right off the cover of a Neiman Marcus catalog, and yet Genia had overheard her say to Celeste Hutchinson that she did all her shopping at a certain store which was the Rhode Island equivalent of Filene's Basement in Boston. The implication was that she could afford good quality clothes because she knew how to shop for great bargains. After more than six decades of living, it was Genia's private opinion that a person could go broke on bargains.

"Thanks, Genia. Did you hear the awful news about Stanley?"

"Yes, I'm sorry to say."

Lindsay grasped one of Genia's wrists and pulled her aside into the shade under a shop's canopy. "What do you know about it?" Without giving Genia time to reply, Lindsay blurted out, "I called Harrison, and he said all he knows is what they have in the newsroom, which isn't much. Just that the police say Stanley was murdered by somebody who bashed him in the head with something. Have you heard any more than that?"

"That's all I know, too, Lindsay."

"I just can't believe it happened like that! To Stanley! It's just too creepy. There he was on the way to dinner at your house, and now he's dead!"

Although Genia could have lived without the juxtaposition of those two events, she nodded sympathetically. She hoped the fact that Stanley was bound for her house didn't actually have anything to do with his death.

"Did the police interview you?" Lindsay whispered, after looking around to see if anybody was listening.

"They came out to my house this morning."

"Well, they called to ask us to come in after Harrison gets off work. They told me that they want to talk to everybody who was at your dinner party! We want to help, but we don't know a thing to tell them. Did you?"

"No, I didn't, either." Genia decided not to gossip about Ed Hennessey. "Oh, I do know one thing, though. I spoke to Randy Dixon, and he said that he and Nikki will be staying at the Castle. There will probably be a memorial service this week."

"Really? Harrison and I had better drop by there."

"Do you know Nikki very well?"

"Well, no, actually, I don't know her at all, but it seems like the nice thing to do. I knew Stanley well enough."

Genia thought that last was said with a dry twist.

As if she had heard the same note in her voice, Lindsay immediately followed that by saying, "It's just so sad. I was crying all morning, just thinking about poor Stanley." She didn't look it, Genia thought; her eyes were clear and happy; her skin was smooth and firm below them. And yet Lindsay turned her mouth down, making a sad face. "Now he won't get to see the art festival happen out on his island. I thought it was a terrible idea, but I feel sad for him because it was something he wanted, and now he won't get it."

"Do you think there won't be one now?"

"Oh, I don't see how. I mean, it was Stanley's island, after all, and where would they hold it, if not out there?"

A bit mischievously, Genia suggested, "Maybe his daughter will take up the cause in her father's memory."

"Nikki?" Lindsay's sunny mood seemed to darken a bit. "But she doesn't even live here anymore; why should she be interested in having all that fuss and bother on her island?"

"I don't know that she would," Genia admitted.

Lindsay nodded, as if that was much the better answer.

Looking cheered up again, she chatted for a few more minutes, telling Genia about an upcoming arts council meeting on Thursday and inviting her to come. Then she was off, floating away like a lemon meringue confection, Genia thought. She watched as Lindsay swung her trim, fit body into a red Saab convertible and then drove slowly down the street. Genia saw her wave at a tableful of diners at a sidewalk cafe. She looked more like a homecoming queen on parade than like a young woman saddened over the death of an acquaintance. For a moment, Genia felt offended by Lindsay's superficial responses, but then she brought herself up sharply: *She is young,* Genia reminded herself, *and Stanley probably was more of an acquaintance than a friend. Lindsay shouldn't have to feel this as deeply as I do. Let her be young and happy; don't force suffering on her just because you feel bad, Genia.*

At Swamp Yankee's grocery, she picked up lobster salad, rolls, clam cakes, and jonnycake meal for white cornmeal pancakes. While standing in the checkout line, Genia overheard the checkout girl tell the boy bagging groceries that she'd heard that Mr. Parker had *many* enemies among the East Coast Mafia. But then the boy countered that Jason Eden had probably smoked some bad weed and done in the old man.

Genia couldn't let that pass.

"Jason Eden did no such thing," she said in her most authoritative voice, looking the boy straight in the eye. "I'm his great-aunt, and I ought to know."

The boy looked embarrassed as he handed her purchases to her.

But as she walked away, she heard the two teens snicker, and the boy said softly, "Yeah, right, like Jason would tell her."

Genia didn't mind the disparagement of herself—she'd had a similar low opinion of grown-ups when she was their age—but she minded very much the slander on her nephew's name. She had started to think, *on my nephew's good name,* as the old saying usually went, but then she had to sadly amend that to the shorter version. The truth was that Jason had already besmirched his name in his hometown. With a sinking sensation, his aunt realized that whether it was fair or not, more than one aspersion might be cast on Jason's name this day. *Oh, Jason,* she thought as she got back into her car, *please don't get into any more trouble of the kind that makes people say cruel things about you.*

She had been going to stop at a Del's Lemonade Stand for a cup of the famous Rhode Island beverage that had a lemon peel in every drink. Now she only wanted to get away from all of the gossip and go home. *Stanley,* she thought as she drove away, *you would have to have had a cat's numerous lives—and deaths!—to satisfy all the theories being tossed around in Devon today.*

10

Cooking up a Storm

That afternoon Genia made her second trip of the day to the
Castle. This time she drove her car along the paved road of
the cul-de-sac, accompanied by her grandniece. They had
fixed a big pot of quahog chowder and two dozen muffins
made from the season's last fresh blueberries.

"I'm overdoing it," Genia admitted to Janie as they loaded
all of the food into the car, "but cooking has always been my
favorite way to cope. My children tell me they always knew
they'd eat well if there was something to celebrate or somebody died. I don't know, I just seem to think best when I'm
cooking large amounts of food for other people. It makes me
feel better."

"I wish my mom felt that way."

Genia glanced at her niece, and they both laughed.

"Did I tell you that your father loved the bisque we made
last night?"

"He did? I didn't really do much, though."

"Well, you cooked it. I didn't even stir it. I just told you
what to do."

"It was easy, except I almost boiled it over."

"*Almost* is not the same as *did*."

Janie grinned at her. "Yeah, but that works both ways, Aunt Genia. That's what Jason's teachers say when he *almost* gets his homework in on time."

Her aunt smiled at her, appreciating her wit.

"But you always do, don't you?"

"Jason could, too, if he wanted to."

Genia looked up at the defensive tone in Janie's voice. "Oh, honey, I'm sorry. I shouldn't have compared you to him. I know your brother is plenty smart, and he can't help it that he has dyslexia. I know it makes it harder for him."

Janie's face still looked flushed with resentment. "I'm sorry, too. I just get this knee-jerk reaction when somebody tells me what a good student I am, 'cause when Mom says it what she really means is what a good student Jason isn't. Sometimes I hate getting good grades. It just makes life harder for him."

Genia reached over to grasp one of Janie's hands and pull her around to face her. "Sweetheart, let me tell you something. First of all, your mother loves both of you more than you know." When Janie started to interrupt, Genia held up a hand to silence her. "And second, I am not worried about either of you. You will do just fine in this life, and so will he, honey. I should know. I got to see him in action down on the ranch, remember? He worked hard, he got along well with everyone he met, and he was smart as a whip about catching on to things."

She had a feeling that Janie wouldn't feel so defensive of her twin if the girl herself had more genuine confidence in him. Her words, as she hoped they would, seemed to buoy up her niece, and Genia felt Janie's arm relax a little in her grasp. Gently, she let her go.

"Sometimes I feel like I'm his mother," Janie muttered.

"I know you do," Genia said kindly, "and the hardest thing a mother ever has to do is let go of her child."

She smiled at Janie and suddenly got a lopsided grin in return.

"Weird, huh?" the girl asked, with a little laugh.

"Normal," her aunt pronounced.

"Oh, gross, just what I want to be, normal!"

They both laughed at the very idea of it.

When they arrived at the Castle, Nikki herself answered the door, looking, to Genia's sympathetic eyes, sweet and young and very sad. Stanley's only child wore a long pink cotton skirt, a white cotton blouse, and sandals. As she tucked a loose strand of her brown hair behind an arm of her eyeglasses, she smiled tiredly at Genia and Janie. Under the glasses her eyes were puffy, as if she'd been crying a lot.

"Genia, you sweetie. Look at all this that you've brought for us." The young woman reached for one of the packages. There was a catch in her voice. "My dad was right, you're really a dear person. This is wonderful. This whole town is wonderful. People are so kind and generous. I do believe we've got enough food to feed the whole state. It's a good thing, too, because it's beginning to look as if everybody in Rhode Island is going to show up. I think Dad knew everybody!" As she held open the door for them, she said, "Randy told me you called earlier."

"Nikki, I'm so sorry about your dad," Genia told her, pausing in the doorway to say it. "It's such a terrible thing." She hesitated, and then added, "Did Randy tell you about Ed Hennessey?"

"Yes, but I can't do anything about that right now." Nikki looked harried, overwhelmed, and ready to burst into tears, and Genia felt guilty for overburdening her. She stepped into the foyer in order to let Nikki and Janie in, too. "I need somebody to take care of the grounds, and there's no time to hire anybody new until all this is over."

"Nikki, do you know my grandniece, Jane Eden?"

Janie nodded her head politely above the load of packages she was carrying for her aunt, and explained, "I'm Donna's daughter."

"And Kevin's," Nikki said, with a warm, quivery smile for the girl.

As they followed their hostess back into the Castle's kitchen, Genia thought about how Stanley used to call his daughter "soft," and "a pushover." Genia wondered if the truth might be that Nikki was just plain nicer than he. Stanley had always said exactly what was on his mind, often to a fault, and frequently mowing over people's feelings in the process. "They shouldn't get their feelings hurt so easily," he'd say, thus neatly absolving himself of any responsibility for being kind. Genia had a feeling that his daughter would never do that. Maybe that made Nikki weak, or maybe it made her good.

They walked by groups of visitors in the central living room to the right and the library to the left. Genia recalled how very "masculine" this residence had seemed to her the first time she had walked into its massive foyer with its thirty-foot ceiling, walnut balustrade, and dark paneling. Stanley had appeared quite naturally at home in the vast rooms with their dark brocaded draperies that shut out the light, but she had wondered how Lillian had stood it for all of those years of their marriage. If there had been suits of armor standing about, it could not have seemed any more like a "castle" or any less like a home for a queen.

This was a king's castle, no doubt of it.

Genia looked curiously about her: There were many faces she recognized, people who smiled or nodded to her courteously, and she to all of them. Some of her dinner-party guests were there, as well as people she recognized from town. Was one of them a murderer, come to pay sardonic tribute to the victim? It was a terrible thought.

"Hello, Mrs. Potter!"

She looked up to see Randy Dixon coming down the main staircase from the second floor. The young man looked confident and at ease in a way Genia had never seen him look around his late father-in-law. He was a physical type that girls through the generations had always labeled "cute"—below average in height, but broad shouldered and slim waisted, with lots of curly black hair, outrageously blue eyes, and an infectious grin.

"Hello, Randy," she responded, stopping to see if he wanted to talk.

But he merely smiled in a welcoming way, and strode past her into the living room to greet the important guests for whom he was now the host.

In the vast kitchen Nikki briefly removed her glasses and Genia noticed again the pillows beneath her brown eyes. Suddenly Nikki turned around and cried out in tones of deep distress, "Genia, they're saying my dad was murdered! No one would murder my father! You don't think it's really true, do you?"

"Oh, my dear," Genia said, with deep sympathy.

She had certainly never expected to stand in this familiar kitchen having this kind of conversation. Everywhere she looked were reminders of Stanley, because it was he—not Lillian—who had planned every inch of this cooking space, and he who had used it the most, apart from their hired cooks. From the stainless steel of the custom-made counters to the wide window above the triple sinks, from the cast-iron utensils to the industrial stove and oven, it was all Stanley's design.

"The police have been here!" Nikki said, a look of disbelief on her face. "The police! The way they asked Randy and me questions, you'd have thought they suspected we murdered my dad for the inheritance! But Genia, I've always known I would inherit almost everything! Randy has, too, and if we were going to kill my dad for the money"—she looked utterly dismayed by her own words—"why would we wait to do it now? I mean, sure Randy's out of work a lot, but that's the nature of what he does! We've always gotten by, with some help from my dad. So why would we do such a thing now? And, anyway, I loved my dad!" She smiled, and her mouth trembled. "He claimed I nearly killed him when I married Randy. But for me to really kill my own father? It's so impossible; I told the police that. And they know me, for heaven's sake, I went to grade school with most of them. I told them I hope they're looking for the person who really did it."

Her words reminded Genia painfully of what Kevin Eden had said the previous night in her own kitchen, about how the Devon police knew him, too, and ought to know better than to treat him with suspicion. These things were especially hard in a small town if neighbor turned against neighbor, and longtime friends against their own school chums.

Genia put an arm around Nikki and led her to a chair to sit down.

A woman suddenly burst into the kitchen, holding a casserole pot in her hands, but paused when she saw the emotional little scene. She put her contribution down on a counter, murmured, "I'm so sorry," threw a compassionate look toward Nikki, and then tiptoed back out again. Janie walked right over, picked up the casserole, and placed it in one of the two large refrigerators. Then she busied herself with the things that she and her great-aunt had brought. Genia felt proud of the girl for trying to be so tactfully helpful, when many teenagers might have hung back or fled from the scene.

Just then the doorbell rang, causing Nikki to rise halfway up from the chair instinctively. Genia placed a hand on her shoulder and gently pushed her down again. "Just sit here and rest for a minute, Nikki. There are lots of people out there who can answer the door for you. Janie, let's you and I get some of this food out into the dining room."

While Nikki sat at the table, her face buried in her hands, Genia put Janie to work layering clam cakes on lettuce on a platter and arranging the gingerbread in a basket. Periodically, the three women were interrupted by other people coming in to deposit more food and to give Nikki hugs and words of sympathy. Foodstuffs were piling up, so Genia started dishing a few of them up and then making room for the others in the refrigerator and along the countertops. From spending time in this kitchen with Stanley, she knew right where to go for serving spoons and napkins, glasses and pickle forks. She plugged in the big stainless coffeepot that Stanley had used for large groups and she uncorked several bottles of wine. And through all her tasks she wondered if Stanley would approve.

"*There you have it, Stanley,*" she said silently to the spirit of her friend. "*The imported cheeses are for you, of course. God forbid we should ever serve processed cheese in your house. We're fresh out of caviar and toast points, I'm embarrassed to say, so you'll have to put up with ham and store-bought egg rolls. We weren't exactly prepared for this, you know. . . .*"

Suddenly, Genia felt like crying herself.

She stopped working and sank down into a chair near Nikki.

Janie had been keeping busy at the kitchen table, putting ham sandwiches together, but suddenly she was kneeling beside her aunt. For the moment there was nobody else in the kitchen but the three of them. Janie laid her cheek against Genia's arm, as if to comfort her. It was a sweet gesture, and Genia quickly put her arms around the girl and hugged her.

"I'm sorry your father died," Janie said to Nikki.

Nikki heard, and looked over at them gratefully.

"You're a nice girl, Jane Devon," she observed. "You take after your aunt Genia."

Genia hesitated, but felt she must say, "Nikki, I'm sorry to trouble you about this, but I feel as if I need to bring up the subject of Ed Hennessey again. Your dad did fire him. And the man behaved in a very threatening way toward me this morning." Genia was worried that the man might steal things right from under the Dixons' noses, or that he might take some kind of nasty revenge on them when they finally did roust him from their property.

"You're right," Nikki said wearily. "I'd better do something."

"Maybe Randy could do it for you?"

Nikki's glance slid away, and she mumbled, "Good idea."

But Genia was left with the impression that Nikki wasn't altogether sure her husband could handle that. It was the only hint of evasiveness that Genia had seen in the young woman since they'd arrived. She knew there wasn't anything she could say to make Nikki do something about Hennessey; she was just going to have to leave the matter of the caretaker in the kind hands of Stanley's daughter. Genia could almost hear Stanley worrying that when it came to Hennessey, Nikki had better not be so kind as to be foolish.

With a tremulous smile Nikki got up from the table, pushing herself up with her hands. She looked girded to reenter her father's rooms and to greet and talk with the dozens of people who would come calling on this first and most difficult day. She straightened her clothes and hair, thanked Genia and Nikki again, and then walked out of the kitchen.

"She's nice," Janie observed.

"Yes, she is," her aunt agreed.

Genia could have sworn she heard Stanley mutter in her ear, "*Too nice for her own good.*"

Judging from the number of people crowding the Castle, it appeared to Genia as if Stanley had known everybody in Devon, if not in the whole state. The mayor was there with a retinue of town council members and other Devon bigwigs. The bank was well represented. Harrison and Lindsay Wright entered with a handsome man whom Genia recognized from the evening newscasts. Although Celeste Hutchinson arrived on the arm of David Graham, he inched away from her when Genia greeted them, as if he realized—better than Celeste—that it wasn't tactful of him to come into Lillian's former home on the arm of another woman. As gently as he did it, Celeste still looked hurt when his arm slid away from her hand. He stepped to one side, a bit closer to Genia. Donna appeared, and also Kevin, though they kept to opposite sides of the room.

Genia observed Nikki as she moved among the groups of guests. Randy Dixon stayed at his wife's side, touching her, getting her water to drink, placing a steady hand on her back. *Look at your son-in-law, Stanley,* Genia thought. *He can't be all bad if he can be as supportive and loving to Nikki as this.*

When Donna appeared Janie hurried to her father's side, and then worked her way around the room to her aunt. Genia could hardly blame her for wanting to avoid her mother: When her children were in the same room with her, Donna just couldn't seem to help but criticize and fuss over them. If it wasn't Janie's hair that Donna disparaged, it would be her jewelry, or her fingernail polish, her clothes, her posture, or the way she carried a tray. Genia thought the girl looked trapped and took mercy on her. "You've been a great help, sweetheart, and you can leave anytime you want to. Get my keys out of my purse over there and you can have my car for the rest of the day."

"But how will you—"

"I'll get a ride with someone, or I'll walk home."

"You sure? Thanks a lot, Aunt Genia. I'll be really careful."

"I know you will. Go have some fun for the rest of the day, dear."

"What will you tell Mom?"

"Why," Genia said, surprised, "I'll tell her the truth, that your job was finished here, and that I gave you my car so you could get home."

"She'll tell you I'll wreck it."

"You seem like a very good driver to me. Have you ever had an accident before, Janie?"

"No, but she'll—"

"Go. Drive safely. I'll handle your mother."

In a flash the girl had grabbed the keys and was gone out the back door, as if she were afraid her aunt might change her mind if she took too long to leave. When Genia reentered the dining room and Donna approached her and asked where Janie was, Genia said, "I sent her home with my car."

"You trust my daughter with your car?"

"Yes," Genia said firmly in a voice that brooked no argument. "I do."

Behind her back she crossed her fingers and hoped for the best.

Suddenly she felt the weight of the long night and day. If she didn't get home soon, she'd collapse right there, she thought. When Donna turned away to chat with someone else, Genia began to work her way through the crowd toward the front door, trying to be unobtrusive about it.

"Genia, wait up!"

She turned around to find that Nikki was hurrying toward her through the throng of visitors in the entry hall.

"I have something for you!"

Nikki thrust a thick, familiar, dog-eared cookbook into her hands. Genia recognized it instantly as Stanley's everyday favorite. "Oh, Nikki," she said, feeling touched by the gesture. "I couldn't possibly—"

"Yes, you can, and you should. I don't like to cook, and I know Dad left me a whole slew of valuable antique cookbooks, so I sure don't need one more. It ought to be in the hands of somebody who will appreciate it. Like you. It would please me so much for you to have it."

Others, gathered in the foyer, listened to their exchange.

Genia ran a finger over the ragged edge of the cover where it was beginning to separate from the spine.

"I'd feel guilty taking it from you, Nikki."

"Oh, you shouldn't! Look how greasy and yucky it is. Really, I ought to be ashamed to offer it to you. Do you mind that it's such a mess?"

"Mind? It's perfect. It will be like having him right there cooking with me. Thank you, Nikki. I will cherish this, but if you ever change your mind and want it back, it's yours."

With the others looking on, Genia said her good-byes, tucked the cookbook securely under her arm, and walked outside. Then she had to laugh to herself: She had forgotten she didn't have her car! She'd given it to Janie to use. Well, that was all right, she could walk home.

But when she saw Ed Hennessey lingering in the shadows near some of the parked cars talking with Randy Dixon, she changed her mind. The two men appeared to be arguing about something—which Genia took as a good sign that Nikki and Randy were finally doing something about the problem of the fired caretaker. Nikki must have changed her mind about whatever hesitation she had felt in asking her husband to deal with Hennessey. *Or maybe I only imagined that,* Genia thought.

The sight of Hennessey's angry face forcefully reminded her—and if she weren't so tired, she wouldn't have needed reminding!—that a murder had been committed in those woods last night. She was worn out from the tumultuous events of the past twenty-four hours. She wasn't thinking straight. And suddenly, again she felt ready to drop where she stood. When David Graham and Celeste Hutchinson came out, she asked them if they'd mind dropping her off on their way back to town.

"I'd be honored to, Genia," David assured her.

"Take her home first, David." Celeste wobbled a bit on her high heels and reached out to cling with both hands to David's arm. Genia would have felt like a third wheel, except that it was obvious that David felt embarrassed by Celeste's behavior. She was more than a little drunk, and she was acting as if this handsome man belonged to her. When he walked Genia to her front door, leaving Celeste in the front passenger's seat, which she had claimed, he said, "It's been a shocking day, hasn't it? Are you sure you'll be all right?"

His tone was so kind, so understanding, that Genia felt tears spring to her eyes. "I'm just tired," she said quickly. "And I need a good cry about Stanley."

The sadness in David's eyes mirrored her own feelings for a moment, and he said softly, "The only good thing about this is that Lillian isn't here to see it." He stepped down from her front stoop. "I hate leaving you alone out here. Are you sure you'll be all right?"

"Yes. Promise."

When she closed the front door behind her, she felt just a little bit better.

11

SPECIAL RECIPES

A long soak in the deep, skylit bathtub in the master bathroom helped Genia to ease some of the tension out of her body and mind. Afterward she slipped into a cotton nightgown and padded back to her bedroom in her house slippers.

She'd left Stanley's cookbook on top of the nightstand.

A nightcap and a good book, that was just what she wanted.

She picked up a small glass of sherry that she had poured earlier and set it beside the bed. Then she got in between the sheets and lay back against plump pillows. First she reached for the book and then for the sherry.

She opened the precious, dog-eared cookbook.

No antique cookbook worth hundreds of dollars could possibly have meant as much to her as this one. Genia couldn't count the number of times she had sat across from Stanley in the past few months, watching him scribble in this book, listening to his strong opinions about food and people and life. And it wasn't merely a cookbook, she saw as she opened it, it was also a diary of the recipes he served and to whom he served them. She found odd bits of paper stuck in it—a postcard here, a grocery receipt there, all wedged between pages. Some such scraps appeared held in by the "glue" of a spot of grease, or what she suspected might be honey.

Stanley's bold, penciled notations were everywhere. They were scribbled in margins, in between recipes, written on divider pages, and in the index. Some recipes he had crossed out entirely, as if they weren't even worth the paper they were printed on. Others he had circled, or starred. He commented on ingredients, added his own inventions, listed who came for lunch.

Sometimes his notes had nothing to do with the recipes at all:

> Served to Genia and Celeste June 2. Delicious! Celeste brought a California Cab., and G. brought a cheese bread that could have used a zinger like red peppers. Told her so.
> June 10—Nikki and what's-his-name, crazy about these rolls. Next time, serve him something he hates, so he won't come back.

Beneath a recipe for deviled chicken there was a wickedly funny note: For David Graham! Genia smiled at Stanley's humor, knowing he had remained more jealous of Lillian's second husband than he liked people to know.

There were also notes beside recipes that Stanley had not yet tried, and finding those, Genia felt especially melancholy. There were suggestions to himself that he invite particular people over to try one recipe or another. She came across her own name several times and fondly recalled the meals and conversations that it signified.

Stars, asterisks, and circles denoted a rating system that Genia didn't begin to understand. Here and there a Post-it note elaborated a recipe's usefulness: Serve cold for picnics, hot for Oktoberfests, lukewarm for what's-his-name.

His dislike of his son-in-law glared from the pages.

"Stanley, Stanley," Genia murmured, chiding his ghost.

A faintly sour smell wafted up from the pages, from wine stains, grease splotches, and even bits of shaved cheese that clung here and there. She pictured him grating cheddar over a bowl while simultaneously checking a recipe from the cookbook.

Genia's fingers paused on a recipe for sautéed veal chops. Stanley had circled it, but that wasn't what stopped her. Above it, he had scribbled a date and initials: "8/8" and "C.H." There was a strip of plain white paper, serving as a bookmark, stuck in the crease of the book, and it bore the same notations: "8/8" and "C.H." Celeste Hutchinson? Had he served these chops to Celeste? Many of the scribbles in the cookbook had faded or smeared with time, but these hadn't. If he'd meant August 8 of this year, that would have been only last week. Genia didn't remember Stanley mentioning having Celeste Hutchinson over for a meal, however. Not that Genia had expected him to tell her all of his engagements, it was just that he had usually seemed to do so while they planned and cooked. She would ask Celeste about it, she thought, and find out if she'd liked the chops. But then she realized that the recipe must not have been sufficiently outstanding to adapt for the cookbook, or Stanley would surely have mentioned it to her.

Stanley's "suggestions" had been more in the nature of fiats, but she'd learned to maneuver around them whenever she strongly opposed them. It was not worth arguing with him, because Stanley never backed down from a fight. If someone tried to argue, he just escalated, and kept that up until his opponent threw in the towel. That had been no hindrance to Genia, however. In her opinion anybody who had ever been a mother to teenagers could handle a man like that.

With sad pleasure she read through the list of marvelous ingredients for the veal dish, both the original ones and some Stanley had added: garlic, butter and cream, thick loin chops, fresh tarragon, and the finest dry French vermouth. That last was "a Stanley touch." She could almost taste the food, smell the aroma of the herb, hear the sizzle of the butter and garlic in the pan.

Genia sighed and closed her eyes briefly.

She felt very tired all of a sudden.

When she opened her eyes and her glance fell again on the closed book, she recognized several other bookmarks just like the one that had fallen down in the middle of the page by the veal chops. She hadn't paid any special attention to them before, because there were many other bits of paper stuck in the book, too. But it dawned on her now that these all had a newer and similar appearance. Curious, she opened to the first one, and discovered it was for a lamb curry salad. On the bookmark itself, he'd written "8/7," and then "Lindsay, a little lamb."

She turned to where another white strip marked a place and found a recipe for a Caesar salad that used seafood instead of the usual chicken. That bookmark also bore a date, 8/11, four days later than the one for Lindsay Wright (Genia assumed she was the Lindsay he meant), and then: "what's-his-name, hates salad."

After that she found garlic steak stir-fry for "Larry, 8/6," and chicken satay for "David, 8/9," Thai pizza for "Kevin, 8/10," and saffron egg salad for "Donna, 8/5," duck with honey, date, and walnut sauce for "Nikki, 8/12."

She also found one that read "S.S., 8/19," which was the only other one for this month. She couldn't think of any of Stanley's acquaintances—at least among the ones she'd met—who had those initials. Perhaps it wasn't a person at all, but an event of some kind, although she couldn't think of anything except "summer solstice," and she knew that wasn't on August 19, which was only a few days away. Except for the "S.S." entry, all of the other white markers denoted last week's dates, leading right up to her dinner party.

And to his murder.

It looked very much to Genia as if Stanley Parker either had—or planned to have—every one of her dinner guests, plus his daughter and son-in-law, over for a consecutive series of private meals with him at the Castle. *If* these dates actually did refer to this year, and not to some other year. Genia thought they did, or why else would the bookmarks still look so clean?

Her guests, all in a row, in the week before he died.

Genia listed them in order on a separate piece of paper:

Aug. 5, Donna
      6, Larry
      7, Lindsay
      8, Celeste
      9, David
     10, Kevin
     11, Randy
     12, Nikki

There was that stray one for 8/19, but except for the fact that it was marked by a white strip of paper, it didn't seem related to these eight, so she forgot about it for the time being. Randy and Nikki were the only ones who had not also been invited to the dinner party, nor could Genia recall that Stanley had ever said he wanted them to be. She would have been happy to include them if he had asked her to.

Why those people? Why last week? And why had he not said a single thing to her about them, even though he and she had talked every day about their cookbook project? He must have been exhausted to have cooked that many lunches for that many people all in a row. No wonder Stanley had seemed to move ever more tiredly and painfully as the week progressed! Genia recalled that she had seen much less of him last week than usual; he had claimed that business appointments and civic meetings were eating up his time. She'd accepted his word without question, for why should she not? Was that what all these luncheons were about? Business and civic matters? It appeared that he had deliberately failed to discuss any of this with her. If all he was doing was discussing—say—the art festival with these people, then why not say so?

And why hadn't he discussed with her the food he served them? There had been nothing Stanley Parker enjoyed more than a good debate on the merits of angel hair pasta over fettuccine, or lamb chops over veal. Every other time he had had company this summer, as far as she knew, he had hashed out his menus with her, just for the pleasure of it.

As far as I know . . .

Evidently, she had known him less well than she thought.

It saddened her to contemplate that possibility.

For some reason Stanley had considered it none of her business that he was having a series of luncheons at the Castle for a short list of prominent citizens of Devon. Nor had he seen fit to tell her they were the very same people he had asked her to invite to her house for their tasting dinner.

"Stanley, what were you up to?"

Genia sat up for a long time with his open cookbook on her lap. And then suddenly it occurred to her that maybe he'd only *planned* to have those people over; maybe none of these meals had ever happened. Even though it was very late, she decided to interrupt her niece's sleep by telephoning her with a single question:

"Donna, dear, I'm so sorry to be calling so late—but did Stanley have you to lunch last week?"

There was a long pause on the other end of the line, which might have been prompted only by the fact that Genia had awakened her. Finally, Donna dragged out a word as if she didn't want to say it.

"Yes."

Again, there was a long pause.

"Why, Aunt Genia?"

"Oh, I'm just trying to decipher this cookbook of his, and he had your name written down by a recipe, with the date, but no year. I just wondered when it was. I didn't remember either of you mentioning it to me."

"Well, that's when it was." Her niece's tone was sulky.

"Thank you, dear. I apologize for waking you over something so trivial."

"That's okay. Good night, Aunt Genia."

"What was the occasion, dear?"

"What do you mean?"

"I just wondered why he invited you to lunch with him."

Again, there was a longish pause. "He wanted to talk about Jason."

"Really? To let you know what a good job he was doing?"

"Yeah." Another pause. "And to tell me not to send him to military school. As if it was any business of Stanley's." The sulky, reluctant tone became sharply indignant. "Jason is my son, and I'll do what I think is best for him."

"Did you say that to Stanley?"

"Sort of."

"What did he say?"

That question produced another pause, and then Donna said, "I really don't remember what he said." Genia heard her yawn pointedly into the telephone receiver. "I'm too sleepy."

But Genia wasn't letting her go so easily. "It looks as if Stanley had Kevin out to lunch last week, too—"

"He did? Why, that conniving old—"

"Kevin didn't tell you?"

"No, he didn't tell me. I'll bet you they cooked this plan up together, to get me to change my mind about sending Jason—"

"What plan?"

Donna's torrent of angry words stopped abruptly. "Just . . . well, just the . . . plan for Stanley to . . . uh, try to convince me. Aunt Genia, I don't mean to be rude, but I'm really so tired—"

"Of course. I'm sorry. Good night, sweetheart."

But after Genia hung up and checked her list again, she saw that what Donna had suggested could not be true: Donna had gone to lunch with Stanley a full six days before Kevin did. If Kevin had "cooked up" some plan with Stanley, it hadn't been then.

Why was her niece apparently so loath to tell her about lunching with Stanley? And what "plan" did she think they cooked up? *And why did Stanley invite all of my other dinner guests over to his house that very same week without giving me so much as a clue that he was doing it?* Not so many days ago, she had inquired suspiciously, though humorously, of Stanley, "What are you up to?" Now, in her mind, she asked his spirit: *What were you up to? What was the real point of the dinner party you lobbied so hard for me to have?*

Genia felt terribly disloyal to her own kin when an unavoidable question rose next in her mind: *Stanley, did all of these mysterious goings-on lead in some way to your death?*

12

WARMED-OVER HUSBAND

Monday morning Genia slept late because she'd stayed up studying Stanley's cookbook the night before. Following her morning tea and a brisk walk, she busied herself by continuing the work of testing recipes for the Rhode Island cookbook she had been writing with him. The only way she could force herself to do it was to decide to dedicate the project to him. It was lonely work.

While two recipes simmered, she removed from the refrigerator a tureen of ginger carrot soup that she had previously prepared and warmed some for herself. She didn't feel like eating, but she knew she should, to keep up her spirits. It felt to her as if she had made the soup a lifetime ago, though it was really only two days old. The rich flavors of it—pear and lemon, ginger and carrot—had blended more, so it tasted even better now than when she had first made it.

Sitting at the kitchen table with it, she thought in regard to the soup, *The secret ingredient here is time. Time to mellow and time to deepen.*

Time. Which Stanley had run out of.

When the bottom of the bowl was visible beneath her spoon, she pushed it aside and pulled out his cookbook again. Slowly, she turned the pages, stopping again at the recipe for sautéed veal, with its mysterious, dramatic message.

The doorbell ringing scattered her thoughts.

When she went to answer it, she was startled to find David Graham standing on her front stoop, looking impossibly debonair in pale yellow slacks, an open-necked white shirt, a blue jacket, and loafers. In his arms he held, rather incongruously, a plastic bag with the label of a gourmet grocery shop in town.

"David!" To her own ears she sounded insincerely warm and enthusiastic; she hoped she didn't sound that way to him. Here on her front stoop was one of the very people whom Stanley had had to lunch last week, and for what reason? she wondered now. Why in the world would Stanley ask Lillian's second husband to dine with him on chicken satay? With an effusiveness born of surprise, she exclaimed, "How nice to see you! Won't you come in?"

"I didn't think you were home." He looked really pleased to see her standing there and he also appeared to accept her greeting as a genuine welcome. "Where's your car, Genia?"

"My car? Oh! I forgot that I lent it to my niece yesterday."

"I didn't know if I should come by without calling first, but I took a chance."

"I'm glad you did. Won't you come in?"

He stepped into the foyer, where the coral roses he had brought two nights earlier now stood in full bloom in their vase on the table.

"I saw you being helpful at Nikki's yesterday, Genia."

"I didn't do any more than anyone else—"

"That's not what Nikki told me." He smiled gratefully at

her. "She said you brought chowder and clam cakes and gingerbread, and then you took charge in the kitchen and got everything laid out for the guests. She was very grateful, and I am, too. You know, I think of her as my own daughter. Anyone who helps Nikki is a good person, in my book."

"She's fortunate to have a stepfather who cares about her."

"I love her as much as if she were my real daughter. Anyway," he said with a charmingly modest air, "I was in the Red Rooster Deli this morning, thinking about you being so nice. And it occurred to me that you had all of us over Saturday night, and then you did all that work for Nikki yesterday, and when did you have a chance to take care of yourself? So I've brought you a few things."

"Why, David...!"

He smiled in a self-effacing way that made light of his spontaneous gesture. "Now, don't be impressed. It's nothing at all. Just a little bread, and wine and cheese. The basic foodstuffs, you know."

Genia laughed, and he did, too.

"That's so true," she agreed. "A person could live a long time on bread, wine, and cheese. You'll help me eat some of it right now, won't you? Normally, at this time of the morning, I'd be in the kitchen working with Stanley, and I'm feeling so blue to be here without him. I'm really glad to have some company."

"I think we all feel that something vital has gone out of the town."

Leading the way into her rental kitchen, Genia thought that had been a very perceptive—and diplomatic—thing for David to say. There were lots of things in the world that were "vital," including floods and hurricanes, but that didn't necessarily mean you'd miss them. Lillian's second husband

had found just the right thing to say about the death of her
first husband.

With a bread board and bread knife between them, Genia
asked David Graham how his stepdaughter was holding up.

"I think she's doing fine, thank you. Randy is standing by
her. The truth is he's probably relieved that Stanley's
gone—"

"Oh, David," Genia couldn't help but object.

"Well, he's only human, after all. Stanley could make life
miserable for people, Genia. You might not have seen that,
but it's God's truth. Any man who was bold enough to take
his little girl away from him was doomed, right from the day
of the wedding. I hope you don't mind my saying this. I mean
no offense to Stanley, but he could sure be hard on people."

"So I'm learning. Was he hard on you, David?"

His response was a wry smile. "Not to my face, which he
avoided seeing as much as possible."

Genia couldn't help but laugh a little.

• David smiled back at her. "Lillian used to say that Stanley
didn't mind me marrying her nearly as much as he minded
that now Nikki had a stepfather. We decided that since Nikki
was a grown woman and she already had a father, I should
take the role of friend and just forget the stepdad business if
it bothered Stanley so much. It seemed to work all right."

"That was tactful of you, David." Genia hesitated and
then plunged in. "Were you surprised when he asked you to
lunch last week?"

David looked surprised right at that moment, she
thought, and then he laughed out loud. "Surprised? That
doesn't even begin to describe it, Genia. Shocked was more
like it. Did he tell you why he asked me to lunch?"

She shook her head no.

"He didn't? That rascal, I thought he'd tell everybody."

"What, David? Honestly, he never said a word to me."

"He wanted money, Genia." David looked squarely at her, and then he, too, shook his head as if he could hardly believe his own words. "Stanley had decided that I wasn't married long enough to Lil to deserve to inherit half of her estate. He wanted it back! He said that I didn't have any right to all that money, or to the house, and that I should sign it all over to Nikki."

Genia's mouth nearly dropped open.

"I told him," David continued, "that what Lillian did with her estate was none of his business anymore. I told him that I had loved her better in those three years than he had in the whole thirty years they'd been together. I know it was cruel, but damn it, the man infuriated me. He treated her like a fancy housekeeper most of the time, and then he thought he could control her even after she was gone." David took a deep breath. "I'm sorry, Genia, I'm sorry if I've offended you."

"I am flabbergasted," she admitted to him.

"So was I. I didn't stay for the lunch he cooked for us. I just got up from the table and walked out of that house, and . . ." He suddenly looked a little pale. "And I never saw him again."

"I don't know what to say, David."

But she knew what she was thinking: *No wonder Stanley had not ever mentioned that luncheon to her; if he had, she'd have told him he was out of his mind to ask such a thing of Lillian's legitimate widower.*

David, looking anxious to find something else to talk about, stared around the kitchen as if searching for a subject of conversation. His expression brightened. "Say, isn't that the cookbook Nikki gave you last night?"

"Yes, bless her heart." Genia felt she'd been quite nosy enough for one morning; she latched on to the change of subject as gratefully as he. "I feel a little guilty having it, though. You might tell her for me that if she changes her mind, she can have it back."

"Oh, I don't think she will, Genia. Honestly, it may be something special to you, but I think that to Nikki it's just a dirty old cookbook. Besides, she's got his whole collection of antique cookbooks, and she is quite proud of those. Still, would you like me to take it back to her, to see what she says?"

"Well, I'm embarrassed to admit that I'd like to keep it around for just a little while longer, David. I am enjoying going through it and reading all of Stanley's notes to himself. It's like being with him again."

Her guest reached for the book and drew it to himself.

"What's in here, anyway? It looks more like a scrapbook than a cookbook."

"It really is. There's a little bit of everything, I guess."

David pointed to a bit of dried cheese and smiled. "And a taste of it, too."

Genia smiled. "A health hazard, no doubt."

"Only if you eat it instead of just read it." He leafed through a few pages, then closed it and looked over at her. "I'd better not overstay my welcome, especially since I arrived like an orphan on your doorstep. But I was wondering if perhaps we could have dinner together sometime?"

She blinked, not at all sure what he was asking.

"Wednesday night is lobster night at the Yacht Club," he continued. "All you can eat, and what you can't eat you can take home. Will you join me?"

It was awkward. She didn't know the context in which he

was inviting her: Was it strictly as a friend, or was it as a date? If the latter, should she mention that she already had a gentleman friend who lived in Boston? And would going out to dinner with this handsome man be an act of disloyalty to her friend Jed? In a small town like this would people talk; would they make up gossip about the handsome widower and the widow from Arizona?

She couldn't just sit there gaping at him. "I'd love to, David."

"I'm so glad," he responded warmly, and suddenly, she was glad, too.

"Did the police come out to talk to you?" he inquired at the front door.

"Yes, but I'm afraid I couldn't help them."

"Nor could I," he said regretfully. "You and I didn't have anything to gain from Stanley's death, but it appears that someone must have thought they did. Do you have any idea who that might be?"

The obvious answer was his own stepdaughter, Nikki.

Genia didn't say that. "No, I don't, David, do you?"

"No, but I hope they catch him soon, whoever it is." He looked at her closely for a moment. "You'll be careful, won't you? I hope it's safe for you to stay here. What do the police say about that?"

"They didn't tell me not to. I think it's all right. I'm not afraid."

And that was true, she didn't feel much fear. And she wasn't entirely sure that made sense. If a murder occurred only a few hundred yards from a person's front door, shouldn't it make that person just a little nervous? Hardly anybody locked their doors in Devon; she supposed that now she ought to, just to be on the safe side.

"Could you stay with your niece, Genia?"

"Yes, I could do that," she said, without indicating that she would.

"I don't want anything to happen to you," he said rather sternly. And then he smiled, looking a bit embarrassed. "Not that it's any of my business to say so. I hope you don't mind. I'm just concerned, that's all."

After he had departed from the house, a scent of his aftershave lingered. It was a clean, musky smell that Genia found pleasant to sniff as she followed it back to the kitchen. When the doorbell surprised her by ringing again, she half expected to find yet another dinner guest standing there at her front door.

But it wasn't a guest. It was a policeman looking for her nephew.

13

ALWAYS HUNGRY

The uniformed officer stood on the brick steps of her rented house, his badge glistening in the sunshine. To Genia's eyes he didn't look much older than the boy he said he was looking for.

"Mrs. Potter, I'm Officer Cecil Patterson. I'm sorry to bother you, but I'm looking for Jason. His mother told me I might find him here."

"Donna did? May I ask why you want him?"

"Just part of his diversion program, ma'am. Random drug test. He knows this could happen at any time. Today just happens to be a day that was good for me to check him out. Is he here?"

"No, Officer Patterson, Jason's not here—"

But then suddenly he was—pulling up into her driveway behind his sister, who was at the wheel of Genia's car. From inside the screen door of the house, Genia and the policeman could see the exact moment when the twin in the first car got her initial glimpse of the police car parked ahead of her. Janie put on the brakes so fast that her brother almost ran into her from behind. Jason tapped his horn at her. She stared toward the house—they could see her do it.

Obviously, she and Jason were "trapped," and so Janie slowly pulled forward and parked. Jason did the same. The twins got out of their separate vehicles and walked up to the house as if they were walking through wet cement. When they opened the screen door, Janie's face hardened into an angry look, but Jason grinned and said, "Hey, Cecil, t'sup?"

The policeman smiled and turned to Genia. "This is what comes of being a cop in a small town, you know. Everybody calls you by your first name." Pretending a fierce officiousness, he growled at Jason, "That'll be *Officer* Cecil to you, kid."

Jason laughed, but behind him Janie did not even smile.

"You know what's up, Jason," the policeman continued in a casual tone. "I know it seems like a crock to you, but them's the rules, kid."

"Urine check?"

"Right."

"Here?" Jason's voice rose a little. "At my aunt's house? This is embarrassing, man! Why can't we do it like in other cities, where at least I'd have to go someplace else, like the police station or something. Why do you have to come out to my own house? Or my aunt's house?"

"Because that's the way we do it here, son."

Unmoved, the cop handed Jason a plastic container with a lid on it, and a plastic bag in which to put the "evidence" and seal it so it couldn't be opened until a lab technician tested it.

"Find a bathroom. Just do it. And then I'll leave you alone."

While Jason trudged off to follow the humiliating instructions, Officer Patterson shrugged apologetically to Genia. "Sorry about this."

"It's ridiculous!" Janie burst out.

He glanced at her. "We're just trying to keep your brother clean, young lady."

"It's so unfair. He's not a criminal—"

"Well," the officer interrupted, "yes, he is. He broke the law, and I hate to tell you this, but that's what a criminal is. Next time, he could get jail time. Do you want that to happen?"

"No, but—"

"That's what we're trying to prevent."

"You're just fascists—"

Genia stepped in quickly before her niece could land herself in trouble as big as her brother's. "Sweetheart, come back into the kitchen with me. Officer, I'm sure you understand. My niece is upset for her brother. If you'll excuse us..."

Grabbing Janie by the wrist, she tugged the girl away from temptation.

"I knew it!" Janie exploded in the kitchen. The words tumbled over each other. "I knew that's what he was here for as soon as I saw that cop car. I hate this! All Jason was doing is what every kid does. He was just experimenting, but he got unlucky and got caught. It could have been me, Aunt Genia! I've tried pot, and other stuff, too. So has everybody I know. And the cops and the court, they treat him like he's an ax murderer or something, when all he is is a normal kid like anybody else. It's so unfair! That cop out there, I'll bet *he's* tried pot. I'd bet you anything he has! And he probably drinks, but adults don't see that as a drug. Oh, no," she said with deep bitterness, "alcohol doesn't count, that's not an addictive drug, not unless a kid drinks it, of course. Then suddenly it's illegal and they throw the book at him. I hate it, it's so hypocritical and unfair!"

Genia let her get it all out and didn't argue with her.

But when Janie plopped down into a kitchen chair and put her face in her hands, Genia sat down near her and said, "You're right about a lot of things, sweetheart. It's true that grown-ups are the most hypocritical creatures on the face of the earth. I don't know if the officer out there drinks, or has ever tried drugs. I do know there are certain laws in this state and this country, and anyone who breaks them takes the risk of getting caught and punished. Just like Jason. That's how it is. You know that. We can change laws we don't like, but as long as they're on the books, there are consequences to breaking them. I love the fact that you care about your brother so much, but you won't help him if you make enemies of the police."

The girl looked up, her face tear-stained.

"Do you understand what I'm saying, Janie?"

Her niece nodded, though her face looked mulish.

Genia got up to make them both a cup of tea. "Have you eaten anything today?"

"I'm not hungry."

Her aunt started getting out a large skillet anyway, and then she pulled out all she would need to fix up "a mess"— as her Arizona neighbors might say—of scrambled eggs, bacon, hash browns with onions, and pancakes on the side. It was her opinion that low blood sugar made almost anything seem worse, and also that there was no such thing as a teenager who wasn't hungry.

When Jason came into the kitchen a few minutes later, looking cheerful enough, he appeared delighted to smell breakfast cooking, even if his sister still sat at the table looking as if she'd like to kill somebody.

"Sorry about that, Aunt Genia," he said, with no real rancor in his tone.

"How much longer, Jason?" she asked him.

"One more week, then I'm free at last." He spread his arms expansively and grinned at them. "Then I can smoke all the dope I want. Just kidding! Just kidding!"

He and Janie had already turned eighteen, which the family had quietly celebrated with a cake at their mother's house. If he broke the terms of his diversion now, he would be held accountable as an adult and be subject to a possible prison term. Genia realized that she only had to hold her breath for one more week, until he had completed his "sentence." Then she had only to worry about the rest of his life! At this moment, Jason certainly didn't look as if he had any fears about this last drug test. She felt so proud of him for staying "clean" and for working so hard at the Castle during this difficult summer.

When his sister stubbornly refused to come out of her unhappy mood or to eat a bite that Genia fixed, Jason gobbled up her share, too. With the resilience of youth, he seemed to be doing fine in regard to Stanley's death. Maybe he had let out his emotions in private, Genia thought, so that now he felt better. She hoped so. It wouldn't be healthy for an eighteen-year-old boy to grieve too much over the death of an old man, no matter how much he liked him.

Looking over at both of them, Genia admitted to herself that if she had to choose which twin worried her most at the moment, it wouldn't be Jason. It would be sensitive, emotional, unhappy Jane.

"I think I'll stop by to see your mom today," she told them.

"You can't," they warned her. "Mom's gone to Providence, and she won't be back until time for the memorial service tomorrow." The twins told her they were going out to Parker's Island to spend the night with their dad, because, as Janie bitterly said, "Mom doesn't trust us to stay on our own for one night."

"But at least if we go to the island to see Dad, we'll get away from Mom," her brother pointed out. He looked up at his great-aunt and grinned. "All Mom has to do is look at a boat and she pukes."

"Runs in your family," Genia told him. "Your uncle Lew was like that, too."

For once Genia agreed totally with their mother's decision. Without a parent around to supervise, teens could find themselves in big trouble they didn't ever intend to happen. Much better for these two to be secluded out on the island with their father, especially considering the fact that unless Stanley's murderer was some stranger who'd already fled, there was a killer still on the loose in their hometown.

"Janie, eat something," she pleaded with her niece.

"I can't," the girl complained. "Jason ate it all."

"You snooze, you lose," he shot back at her.

"I have more eggs," their great-aunt promised, and she turned to crack two more into the skillet. A few minutes later, she watched with pleasure as Janie chowed down on scrambled eggs, toast, and bacon. Genia knew she was foolish to think food always made everything all right, but sometimes, it surely made things better.

14

FOOD FOR THOUGHT

Nikki Parker Dixon didn't wait for her father's murder to be solved to hold his memorial service. On the Tuesday morning following his murder, almost six hundred persons filled St. Anne's parish church to hear their celebrated citizen eulogized by mourners ranging from the lieutenant governor to an ex-convict who had gone straight under Stanley's sponsorship. The weather changed from clear to overcast that very morning as the limousine pulled up in front of the church with Nikki and Randy inside.

Within the church the people who had attended Genia's dinner party sat near one another, as if drawn together by something in common beyond the fact of their mutual acquaintance with the deceased. Harrison Wright held his arm around his wife throughout the service. Celeste Hutchinson sat in the front row with the mayor, Larry Averill. David Graham slid into a row beside Genia. They shared a hymnal, and he whispered to her, "I hope you still want to have dinner with me tomorrow night?" *Why did I agree to that?* she thought. Nevertheless, she inclined her head in acceptance. The church was no place, and this service was no time, to back out now. Beside her the whole Eden family sat together, the twins sandwiched protectively between Kevin and Donna.

As Genia nodded her hellos to all of them, she thought of the names on the white bookmarks in the old cookbook, and she wondered, *Why did he invite you to lunch at the Castle? Why did he make me invite you to dinner?*

Ed Hennessey, dressed in a suit, stayed outside and smoked.

As Genia listened to one speaker after another extol her late friend, she thought unhappily, *Was he killed last Saturday by someone who is eulogizing him today?*

Genia had just finished changing from her black funeral suit into a comfortable pair of slacks and a blouse when a brand-new crisis exploded, forcing her attention in another direction. She had spent an hour at the Castle with other invited mourners. Now, middle of the day or not, she wanted to pour herself a glass of the wine and indulge in some of the creamy French cheese that David Graham had given her. Then she wanted to retreat with her snack to a covered section of the deck, blessedly alone, to watch the rain begin to fall.

The crisis call came from Donna.

"The police just called, Aunt Genia. It's positive." Donna's voice was rough with anguish.

Alarmed, but not understanding, Genia asked, "What is, dear?"

"Jason's drug test!"

"Oh, no! Does he know?"

"Jason? Aunt Genia, it was Jason they tested. Of course he knows. He had to know it would be positive. He couldn't have smoked the stuff in his sleep."

"No, of course not." Genia felt a rush of sympathy for her

overburdened niece. To make matters worse, he was now eighteen. "You must be worried sick. Where is he now?"

"I don't know! He raced off in his car, and I haven't seen him since. The court date is already set. It's in three weeks. How could he do this? He knew what would happen."

"Did he say anything to you before he left?"

"Oh yes. My son said, and forgive me, but I quote, 'Those assholes, I didn't smoke pot, I'm clean.'"

"Well, then, we need to find out what went wrong."

"Aunt Genia, you don't believe him, do you?"

"Well, I don't think we ought to take it for granted that he's guilty. He may be. But drug tests are often wrong. There can be false positives and false negatives."

For a moment, Donna seemed to forget her own troubles, as she exclaimed, "Sometimes I wonder about you, Aunt Genia! The things you know that I would never expect you to know ... well, if Jason shows up there, tell him to come home so that his mother can kill him. And tell him if I don't, his father will."

Within the hour, Jason showed up at Genia's back door. She let him in, observing that his young face looked shadowed with concerns that no one his age should have to carry.

"Come in, dear." She ushered him directly to the kitchen, the room in any house where troubles, if they could not be solved, could at least be salved. After the call from his mother, Genia had never poured that glass of wine. Instead, she had water on the boil, and so she poured for him and herself cups of herbal tea that advertised itself as "soothing." That was what they needed, she thought, a little warm and calming comfort. To the tea, she added honey.

"Here, Jason, drink this."

"Did Mom call you?"

Genia nodded.

"For what it's worth—probably nothing—I didn't do it, Aunt Genia. There's a mistake, there's got to be."

His aunt released her breath in a long sigh.

"It doesn't make any sense, I know," her nephew admitted. "I can't explain it. But I swear to God, I swear on Mr. Parker's grave, I didn't smoke any dope. I know what will happen if I do, I'm not a total moron. Even if my mother thinks I am. Does she really think I'm so stupid I'd risk going to jail? For a joint?" His voice was choked with anger and hurt feelings, and the sight and sound of him hurt Genia's own heart.

"I don't think you'd do that."

He lifted his head and stared at her. "You believe me? Really?"

"Of course I believe you." Genia said the words stoutly, as if they were completely true, but inside she quailed a bit, hating the soupçon of doubt she felt. "If you say you didn't, you didn't. It's true that it doesn't make any sense, but there has to be an explanation. Perhaps a mix-up in samples. Mislabeling. Something simple." She reached over to lay her hand on his arm, and she could feel how tight his muscles were.

"There's more." He paused, and gulped in air. His body looked all bunched in the chair now, as if he were pulling himself in tight. "The cops think ... Eddie told them ... they think I smoked pot ... because he told them I was growing a bunch of it in Stanley's greenhouse."

"Oh, Jason. Were you?"

He lifted his head again and stared directly into her eyes. "Well. Sort of."

Genia felt her heart sink. "You were? Did Stanley know?"

Suddenly the boy's gaze shifted away from her. "That's what the cops want to know, too. What do they care if Mr. Parker knew?" His tone became deeply sarcastic. "Are they going to arrest him, too?"

"I have to ask, Jason. Why did you grow it?"

He shrugged and avoided her gaze. "I just did. I never meant to smoke it."

"Or sell it?"

"No way!"

"Then . . . why, Jason?"

"Does there have to be a reason for everything?"

"Well, there usually is," she replied gently.

"Yeah, well, I don't know what to tell you."

The police will not be satisfied with that, Genia thought.

They finished their tea in a tense and worried silence, until her nephew said, "I'm sorry, Aunt Genia."

She clasped one of his hands. "We'll get you through this."

"I'm really glad you're here. I don't know what I'd do—"

"The main thing is, you didn't smoke it, and that can't have been your sample they tested. Let's get that straightened out first, and then we'll figure out what to do about the pot in the greenhouse. You say the police know about that?"

"Yeah. Yes."

"We're going to need to talk to your lawyer, Jason."

The boy's eyes filled with tears, which he angrily wiped away.

"Life sucks," he blurted out.

She hated very much to hear him say so. "I hope one day you'll be able to change your mind about that."

"Don't count on it, Aunt Genia," he said bitterly.

But she did count on it, with all of her heart.

And now she deduced what Kevin Eden was doing at the greenhouse the morning after Stanley's death: He wanted to destroy the evidence of his son's illegal crop.

"How did your father know you were growing pot?"

"Janie told him." This was said without surprise or rancor. "Remember when she was so mad at Mr. Parker? She saw it in the greenhouse when you sent her up to the Castle to look for him. She was so mad at Mr. Parker and me that she called Dad out on the island. She called him from right there in the greenhouse and told him."

"*That's* why she was so mad at Mr. Parker?"

"Yeah. Janie was pissed! Excuse me."

"That's all right. I'll bet she was! I am, too!"

"Don't be mad at him, okay?"

"Why not? Look at the trouble you're in now. He should never have allowed it, and don't tell me that Stanley didn't know anything about it. He knew every plant by sight. He would certainly have noticed a marijuana plant growing in his greenhouse! Honestly, if he weren't already dead, I think I would kill him myself."

"My dad was sure mad enough to kill him."

Suddenly great-aunt and grandnephew stared at each other in mutual dismay at those words.

"No!" Jason protested. "I never meant—"

"I know, honey. But tell me something. Is *that* why your father was here that night, Jason? He wasn't really coming to my dinner party, was he? He was coming to give Stanley a piece of his mind, wasn't he?"

"Yes, but Aunt Genia, my dad wouldn't . . ."

She covered one of his hands with her own again. "Of course not, but we have to know the whole truth so that no one can surprise us with it, don't we?"

She waited, but Jason didn't respond.

"*Is* that the whole truth, dear?"

He nodded without looking at her.

"And nothing but the truth?"

"So help me." But he said it bitterly, and it sounded to Genia more like a prayer than a vow.

The next evening, while getting dressed to go out to dinner with David Graham, Genia thought wearily, *Why in heaven's name did I agree to this?* She didn't want to go out with a man she barely knew and pretend that everything was just fine; she wanted to stay home and think about how to help her family. Plus, now that push came to shove, she felt a little uneasy about going out with a man other than her friend Jed White, who lived in Boston. Not that she and Jed had any claims on one another, but neither had they gone out with other people, either.

Jed had been her first true love, a college friend who had appeared back in her life a year ago. When she had first arrived in Devon, Jed had driven down from Boston to see her that week. They had met in Newport, where they had dined at a charming coastal restaurant owned by a friend of his. They'd sat outside on a heated deck, under a sky packed so full of stars that Genia accused Jed of ordering them from a catalog, just for the evening.

"It's wickedly extravagant of you," she'd teased him.

"For you, anything," he'd said with a wide smile.

Their meal had been memorable, though not entirely in a good way. It had started well enough, with delicious baked lobster stuffed with wild mushrooms, corn so sweet it took her back to her Iowa roots, and exquisite Key lime pie for dessert. It was their conversation that had soured the evening for her, and which made her still feel uncomfortable when she recalled it.

It had started when she told him the outcome of Jason's hearing for possession of marijuana.

". . . has to remain free of drugs and alcohol."

"No jail time?"

"Thank goodness, no. He's only seventeen, Jed."

"Old enough to know better, young enough to be taught a lesson."

"Surely you don't think an ordinary seventeen-year-old high school boy...who has never been in trouble before... deserves to be sent to jail...do you?"

"It would be convincing, Genia."

"It might be a good deal more than that, Jed. It might also be dangerous. I can't believe you really believe what you're saying. Marijuana is not harmless, I know, but neither is prison. In fact, I suspect it holds a great many worse dangers for a young boy than marijuana does."

"Are you a hippie, Genia?"

"No, Jed," she had retorted. "I am a grandmother."

"Soft-hearted," he'd pronounced with a patronizing tone.

"Realistic," she had snapped back.

Their evening had never got back on course after that.

Since then they had chatted by phone, but there always seemed to be some reason to cut their conversations short. Jed's business and travel schedule—and her cooking schedule with Stanley—had made it impossible for them to meet again. They were so near to one another, and yet so far. And that might be true in many ways, Genia suspected. She hated to think what he might say about Jason testing positively for drugs. As the weeks passed for her without seeing Jed again, she wondered if it was the man she missed, or only the dream of romance.

Dinner with David Graham would not be the same thing at all.

It was a reassuring thought that did not prevent her from feeling just a bit disloyal, and not only to Jed White, but also to Celeste Hutchinson. *I hope Celeste isn't at the club tonight.* However little this dinner meant to Genia, she had an uncomfortable feeling that Celeste might read it differently.

Celeste was more likely to look at it as competition for David.

"But that's silly," Genia assured herself as she fastened pearl earrings onto her earlobes. "It's just a dinner date. It's not as if I want to marry the man. Celeste is welcome to him, if he's interested in her."

Before she left she looked around the bedroom again.

"Oh, I wish I could find Grandmother Andrews' brooch," she said to herself.

15

DINNER FOR TWO

Genia wore to dinner a simple black summer dress, one that draped easily over those small bulges that seemed to appear in spite of her daily walks. Glancing in the side mirror of David's car, she checked the light sweep of blush across her cheeks, the touch of gray eye shadow, her lipstick. Over her shoulders, she wore a soft, handwoven shawl to ward off the possible chill of air-conditioning at the club. The shawl was black angora, shot through with pearly threads that picked up the luminescence of her earrings. A strand of pearls around her neck and black watered-silk pumps completed her ensemble, in which she felt a great deal more dressed up than usual.

"You look lovely, Genia," her date greeted her.

At first they drove to the Devon Yacht Club in a silence that seemed to acknowledge that they'd both had a very long week. Genia enjoyed being squired, and watched the view roll by while David remained attentive to his driving.

She stroked the buttery yellow seat of the car.

"This is very nice, David."

"It's a Lexus."

"I'm more accustomed to pickup trucks."

"It's hard to think of you as a rancher, Genia."

"Why is that?"

"Well, you hardly look like one." He glanced at her and laughed. "Where are your cowboy boots? Where's your horse?"

"The boots are back home in my closet, the horse is in the stable."

He smiled. "Maybe you are a rancher, after all."

"I love it there," she said, as she stared out the window. They were just pulling into the club, where there was a wonderful view of the ocean on three sides. "It's where we raised our children. It's home."

"A ranch must be worth a king's ransom these days."

"I don't know about that, but ours is certainly priceless to us."

"Ours? I'm sorry, I was under the impression that your husband—"

"Oh, yes, Lew died about twelve years ago. I just meant the children and me, our family."

"I see. I wish I could say the same about children of my own."

"Were you not ever married before, David?"

"No, not until Lillian."

David let a valet open the doors for them and take the car. He offered his arm to her when he came around to her side. They strolled together up the stone walkway to the club. Halfway there, an outburst of noise at the edge of the parking lot drew their attention.

"There they go again." David shook his head. "Drunken sailors."

Genia saw two men squared off. "Are they fighting?"

"Usually. Wednesday is half-price night at the bars down there."

A small crowd of men and women had gathered around the two would-be combatants. Genia stiffened when she thought she recognized Ed Hennessey, Stanley's fired handyman. And the traitor who had told the police that Jason was growing pot in the greenhouse. She could have sworn that he was staring right back at her, and she would have bet her bottom dollar he was smirking at her.

"I'd like to knock *his* block off," she muttered.

Her escort looked startled, amused. "Whose?"

"That man . . ." Genia pointed. "Stanley's handyman."

"What did he do to make you so mad at him?"

"It isn't what he did to me," she said, but then said no more.

When David tried to get her to explain herself, she squeezed his arm lightly and turned him in the direction of the entrance to the club. "I promise not to make a scene," she said lightly. "No fistfights, I swear. Not unless he starts it."

David burst out laughing. "You surprise me, Genia Potter."

If there was anything she couldn't forgive, it was somebody who hurt her family, especially the children. Aloud, she merely said, "Why, David, it's lovely in here."

"You've never been before? I thought surely Stanley had brought you."

He looked surprised and delighted to be the first to show her around. Genia tactfully refrained from telling him that Stanley had told her he wouldn't set foot in the Devon Yacht Club once Lillian and David made it their favorite place for drinking and dining.

By eight o'clock that evening Genia felt glad that she had accepted David's invitation to dinner at the Yacht Club. Seated amid elegant surroundings, with a moonlit view of the bay, Genia enjoyed being able to relax for a few hours in the company of a handsome, gracious man. His own affection for his stepdaughter, Nikki, made him sympathetic to her niece's and nephew's growing pains.

"They seem like great kids to me," he commented at one point. "Almost everybody goes through a rough time at that age, don't you think so? As long as they don't get killed, or end up in jail, or hurt anybody else, or get pregnant, I say they've done just fine." His smile was rueful. "Modest goals, perhaps. But it looks like hard work to me to navigate teenagers through the shoals of high school these days. My hat is off to all of you for trying so hard to do it right."

"Thank you, David."

Genia felt warmed by his kind words, and also by the wine, and she couldn't help but compare his empathy with the harshness of Jed White's attitude toward Jason, a boy Jed didn't even know.

Then, for over an hour, they talked of almost nothing but Stanley, of his life, his murder, his funeral. There was much to say, and there were many speculations to lay on the white-covered table. Cold stone crabs with remoulade sauce came and went, followed by Caesar salad made with fresh eggs and anchovies, and twice they emptied little plates of thin, crisp, buttered, crustless toast. Genia declined David's generous offer of champagne, but was happy to accept a glass of delicious, fruity white wine.

Her host raised his own glass of wine.

"To Stanley, of whom many fine things may be said, but the finest of all is that he was loved by Lillian."

"Why, David, what a sweet thing to say."

They touched glasses.

"Did you know her, Genia?"

"I only met her a few times, years ago."

He smiled, looking as if he were remembering something sweet. "I hope you don't mind it if I talk so much about my wife...."

"I enjoy hearing about her."

"She was beautiful, in every way. I fell in love with her the first time I saw her. You know"—he glanced frankly at Genia—"the rumors were that we had an affair before she divorced Stanley, but that is a slander on a good woman's name. I won't say that I would have had any scruples, but she certainly would have. The fact is, we never even met until after her divorce. And if we had met before then, I doubt she would have noticed me."

Privately, Genia thought it unlikely that any woman would fail to notice David Graham. He had the looks and charm to attract the attention of people of any age.

"When did she finally notice you?" Genia teased gently.

He smiled, looking pleased. "At an art auction in New York City. I bid on a Chagall print, just an inexpensive little thing, and she counterbid, and I bid again, and she beat me. I walked over to congratulate her and fell in love with her blue eyes. Lillian used to tease me that the only reason I married her was to get my hands on that print." He laughed out loud, and Genia found herself feeling charmed both by the man and by his story.

A little later, Genia found a tactful moment to ask:

"David, is it true that she drowned?"

"Didn't Stanley tell you about it?"

"No, he wouldn't discuss it."

"Really? Not at all?"

"Not at all."

"That's interesting, because I've always thought he blamed me."

"Oh, he probably did," she admitted ruefully. "But he still never talked about it, at least not to me."

"Yes, she drowned on her birthday."

"Oh, David! How awful!"

"She had a little sailboat that she loved, and she took it out for a solo cruise late that afternoon." His face darkened, and an expression of such sadness crossed it that Genia wanted to reach out to grasp his hand. "I'll tell you something I don't tell many other people. We'd had an argument that day, on her birthday, just to make it worse. I think we'd had too much wine for lunch. Usually we never argued. Never. But we did that day, and that's why she took the boat out alone. To get away from me—"

"Oh, David . . ."

"Not that she didn't love me. She did. The argument would have blown over. It was nothing. But she left angry, and maybe a little drunk, and the current was a little more than she was used to handling, only neither of us thought about that at the time, and . . ."

He sat quietly, staring down at his dinner plate.

After a moment, he continued. "She had promised to be back by six, because we had a dinner party to attend. When she didn't show up, I called her on her cell phone. It was a birthday gift. Actually, that was what the argument was about. She accused me of thinking she was an incompetent sailor. She said if I really trusted her ability, I wouldn't feel the need to reach her by telephone. I got defensive about it and said that was ridiculous, that there could be a million reasons why I might need to talk to her on the boat. But she was right, of course. It wasn't that I didn't trust her ability or her judgment, it was just that she hadn't been sailing long enough to have a chance to develop them. I hated it when she took the boat out alone. So, yes, I admit it, I got her the cell phone to make myself feel better, so I could call her and hear her voice when she was out on the sea.

"I called once. Twice. I knew she could have her hands full with the sails, I prayed that's why she didn't answer." He shuddered visibly. "That was the worst feeling I ever had, listening to that cell phone ring and ring. The damn thing was waterproof, because I got it *for* the boat. It was this elegant little teak thing, custom-made for sailors, with the name of her boat embossed on it, and it could have been ringing at the bottom of the ocean by then." He made a fist with his right hand and silently and slowly pounded it on the white tablecloth, as if crushing something. It was one of the most poignantly impotent gestures Genia had ever seen. "She never came back. They found the boat, capsized. I don't know if the boom came around and struck her, or if waves swamped her. It doesn't matter now. She's gone, and I couldn't even bury her. It seems horribly ironic now that we named her boat *Waterlily*."

When she heard that, Genia had to suppress a shiver of her own. This time, she did reach over and briefly grasp his hand. Under her touch, the tightened fist relaxed a little.

"I've never been that frightened, when she didn't answer."

"I can't even imagine it." But then Genia realized she could exactly imagine it: That's how scared she had been after Lew had collapsed with his heart attack. Like the man seated across from her, she had feared the worst, and the worst had happened to her.

"One of the most awful parts of it was telling Stanley," he said unexpectedly. "He wouldn't believe me at first. Did he think I was making it up to torture him? No, that's unkind of me. He didn't want to believe it, any more than I did. I just let him rail at me. Maybe I thought I deserved it. If I hadn't encouraged her to learn to sail...if we hadn't argued..."

"If life weren't what it is."

"Yes." He grimaced as if he'd had a sudden sharp pain. "As far as Stanley was concerned, I thought, if it makes him feel better to hate me, then let him rant at me. I knew how he felt. I wished I had somebody to blame, too."

"That was very generous of you, David."

He shrugged off the compliment. "Anybody would have pitied him."

Genia didn't think so; she thought it took a special kind of second husband to be so understanding of a hostile first husband. She listened as David added, "I think Stanley was in worse shape than I was, Genia. He really loved her, I believe. He just didn't have any talent for showing it. Lillian never quite believed that he cared as much about her as he did about himself and his many other interests."

"Do you think she was wrong about that?"

This time his smile was a little embarrassed. "Well, if I did, I never tried to argue her out of it."

Genia laughed a little. "I understand. You're only human, after all."

"All too!" He sat up straighter and made an obvious effort to smile and to inject some cheer into his voice. Rather incongruously, he inquired, "How's your lobster?"

"Perfect. But I can't eat another bite."

Genia took his cue that he had said all he could about Lillian.

"But it's all-you-can-eat!"

"This," she said, smiling, "*is* all I can eat."

16

POSTPRANDIAL

Genia! Oh, David!"

Genia looked around at the loud sound of their names, but David did not. He seemed to freeze where he sat, his right hand holding a water glass in midair. When Genia spotted the source of the greeting, she saw it was Celeste Hutchinson, perched at the bar on a tall stool, a drink in her own right hand, posed in a salute to them. She wore the same floral print dress she had worn to the dinner party; when she slid down off the stool, the back of the dress caught, hiking it up above her knees for an instant, though she didn't appear to notice.

With a feeling of dread, Genia watched her weave their way.

Celeste's gait was unsteady, her smile a bit loose.

Politely but slowly, David got up and stood beside his chair.

"Celeste," he said in a tone of resignation. "Join us?"

Genia would have felt embarrassed to be the recipient of such reluctant courtesy, but Celeste accepted the invitation cheerfully, plunking herself down at their table and then emitting a big sigh, like someone whose feet hurt and who had finally got to rest them.

"Why thank you, darlings!" Celeste had sat down too hard in the chair that David held out for her, and her body took a moment to realign itself on the cushion. She plopped her drink down hard, too, so that still more of it splashed out. There was a slur to her voice, and she was talking loudly enough to cause other diners nearby to turn their heads to look at her. With a coy lilt, she inquired, "Am I interrupting something private?"

"Not at all," Genia said with a reassuring smile.

Celeste cocked her head coquettishly at David. "A little tête-à-tête, a dinner date for two?"

"I'll order something for you to eat," he said bluntly.

Genia thought that was a good idea, but an expression of hurt crossed Celeste's expressive face. She looked indignant and martyred. "You don't have to feed me, David. I'm not a beggar here. I can take care of myself." She started to get up, but then gave up the struggle. The anger disappeared as quickly as it had come, and she giggled drunkenly. "Later. Oysters. And crackers. That sounds good. 'Long as you're paying."

She giggled again, and winked at Genia.

"Here's to Stanley Parker," Celeste said then, raising her glass high again. Her flushed face grew even redder. "Rest in peace, you lousy bastard."

Genia felt every ear in the place upon them, and she glanced rather desperately across the table at her host. "Take it easy, Celeste," David said harshly. "Everybody can hear you."

"Don't give a damn," she muttered into her drink. "Don't give a damn about anything now." She slugged the rest of it and then pointed at the empty glass while looking at David, as if to tell him to get her a refill. But when a waiter came over to take the order for oysters and crackers—to which David added a request for clam chowder—he neglected to order the drink.

The waiter walked away, looking glad to escape.

"David! You forgot my drinkie-poo."

"You've had enough to drink, Celeste."

Genia tensed at the abruptness of it, but neither did she blame him for saying it. They would do Celeste a kindness if they could keep her from making a bigger fool of herself.

Celeste glared at him. "Who do you think you are? Mr. High and Mighty Stanley Parker? Godalmighty Parker? I'll drink as much as I damn well please, and I don't want any damned clam chowder, either." She turned to Genia, her lower lip stuck out like a pouty little girl's. "Men all think they can tell me what to do. Do they do that to you? They'll run your life if you let them. As if I haven't run my own life perfectly well all these years. Who says I need any help?"

Genia exchanged another glance with David that Celeste didn't see.

This was getting out of hand, embarrassing for all of them. If they tried to stop her, she'd get angry and make an even worse scene. But if they didn't stop her, there was no telling what she'd do. Genia felt terribly relieved when a distraction walked up in the portly form of the mayor of Devon.

Larry Averill laid a hand on Celeste's shoulder.

"Did I hear somebody ask for help? Well, I could sure use some help from somebody. Evening, Genia. David. You're looking gorgeous tonight, Celeste. But poor ol' me, I could sure use a place to sit down and have dinner. You folks happen to know of an empty chair someplace in this club?"

With a look of relief, David said, "Please join us, Larry."

Instead of taking the empty chair across from Celeste, the mayor grabbed another chair from a table close by and scooted it up to their table right next to her, so he was seated between the two women. Then he took Celeste's right hand and held it firmly in his own left hand, on top of the table-cloth. Understanding that he was trying to keep a grip on his old friend's behavior, Genia scooched her own chair over to make room. It resulted in an odd seating arrangement, but it seemed perfectly satisfactory to her. *Bless his heart,* was Genia's only thought. *He's so sweet to her.*

The mayor took firm hold of the conversation.

"Great send-off for Stanley, don't you think?" he asked them.

"Fit for the king he thought he was," Celeste slurred, and would have added more, except that Larry squeezed her hand, visibly, on the tabletop, and then interrupted her to laugh and say, "Me, I wouldn't ever want to be a king, would you, Dave? Too dangerous. Too many enemies out for your blood all the time. I'll settle for a simple seat in the state leg-islature, and if I can't have that, I'll die happy being mayor of this town."

"No, I wouldn't want to be king," David replied quickly, as if also trying to override anything that Celeste might try to say. "I'm more the courtier type, myself." He laughed, in a self-deprecating way that invited the others to join in the humor at his expense. David smiled over at Genia, and then included Celeste in his glance, too. "I don't want to rule a country, I just want to take lovely ladies to dinner."

"Smart man," the mayor said, just as quickly.

"Well, I want to be queen!" Celeste waved her left arm about, almost knocking David in the head with her hand. Taking a cue from the mayor, David grabbed the free hand and held it down, also, on the tabletop. Celeste flushed and said directly to his face, "So I can yell Off with Their Heads!" She laughed, and it had a nasty sound. "Somebody sure tried to take Stanley's head off, didn't they?"

She put her face up to the mayor's, grinned drunkenly, and asked, "Who do you think that was, Larry?"

Genia wished she could be anywhere but here.

David released Celeste's hand, but Larry held on to her.

"I don't know," the mayor said calmly, "but I do know that daughter of his may have as good a head for business as her father did. I talked to Nikki a little bit, about the art festival, and I think she's going to support it." Genia felt her own admiration for the mayor growing by leaps and bounds; she felt she was getting a glimpse into how this amiable mayor managed to handle people, difficult situations, controversy. As if there weren't anything else in the world to worry about at the moment, he said to her in the most pleasant, innocuous way, "We want to hold it out on Parker's Island, you know."

"Will she let you do that?" Genia asked him, playing along.

"Well, she didn't say yes, but she didn't say no, either."

"She'll do what her father wanted," Celeste predicted in a loud voice. She stared angrily at David. "Just like everybody else did. The cowards." She looked away from him. "But not me. I've never kowtowed to Stanley Parker or to anybody else, have I, Larry, honey?"

"No, Celeste," he replied with pride and affection in his voice. "You've always been your own woman."

"Damn right."

"Nikki's hubby is all for the idea," Larry told them, referring to Randy Dixon.

"I'll just bet he is," Celeste said sarcastically. "She'll give him some highfalutin supervisory job, and he'll never have to work for a living again."

She appeared to be unhappy at losing their attention.

"Isn't anybody going to buy me another drink?"

"No," David said rather coldly, Genia thought.

"Sure, Celeste," Larry said, in a much kinder voice. "I'll buy all of us coffee and dessert. You've never had apple crisp until you've had it here in Devon, Genia. Who wants decaf?"

"Coffee?" Celeste's tone was disbelieving. "Only if it's got scotch in it."

"And then let's take a walk," Larry continued cheerfully, as if she hadn't spoken. "You and me, Celeste, down by the docks. Or, all of us, if David and Genia want to come, too. It's a pretty night, no matter what Harrison Wright says it's going to do later this week. I saw Kevin Eden tying his boat up, just before I came in here. We could go down and talk to him about the art festival, see if we can get him to cooperate." To Genia, he explained, "I guess you know Stanley let Kevin live out on the island for a pittance, and now Kevin doesn't want to be bothered with our festival. Not that I really blame him. I mean, we *will* bother him with all of our preparations, and he would probably need to vacate the island the weekend of the event."

"Is there any benefit to him?" David asked.

"Well, yeah, he could probably sell a lot of his own artwork." Larry smiled around the table at them, his genial gaze lingering last on Celeste. "So let's walk down to his boat and try to convince him to go along with it."

"He doesn't have to go along with it," Celeste blurted out, with an arch look for all of them. "Now that Stanley's dead."

There was a silence while they stared at her.

"Celeste, what are you talking about?" Larry asked her, and for the first time that evening, his tone betrayed a hint of impatience. "What does that have to do with anything?"

Celeste faced them triumphantly, with the air of someone who knows something the others don't. "It has everything to do with it! Stanley had Kevin up to lunch at the Castle, and he told him that if he didn't go along with the festival—and do it gracefully—that Stanley would kick him off the island."

Celeste laughed, and banged her empty glass on the table.

"Of course, Nikki doesn't know that," she said unsympathetically. And then she giggled. "I'm not supposed to know this. Nobody's supposed to know, but Ed Hennessey told me, 'cause he overheard the whole thing. Now that Stanley's dead, Kevin can pretend he never said anything. Unless somebody tells Nikki." She shrugged. "I'm not going to. Why should I? Why should I do a favor for Stanley Parker, who never did a damn thing for me?"

"Celeste," Larry chided gently. "That's not true—"

"You don't know!" she shot back at him. "You don't know a damn thing about it, Larry Averill." She grabbed David's wineglass and downed the remaining contents. "Stanley's dying did a lot of folks a favor, didn't it?"

She stared at each of them in turn, as if daring them to protest.

"Celeste," Genia asked quietly. "What do you mean?"

"I don't have to say what I mean." Celeste's expression looked childishly exultant until she looked over at David Graham. Then her look turned sly. "But you, David, what do you get out of Stanley being dead?" Celeste pressed her fingers to her lips in a false show of suppressing a smile. "Oh, but I guess you already got what you wanted from Stanley out of Lily, didn't you, David?"

A silence, this one chilling, fell on the group.

"Oh, did I say something wrong?" Celeste mocked them with widened eyes. "I'm so bad. Genia, I guess you're the only one here who doesn't stand to benefit from Stanley's death, aren't you?"

The mayor looked flabbergasted by the implications of that question. "Celeste," he started to say, but he was cut off before he could finish his sentence.

"How do you benefit, Celeste?" David asked in a dead-even tone.

"Me?" For the first time, Celeste looked flustered instead of just drunk. "I don't benefit from his death. Not at all. I'm sorry he's dead."

"No," David pressed, "you're not."

"David Graham, that's a terrible thing to say!"

"Do you think you haven't been saying terrible things about us?" he continued, leaning toward her. "How about facing the truth about yourself for once, Celeste? You were furious at Stanley, weren't you? I don't know why, but I know you were, so why don't you admit it to all of us?"

"Take it easy, Graham," Larry Averill objected.

The mayor grasped Celeste's hand again.

She jerked it out of his grasp and attempted to stand up.

Genia stood up quickly, too, and hurried around to Celeste's side of the table. "We're going to the ladies' room," she informed the gentlemen. Firmly, she guided Celeste around her chair, then around the table, and on toward a discreet sign that pointed to "Rest rooms."

When they got into the ladies' room, Celeste began to weep, and she begged Genia, "I've got to get out of here. Don't let David see me like this. I have to go home. I know I'm too drunk to drive. Take my keys, Genia, please? Drive me home? Oh, God, why did I say all those things? Please, please, don't let anybody see me like this."

Genia sat Celeste down in a chair in the rest room and hurried back out into the dining room to tell the men she was taking Celeste home.

"I'll drive her," Larry said, standing up at the table.

But she declined his offer, recalling how pitiful Celeste had looked as she begged Genia not to let anyone see her. "She doesn't want to see anyone right now, Larry," Genia told him quietly. "She's embarrassed. I'm sure you understand. I'll just take her keys and drive her home." Turning to her own escort, she asked, "David, could you pick me up in front of her house in twenty minutes?"

"Of course. I'll follow you."

"Fine, just don't let Celeste know you're doing it, all right?"

Genia reached for Larry Averill's hand. "She'll be okay."

"I wish you'd let me drive her home."

"No, really, it's better this way."

With the discreet help of the maître d', Genia got Celeste out a side door without being observed by very many people, and then into the front passenger seat of the Realtor's red Lincoln Town Car.

Their ride to Celeste's house was brief, as she lived close enough to the Yacht Club to be within walking distance. All of the way there, Celeste cried into the steady supply of tissues that Genia kept handing her from an open box between them on the seat. Once there, Genia got the front door open with Celeste's keys and then helped her upstairs to her bedroom.

"I don't know what I'm going to do," the Realtor kept sobbing. "I don't know what I'm going to do."

*   *   *

Still weeping, Celeste sat down heavily on the edge of her unmade bed.

"Will you be all right by yourself?" Genia asked her gently.

"Yes. No. Are you all right by yourself?" Celeste looked up with teary, mascara-smeared eyes. Genia realized she was interpreting the simple question in a complex way. "Don't you get lonely? I'm not all right by myself, Genia, and I never have been. I don't want to be alone, but what choice have I got?"

Genia thought, *You've always had a choice you didn't want.*

Lawrence Averill, she meant, for it was obvious how much he loved Celeste.

Instead of answering, Genia laid her cheek on top of Celeste's head and gave her a little hug. Then she went into the bathroom to look for some kind of medicine that might mitigate the ferocious hangover Celeste was bound to have in the morning. Finding a bottle of aspirin, she spilled out two tablets into her hand and also filled a glass with water. She took it back to Celeste, who swallowed obediently and then fell back onto her bed.

"Don't you want to get out of those clothes?" Genia asked her.

But Celeste already had her eyes closed.

Genia managed to remove Celeste's shoes, lift her legs onto the bed, and roll the bedcovers over and around her so that she wouldn't get chilled. Winded after that exertion, she stood gazing down at the other woman for a moment, waiting to see if she really was asleep.

It appeared she was, or at least she wanted Genia to think so.

Genia picked up the glass she'd brought in and carried it

back toward the bathroom to fill and leave on the bedside table for Celeste, for the inevitable moment when she awoke with a raging thirst. On her way back, moonlight caught a glimmer of jewelry on Celeste's dressing table and snagged Genia's glance. She saw necklaces, bracelets, and earrings spread haphazardly across the top of the table.

And she also saw something that made her catch her breath.

"No, this can't be," she whispered.

She walked over to the dressing table to get a better look at the contents of the jewelry box. And there it was: a starburst of diamonds and pearls, Grandmother Andrews's pearl and diamond brooch. There could not be two such pieces of jewelry in Devon. Genia lifted her lost brooch from the tangled mess of adornments, glanced over at the recumbent figure on the bed, and then put the heirloom into her own pocket.

Genia was making sure the front door would lock before she stepped out of Celeste's house, when she heard a noise that stopped her.

She looked up toward the ceiling, from where it came.

From above she heard the sound of Celeste moving about in her bedroom, first the creak of the bed as she sat up and swung her legs to the floor, then the sound of her footsteps as she walked heavily to the bathroom. For a moment Genia thought of going back upstairs. Would Celeste be sick? Was it safe to leave her alone? She guessed that Celeste had had a lot of experience with nights like these.

It was probably best to leave her alone now. By morning, the fog of alcohol would lift and give Celeste a chance to explain what looked unexplainable.

David Graham's Lexus was quietly idling at the curb,

where he waited to pick her up. She was suddenly exhausted, and felt he would understand if she asked him to take her straight back home, instead of going anywhere else that evening.

"How is she?" he asked, when he opened the door for her.

"She'll be better in the morning."

"She'll be miserable in the morning."

"I don't know what to do about that."

She decided to say nothing about the brooch.

"There's nothing any of us can do," he said.

"David... ?"

"You'd probably like me to take you right home, wouldn't you?"

"How did you guess?"

"Celeste has a way of wearing people out. Even Larry, who is as devoted as an old dog, said he was going home to bed. And I didn't think politicians ever got tired." He smiled over at her, looking almost as weary as she felt. "It was very nice of you to help her, Genia."

"Anyone would have done the same."

"Not I." There was a stern set to his jaw. "I would have left her there to get herself out of the mess she got herself into. That may sound heartless, but nobody ever helped a drunk by making it too easy for him."

Genia didn't reply, but she didn't entirely blame him, either.

It sounded to her as if perhaps David Graham and Celeste Hutchinson had a bit more of a history together than most people knew. Genia didn't know how many times they had gone out together, although she had the impression it wasn't very often. Possibly he had witnessed similar scenes before this, and that's why he was no longer as interested in Celeste as she was in him. Genia didn't judge him harshly for that, any more than she judged Celeste for being an alcoholic.

She would have liked to help, but didn't know how to do that.

David walked her to her door, left her with a polite kiss on her cheek, and said, "I hope you'll allow me to start all over again, Genia. Maybe we can pretend this evening never happened and go out to dinner again very soon?"

"I'd like that, David."

As she said it, she was surprised by how much she meant it.

17

SECOND SERVING

Eddie Hennessey leaned against the wall of the crowded, smoky bar—his usual hangout—and wondered if he would ever come back here again. After tonight he would be able to afford a better atmosphere than this, hang out with a better class of people, drink better booze.

It all depended on a telephone call.

Before tonight he'd never really noticed how bad this place smelled. He wrinkled his nose in disdain. Stale beer. The sweaty smell of frantic people. He wondered how he'd ever thought this was such a great place to spend his time, in this noisy bar full of drunken fools.

He was on his tenth drink of the evening, and it tasted fine, because this particular drink was a taste of the good life to come. In anticipation of his coming good fortune, he had spent almost the last of his final paycheck on Wild Turkey instead of his usual rotgut. His stomach was warm, his chest felt the glow of good bourbon, and he even had a second glass—imported dark ale—to chase it down.

As he savored his own excellent taste, he regarded his usual drinking buddies with a newly discovered disdain. He'd always known he was better than these bums. They'd be jealous as hell when they heard he'd won big at a casino— which was the story he was going to tell them—but he wouldn't even come back to toast his own luck and buy them a round. *Let 'em buy their own damn beer, bunch of drunks,* Eddie thought. As soon as he got his fresh start, with his fresh wad of dough, he was through with joints like this, and with lowlife people.

"I could join the Yacht Club," he proposed to himself, and then he voted himself into membership by acclamation. "Yeah, and I'll get a yacht." It suddenly struck him as very funny that there could be members of that snooty club who didn't even own a yacht. But he knew there were. Stanley Parker was one; the old man thought sailing was a bore and big boats were a waste of money. "If I want a fancy cruise, I'll call one of my foolish friends," he used to say. "All a person needs is a runabout to get them from here to there on the water."

And who's the fool now? Eddie thought, with a private smirk.

He spent a few minutes imagining the kind of boat he'd buy first: a real man's boat, something flashy and loud that he could roar around in with sexy women stretched out on the back of it. Monster dual diesel engines. He'd stock it with the finest whiskey, beer, and scotch. Cruise it down the Intracoastal Canal all the way to Miami. Hell, you could live in a boat like that; the best ones had all the comforts of a first-class apartment, and they'd rock and roll you to sleep.

"Hey, Eddie, you got a telephone call!"

His heart felt jolted, his hand shook. This could be it.

A bartender held out the receiver to him, past the faces of two women who glanced back curiously, saw Eddie, and immediately turned back to the other men seated on either side of them. He snatched the receiver, stretching the cord past the long, messy black hair of one of the women, and had to restrain himself from wrapping it around her stupid neck. Pull her clear off the barstool, that's what he'd like to do, choke her with the cord, see if she ignored him then. She'd be interested in him tomorrow, oh yeah, but he wouldn't give her a second glance by then.

"Yeah?" he said into the receiver.

"All right. You win," a voice said. It was a disguised voice, which amused the hell out of Eddie. No one listening in on an extension would have been able to tell if it was a male or a female who had called him. With a triumphant grin, Eddie replied, "Like, you had a choice."

"Public docks," the voice said, sounding angry. "One A.M."

"Hey, I'll be the one who—"

But he was talking to a dial tone. Dammit, he was supposed to be in control now, he should be setting the time and place to meet, not this loser on the other end of the phone. Flushing with anger, and embarrassed because one of the women had seen that somebody had hung up on him, Eddie tossed the receiver back onto the bar so that it barely missed hitting her.

"Hey! Watch it!" the woman protested.

Eddie muttered an obscenity at her and walked away quickly.

The men seated near the women were bigger than he was, and this wasn't a good night to be picking a fight with anybody. Now the bartender was pissed at him, too, for doing the telephone like that, and he was yelling something at him.

Eddie muttered a series of curses under his breath.

It didn't matter what these losers thought of him anymore. What mattered was what they'd think of him tomorrow when he was the big new winner in town. Women wouldn't snub him then. He could say what he wanted to them, do what he wanted, and nobody could stop him, because people with money got their way in life. He'd just roar off in his new cigarette boat, and leave them choking on exhaust fumes.

Suddenly, remembering the best part of the telephone call, he felt a pleasure so deep it hurt. "You win." They were words he'd never heard before. He hadn't really believed it would happen this quickly. But this was it, tonight! He looked at his watch. In less than an hour, he would be a rich man, a new man. Damn, he needed something special to celebrate. Holding his bourbon high in one hand, he fished in his pockets with his other hand, finally coming up with two five-dollar bills. This was it, the only money he had left from his bad old life.

Eddie weaved back through the crowd to the bar, but farther down, where another bartender was pouring drinks.

"I want a bottle of champagne," he told the guy.

"You?" The bartender barely glanced at him and laughed when he did. "You ain't the champagne type, Eddie. Try a draft beer, why don't you?"

"I said I want champagne." He wanted to toss his drink in the smart mouth's face. "I got ten dollars. Give me a damn bottle of it."

The bartender grinned at the people on either side of Eddie. "Wow. A ten-dollar bottle of champagne. Man, that's a first-class party. When you go, you go all the way, don't you, Eddie? Okay, you want some champagne, I'll give you the best we got that ten dollars will buy." He turned away, knelt down, and opened a cabinet. After moving some bottles, the bartender fished out a dusty bottle with a champagne label. He put out his right hand, palm up, and Eddie slapped his money into it. Only then did the man release the bottle into his custody. Around them, other drinkers were laughing and joking with each other about the exchange. "Have a blast, Eddie. If you can't drink all of it, you can use it in the morning to clean the fine silver."

A burst of hilarity greeted that mockery.

With his head full of booze and hatred, Eddie turned away without a word, because he knew who would have the last laugh.

The cool night air didn't clear his head at all when he stepped outside.

He pressed the warm champagne bottle against his ribs.

So it'd been sitting back in a cupboard, so it wasn't chilled on ice, who cared? Champagne wasn't supposed to be real cold, anyway. He'd show what a classy guy he was. Classy guys always used champagne to close their deals, that's how it was done.

When he reached the public docks, he looked around for his "mark."

There weren't any security guards here, not like the clubs where you had to prove you belonged before they'd even let you walk onto a dock. Choppy waves banged against the pilings and bottom of Dock A, making it shake, when he walked out onto it. For a wobbly moment, Eddie had to fight to put one foot in front of the other. Maybe he was a little drunker than he'd thought he was, but who could blame him? Eddie made himself stand up straight on the unsteady dock and told himself he was going to straighten up in all ways from now on. He wouldn't screw this up, not like he'd been screwed all his whole friggin' life. Tonight was the beginning of good things. Eddie felt grand as he imagined himself buying the power boat, and also a cabin on a salt marsh. Or a condo right on the ocean. And he was going to need a deep-sea fishing boat, and not one of those puny skiffs like his loser so-called friends owned. A fifty-footer, with a cabin below and a flying bridge up on top. He'd need something big enough to haul red crabs, pull some pots, spear some swordfish, something big enough to cruise the shore, and also go way out to sea. Maybe he'd take it on down to the Caribbean, maybe through the Panama Canal, and over to California. There was no stopping him now.

He reached for a railing, steadied himself, clung to it.

The sky was heavily clouded, covering the moon, not like the night when old man Parker got killed. That night was a miracle, Eddie truly believed, a miracle, the way the moon lit up the path right where it happened, so Eddie could see it all perfectly. The rain had come up soon after that and there were clouds all over the rest of the sky, but there was that one spot where it was clear, where the moon beamed like a spotlight exactly where Eddie needed to see what he saw: the approach. The greeting. The angry argument. The upraised arm. The weapon, and the blow, so strong and murderous it not only knocked the old man sideways, but his motorbike, too, sending both man and bike tumbling over the hill. And then Eddie had watched with eager interest the rest of it, which was horrible and fascinating: how the old man had fallen midway down the cliff and sprawled there, not moving, and then how the attacker had climbed down after him, striking him again and again, and then using the weapon to shove the old man's body until it rolled all the way down to the beach.

The old man had to be dead after the first blow.

But the killer made sure, and the moon made sure that Eddie knew who it was. And that wasn't even all he knew from hanging around the Castle, especially during the last couple of weeks of the old man's life. This was just the biggest secret, the main treasure chest of loot for him. The other things he knew, they were small change he could collect anytime he needed pocket money.

Tonight, he'd go for the big payoff first.

A sudden wind sent an empty paper cup skittering across the dock and into the water.

The sudden noise made him jump.

What time was it? How long had he been standing here? He couldn't miss this appointment! Even if he was late for everything else in his life, he had to be on time for this.

Eddie looked around, feeling worried.

This couldn't be right, this dock was too crowded, there were people in these boats, a few of them still sitting out on their decks. There was a radio playing on one of them, and the sound of soft laughter coming up from a cabin. Eddie turned and weaved back the way he'd come. He'd lost all track of time. He made his way down past the other docks, toward the last one.

Finally, he saw a figure standing in the shadows.

It was the dock where boaters tied up the smallest of the motorboats, not the kind you'd sleep on overnight, and it was empty except for the lone person standing there.

"Hey!" Eddie called out, before he realized it wasn't a good idea to shout. More softly, as he got closer, he said, "That you?"

"Right here," a restrained voice answered. "You're late."

It made Eddie mad to be accused like that by this person.

As he got close enough to see a face, he retorted, "I'm here when I want to be here." Suddenly, he felt a need to hurry. "Let's get this over with. Where's my money?"

"Come on out and I'll give it to you."

"Out where?"

The person walked out onto the dock between the two rows of tied-up motorboats. Evidently, Eddie was expected to tag along, and that made him mad, too. Oh, well, let the fool pretend to be in charge. They both knew who was really running this show and who would be leaving with the cash. When Eddie saw that he was expected to climb into a small boat, he balked, but only because he was already unsteady on his feet, and the idea of maneuvering his way into the hollow of the little motorboat seemed too difficult to contemplate.

"Come on aboard, Eddie."

"Don't want to. You come back out here."

"Oh, come on, I'll give you a hand. It's all here. We can sit down and talk about it. Anybody sees us, we're just a couple of friends on a boat."

But Eddie snubbed the helpful hand that reached up to him.

"Forget that, I can make it on my own."

He grasped a post on the dock with his left arm and let himself clumsily down into the boat, still clutching the champagne bottle under his right arm. The boat lurched just before he let go of the post, and he almost went in the water, in the narrow space between the side of the motorboat and the edge of the dock.

"Damn! Whose boat is this?"

"It's the *J&J.*"

"*J&J*? What's that mean?"

"It stands for Jason and Janie."

"Jason and—" Eddie got it, and laughed. "Perfect."

Once he was in and safely seated, he felt triumphant, as if he'd proved something important. He'd gotten into the boat on his own. He could handle things. He could handle this. "I can barely see you. Don't they put lights on these docks?"

"We don't need any light."

"Afraid somebody will see you with me?" Eddie laughed. "They'll say, 'Hey! Ain't that—' "

"Keep your voice down."

It made Eddie mad to be talked to like that, but that was okay, because getting mad just made him more courageous. "Got us a bottle of champagne to seal the deal. Want a drink?"

"No, I've had enough tonight."

Eddie fumbled with the plastic and wire top on the champagne, his thumbs slipping off it a couple of times before he got the hang of it. He didn't want to look like an idiot. When the plastic cork finally popped, it flew off into the water, releasing a spray of fizz over the top of the bottle, wetting him, his knees, and the bottom of the boat. Eddie licked the wine off his fingers and made a face. It was sour. He'd rather have whiskey or beer. "Got any glasses?" he asked, and then laughed.

"No."

"We'll have to share the bottle."

"I don't want any. It's all yours."

"Aw, come on, don't you want to celebrate?" It was said sarcastically. Eddie raised high the fat bottle. "Here's to us, a great partnership."

"No partnership. A one-shot deal. You shut up. I pay up."

"Yeah, yeah." He took a swig, made a face at it. "Cheers."

"You think it was easy for me to get this money?"

"Yeah, matter of fact, I do. And I think you ought to throw in something else, for all the trouble I'm saving you." This idea had only just come to him, but it seemed so logical and right. "You gotta get me a place to live free. Not over a damn garage, either. I want a nice place, like you got."

"I can't do that much for you."

"Why not? It'd be easy for you."

"You're greedy, Eddie."

"And you're not?" He laughed, took another swig. "You got the power to do things for me."

"I haven't got any power, Eddie."

"Sure you do, and there's lots of things I want."

"First things first. I brought the money."

"Where is it? Give it to me."

"Here."

The other person reached back, grabbed hold of something.

Eddie lifted the bottle again and closed his eyes. He had to laugh. Old Man Parker was always telling him how he ought to grab the opportunities life gave him. Well, this was it. Heaven was opening, and hell was closing up tight. In another minute, when he opened his eyes, there'd be a spread of cash in front of him, more cash than he'd ever seen outside of the cashier's cage in a casino. He groaned out loud with pleasure and anticipation.

Some sixth sense made his eyes fly open.

He saw the arm swinging toward him, holding long, hard metal quahog tongs. There was no time for him to move out of the way. It came so fast it was a blur. He felt an instant of blinding pain when the tongs slammed into his skull and heard a terrible crunching within his own head. The champagne bottle fell from his grasp, spilling its sour yellow contents all over his pants legs, flooding the bottom of the boat with the smell of alcohol. The tongs crashed into his skull a second time, then a third and fourth, but Eddie didn't feel those. He didn't hear the splash when the tongs went into the dark water of Narragansett Bay, and he didn't feel the boat rock when the other occupant stepped out of it.

Nor did he hear the words, "One more job to do."

18

TOO MANY COOKS

Genia's curled, sleeping body felt the noise before it registered in her mind. One of her shoulders twitched, as if it had been shoved by an invisible hand. Instantaneously, her eyes flew open. *What was that?* She shot up in bed, every nerve ending alert.

Did I hear something, or only dream it?

She blinked, fighting to see through the darkness of the bedroom. Although the curtains at the windows were pulled back and the shades were raised, no moon or starlight shone through to illuminate things for her. Either the moon was busy elsewhere, or black clouds covered it tonight. Gradually, she made out shapes of furniture, humped and inhuman in the shadows.

There's nothing in here that shouldn't be here.

At least not that she could see. Genia realized she was holding her breath. She let it out quietly, and just as quietly took in another breath. Her ears strained to catch any untoward sound from this floor or the one below her. Through an open window, she heard the branches of the slender pine tree outside her windows slide against each other as a slight breeze moved them. Everything, otherwise, seemed unnaturally silent, except for the pounding of her own heart, which sounded as if it were beating in her ears instead of in her chest.

She glanced at the small round clock beside the bed: one-thirty. Long enough for her to have drifted off into a deep sleep for several hours. She had fought sleeplessness by reading Stanley's old cookbook until her eyes drooped. Then she had closed the cookbook and laid it down beside the clock. And now a noise—actual, or dreamed?—had jerked her back to wakefulness. She reached for the light near the clock and book, but before her fingers could touch the small brass switch, she heard something. Or thought she did. A muffled sound, partly thud, partly click. It sounded distant but distinct, a real sound coming from downstairs. This was no dream.

I really heard something.

She reached instinctively for her robe, which lay across the foot of her bed. The sound was inside the house, she was sure of that now. Something—someone!—was in the house.

Without turning on the light, she slipped out of bed and into the robe. Standing beside the nightstand, she looked frantically around the room. *Where did I leave the phone?* It was a portable, and the base that sat upon the nightstand was empty. *Where was I when I used it last?* Frantically, she tried to remember, but couldn't. It had been so many hours ago, even before her dinner at the Yacht Club with David. Who had she called before that? Where did she leave the phone? She moved toward the bathroom—terrified of making the floor creak—hoping she had left the receiver on the counter while she was making up her face for her date.

Yes! Oh, thank goodness, there it is!

But when she punched the "on" button—and froze at the sound of the beep it gave off—the hollow, echoing silence of a dead phone line fed her fear.

Now what, old girl?

No 911. No neighbors close enough to holler out the window. No way down outside from this second floor without breaking a leg or my neck. Should I swallow my fear and go downstairs to check things out? No! Stanley was murdered! I must not take any stupid chances. Whoever killed him might be downstairs in this house at this very minute. I'll have to hide, but where?

If she moved from where she stood, with every step, she took the risk of making noise. Another muffled *thud* from down below made her decision for her. She bolted silently into the closet but did not close the door behind her. If the intruder came up here, let him see the open closet door, let him think that meant she wasn't in there. With pounding heart, she crept into a corner of it, covering herself behind hanging clothes.

But as she waited—*for what?*—a sliver of anger worked its way into her chest and began to grow into indignation, then fury, and then into resolve.

No! No one is going to get the best of me like this. How dare they! I will not be killed like a cowering rabbit. I will not die like this, huddled in a corner of a closet! No!

With great care she crept out of the closet, still feeling very afraid but no longer helpless. She grabbed the only potential weapon she could find, an umbrella with a leather handle and a stiletto metal point at the business end of it. *Absurd, but what else is there?* She wrapped her fingers around the handle and tiptoed toward the open door of her bedroom, taking up a position behind the door, the umbrella pointed up, ready to plunge into the chest of any intruder who entered there.

She leaned back just a little, intending to support herself against the wall. Her head pressed against the corner of a framed painting. Before she could stop the movement, the frame thudded against the wall behind her. In the silence it sounded as loud to her as a gunshot. She went rigid with fear, her knuckles weakened, and then she grasped the umbrella handle as if her life depended on it. *As perhaps it does. Did the intruder hear that? Will he come upstairs now?*

Below, there was nothing but silence.

The moments stretched into an eternity. She prayed the intruder would stay below, or if he came upstairs that she would have the opportunity to stab the umbrella into his throat or his face or his groin. *I will not hesitate.* She feared she was not strong enough to do any real harm, but if she could hurt him just enough to make him pull back, she might get precious minutes to race down the stairs and out the front door to her car, to the neighbors, to the police.

I will not be a victim!

From out of nowhere came a memory: she and Lew many years ago, sleeping in their cabin in Maine. A cold night. Lew's body curled around her own to warm them both, her back pressed cozily into his chest, his knees brought up behind her own. They'd been sound asleep with the moon flooding their bed and their bodies with light. And someone—a drifter, the police said after they arrested him weeks later—had broken into their cabin and rifled it of every radio, camera, television that could be lifted through a window into the waiting arms of his accomplice. A sound had awakened them to what was happening only a few feet away from where they slept. Lew had shot out of bed, grabbed a hunting rifle, and plunged into the living room in his pajamas. The intruders ran, with Lew firing over their heads into the cold night air. He hadn't wished to kill anyone, just scare them off. Both he and Genia had insomnia for many nights afterward.

The grandfather clock at the foot of the stairs struck the hour.

Her arms ached from grasping the umbrella. There were no more sounds, and now the house felt empty to her. She felt alone in it again, but could she trust that sensation? What if someone were waiting for her at the bottom of the stairs? What if he had more patience than she?

For an eternity more, she stood there, afraid to come out. *My life may be at stake. I can bear this. I can wait.*

Only when the sky began to lighten did she finally move out from behind the door, so stiff and exhausted she felt like an elephant crashing through the underbrush.

There was no answering noise from downstairs.

She ventured down the carpeted stairs, pausing at each one, waiting, listening, still hanging on to her weapon. Normal noises came to her: the hum of the refrigerator motor, the tick of the grandfather clock, a drip of the kitchen faucet.

Genia stepped onto the first-floor carpet.

From there, she could see into the living and dining area. *Nobody there, unless they're crouched behind the furniture, or lurking behind the draperies.* She moved cautiously into the hallway, checked the front foyer—*The door is still locked*—then walked back toward the kitchen. It took all the courage she had to push open the door, and then walk into that room.

Her purse still sat on the kitchen table.

She went over to it, opened it, found nothing missing.

A radio still sat on the windowsill above the sink. She had not noticed anything awry in the living room. It appeared so far that nothing was missing, nothing stolen, or at least nothing she had seen so far. Everything was as she had left it when she went up to bed. The kitchen door was bolted, just as it should be, as she had taken to doing ever since Stanley died.

Did I imagine this nightmare? Was there never anybody here? Did I exhaust and terrify myself over nothing at all?

The portable kitchen phone lay upside down on the kitchen table beside her purse, just as she had last seen it. She picked it up, listened to the same hollow sound she'd heard on the extension upstairs, and then looked at it. It was "on"! As if it had been left off the hook! *Did I do that? Did I forget to press the "off" button the last time I used it?* It was easy to make that mistake, but she thought she had been careful every time to push the "off" button after each call.

She turned it off now, feeling very foolish.

Everything seemed normal, just as she had left it.

Genia filled a kettle with water, put it on the stove, and turned it up to boil. *I need a cup of tea. Oh, Stanley, am I crazy? Did I only imagine there was someone in this house?* There was no point in calling the police now. Obviously, she had imagined everything. Thank goodness she hadn't called them! A little self-criticism and self-pity started to creep into her mind, but then she reminded herself: *There was a murder in this little town just a few days ago. I am surely not the only person in Devon who has imagined things that might go bump in the night. We're all afraid, it's not just you, Genia.* She forgave herself. But now she felt tired enough to crawl back into bed and sleep for several hours.

After one cup of tea, that was exactly what she did.

19

Sweet Tooth

Three hours later, when Genia went downstairs again to start her morning for real, something felt "off" to her about the kitchen. Even so, she couldn't put her finger on what it was. She shook off the feeling, telling herself firmly, "It's just your imagination working overtime again." Although she was still tired and emotionally edgy, she felt ready to tackle a necessary but unpleasant task.

"Let's get it over with," she told herself.

She took a deep breath and then dialed Celeste's number.

After several rings, Celeste answered, sounding as if she had endured an even rougher night than Genia's. Feeling it might be untactful to ask "How are you, Celeste?" Genia opted for a cheerful, businesslike briskness, instead.

"It's Genia. I'd like to drop by for a few minutes."

"This morning?" The Realtor groaned. "Oh, God, I have such a hangover. Did I see you last night? I did, didn't I? At the Yacht Club, right? What did I do? Did I do anything embarrassing? Oh, God, don't tell me, I don't want to know."

"I'll bring you some coffee, Celeste."

"Oh, heaven! You're an angel. Make it a latté. A double. Skim milk."

"Sweetener?"

"I've got the sweetener, and it's called bourbon." Celeste laughed, a throaty sound that ended in coughing. "But bring me something sweet to eat, will you?"

She abruptly hung up, leaving Genia hanging on to the receiver.

She had actually sounded fairly good-humored, Genia thought with amazement, as if she truly had no idea how she had behaved last night, or how she had looked to the man whose opinion seemed to matter most to her. It appeared that Celeste had no memory of how she got home, either. Would she remember taking a brooch from Genia's dining room?

Genia stopped by Stella's Bakery for a cream cheese and blueberry kringle, a circular delicacy that had become her favorite coffee cake in all the world. Stella's were only one inch high, but that single inch was sinfully buttery with a fresh fruit and cream-cheese filling set into golden brown pastry. It made Genia's mouth water to look at it.

With the still-warm kringle in a white box at her side and two lattés propped up in drink holders, Genia drove south along the wharf area. She noticed police cars, four of them, down at the water's edge. A crowd of people were held back by a yellow crime scene tape that brought all too vividly to mind the last time she had seen such a thing: at the site of Stanley's murder.

Oh, dear, she thought, *I hope those men who were fighting last night didn't kill each other.* Her second thought was to wonder if a boating disaster had befallen someone, or if somebody had gotten drunk and tumbled into the harbor. It probably wasn't "just" an accident in the parking lot, because surely the police wouldn't put up crime scene tape for something like that. Even though she slowed her car to try to see what was going on, she couldn't tell much from where she was driving.

She recalled her own fantasy of terror last night.

It seemed childish in daylight, and especially in view of the scene down at the harbor. That hinted at tragedy for someone, of real fear, and possibly real loss. She offered up a prayer for the sake of anyone who might be involved in it, whatever it was.

She drove on farther south into the section of Devon where Celeste lived. A handful of the colonial and Federal-style homes in the picturesque area boasted small brass plaques that denoted inclusion on the National Registry of Historic Places. She knew that one of them was attached to Celeste's house. Genia had other friends with such residences and she knew how much money was required to maintain them.

Turning onto Celeste's street, Genia admired a profusion of pink and white wild roses climbing over a wrought-iron fence on the corner. The Realtor's home was a Federal-style brick house, old-world and elegant. When Genia had driven Celeste there the night before, she had altogether missed the stately beauty of the house, and now she admired it fully. Neatly trimmed bayberry bushes lined the gas-lit drive and a brilliant array of zinnias and begonias welcomed visitors to the front door. Genia could easily imagine the wife of a sea captain waiting inside to welcome her husband home from his journeys.

Sunlight, bright and hot this morning, reflected blindingly off Celeste's red Lincoln, which Genia had left parked in the driveway. But clouds on the horizon told her that the weather was about to change, just as Harrison Wright had been predicting all week. She smiled to herself, thinking how much ribbing he would have to take when the rain arrived and scared off all the tourists.

Despite her smile, the clouds suited her own mood this morning.

She was worried about Celeste, about her drinking, and about the inexplicable appearance of the brooch in her jewelry box. Maybe there was an innocent explanation, but what if there wasn't? Why would a successful Realtor, a woman who lived in the "best" part of town, take a valuable piece of jewelry that didn't belong to her? For that matter, why did she drink so much? A recovering-alcoholic friend of Genia's had once told her, "It's a progressive disease, Genia, and to stop drinking is merely the first step in recovering from it."

Celeste didn't seem ready to take that step.

Clearly, Larry Averill thought that Celeste was about as fine a person as anyone could be. But even the mayor had acted concerned about her last night. Genia wondered if he had been watching Celeste decline over a long period of time, or if something recently had exacerbated the problem.

Like an unrequited love affair? she wondered, feeling uneasy.

Had seeing David Graham with Genia at dinner been enough to set Celeste off on that humiliating scene?

Genia parked behind the Lincoln and then walked reluctantly up to the front door carrying the kringle box in front of her like a shield, with the lattés in their tall cups perched precariously on top. She saw a "Wet Paint" sign and carefully avoided the shiny black trim around the front door.

Framed in the gleaming doorway, Celeste stretched out her arms. "Genia, come on in! What have you got there, something delicious, I hope? I'm starving! What a marvelous way to start the day, with you dropping by for breakfast."

Genia handed over the lattés, feeling taken aback.

Here was no hung-over, disheveled woman in a frumpy bathrobe.

This was a vivacious dynamo in a gorgeous red silky robe over matching pajamas, with red high-heeled slippers, and her hair combed and makeup on. Celeste looked exactly like the successful Realtor she was, and not at all like the shamefaced, sick alcoholic that Genia had expected to see. If Celeste had felt rotten when Genia called earlier that morning, there was no sign of it now.

As Genia stepped inside the house, she inquired a little wickedly, "Are you feeling all right now, Celeste?"

"I feel marvelous, all I needed was a little hair of the dog that bit me."

Genia hadn't heard that euphemism for alcohol in years. Celeste, it seemed, had already started off her day with a drink.

Moving like a woman of boundless energy, Celeste led her guest through the front rooms, where Genia silently admired a landscape painting above a wonderful fireplace and richly polished ash wainscoting along the walls. "I must have had a touch of flu last night, Genia, otherwise I can't imagine why I reacted so strongly to just a little bit of alcohol. That isn't like me at all! I hope you understand. I've already talked to Larry, and he tells me you brought me home, you sweetie. I'm sure I could have made it on my own, but it was nice of you, all the same. Let's see what you've brought me from my favorite bakery!"

Following behind, Genia decided ruefully that she now had a much better understanding of the concept of "denial." She'd never seen anyone make so fast a recovery from being so inebriated. Perhaps Celeste had started drinking again first thing in the morning—"a little hair of the dog"—or she had taken an amphetamine to counteract the sedative effects of the alcohol. Either way, these were bad signs.

"What is happening to my town, Genia?" Celeste's tone was as dramatic as a diva's as she got busy opening Genia's gift box in the kitchen. "Oh, a kringle, my favorite, and blueberry, too." She touched the coffee cake with the forefinger of her right hand and then licked her finger. "Yum. Hand me a couple of those dessert plates, will you? Isn't it scary? People just being killed right and left? How am I ever going to sell houses if buyers are afraid they'll be murdered in their beds?"

Genia took a seat on a stool at the counter. "One murder is not an epidemic, Celeste."

"One? Haven't you heard the latest?"

Intuitively, Genia thought back to the yellow crime scene tape down at the wharf this morning. "No, what happened?"

"Somebody killed Ed Hennessey." Celeste said it with relish, as if passing on delicious news. "That awful groundskeeper of Stanley's. It happened down at the harbor last night. Or maybe this morning, I'm not sure. Larry told me all about it, but I've already forgotten the details. Can you believe it? Two murders in less than a week? This one's so disappointing, though."

Genia stared at her hostess. "How so, Celeste?"

"I had Eddie pegged as the number-one suspect in Stanley's death!" She glanced over at Genia as she continued cutting the entire kringle into serving-size pieces. "Didn't you?"

Genia had to admit, "Yes, maybe I did."

"Well, I guess it's not him!" Celeste laughed and passed a plate over to Genia, along with a sterling silver fork. "*Bon appétit,* thanks to you. Now, tell me all about you and David Graham!"

Genia felt doubly taken aback, first by the news of the latest murder, and then by the incongruous change of subject. She looked closely at Celeste, who appeared rather studiously blasé, as if the question and the effort of hearing the answer were costing her something she didn't want revealed. Genia felt she was rather callously dismissing a man's death, even if he had been a reprehensible human being.

"There's not a thing to tell, Celeste."

"Bosh. Out to dinner together and nothing to tell?"

Evidently Larry Averill had jogged her memory quite a bit.

"No, honestly, we were just two friends dining out. We were both so glad when you joined us, and then Larry, too."

"*You* may have been glad," Celeste said meaningfully.

Genia didn't want to go down that road, and neither did she want to be sidetracked so easily from the shocking news of Ed Hennessey's death. "Celeste, how did Hennessey die, did Larry say?"

"What do you mean?"

"Was he killed in a fight?"

"Oh, I guess. I heard he was beaten to death."

Instinctively, Genia's hand went to her heart. She couldn't help but feel compassion for the man whose life had been so short and so sordid. "Oh, my. Do they know who did it?"

She half expected Celeste to say it was another drunken man down at one of the bars, and was dismayed when the answer was "Well, they found him in Kevin Eden's boat, so maybe it was Kevin, or that delinquent son of his, what's his name?"

"Jason," Genia said, barely able to get the name out.

"Oh, Genia!" Her hostess turned with a look of such dramatic sincerity that Genia immediately sensed it was false. "I'm so sorry. I completely forgot they're your relatives. Please forgive me."

Genia was unable to utter any such words at that moment.

It was her definite impression that Celeste had purposely set out to be cruel. If so, she had succeeded. Eddie Hennessey's body found in Kevin's boat! Genia felt like weeping at the new trouble that might now be roaring into the lives of her niece and the children. And Kevin, she amended guiltily. She mustn't forget the twins' father, even if he was divorced from their mother.

She put her fork down on the plate, all hunger fled.

"I never should have said that," Celeste continued in the same tone of false remorse. "And I shouldn't listen to gossip, either, but in my line of work, I hear everything, even the stuff that isn't true. Now I know perfectly well that your nephew wasn't growing marijuana up in that greenhouse of Stanley's, was he? And he certainly didn't kill Stanley, did he, Genia? That's just absurd, isn't it?"

Genia felt pummeled by one shock after another as she listened to the ugly words coming out of Celeste's mouth. She knew that Jason was growing pot in the greenhouse? Jason killing Stanley? Feeling sick, she asked, "Is that what people are saying, Celeste?"

"What? About Jason?"

"Yes, that he was growing pot, or that he killed Stanley?"

"Who cares what people say? The important thing is the truth."

"I care what people say about him," Genia said as firmly as she could with a trembling voice. "He's my nephew, Celeste. I want to know who told you these things."

"Oh!" Celeste turned her back for a moment to do something at the sink. "It was Ed Hennessey, if you want to know. He just seemed to know everything about everybody, didn't he? Maybe he shouldn't have." She turned around again, an odd smile playing at her lips. "Maybe it wasn't good for his health."

Genia sat silently, stunned and hurt, trying to absorb all she was hearing. Celeste was implying that Ed Hennessey had been killed because of something he knew about Jason, or about someone else. Celeste was implying many things, any of which might be totally false.

"When did he tell you all this, Celeste?"

"I don't know. Last week sometime."

"Why would he tell *you*?"

For the first time, the other woman looked hesitant. She picked up the sticky knife they had used to cut the kringle and turned around to wash it at the sink. With her back turned, she said, "Why not me? For all I know, he told a hundred other people."

Genia decided to drop her own bomb at that moment.

"How did my grandmother's brooch get into your jewelry box, Celeste?"

She saw the other woman's shoulders tense.

"Your what?"

"I saw it last night, in your bedroom."

There was a long moment of silence, and then Celeste whirled around, her eyes narrowed, her voice loud and furious. "Oh, I see how it is. You're going to tell David Graham that I'm a thief, and it'll be your word against mine. I didn't take your brooch, Genia. It must have fallen off your dress, and it got stuck to my shawl, somehow, and I carried it home accidentally with me. I was going to return it to you, and I just forgot about it. But I didn't steal it. Why would I?" She gestured dramatically about her. "I already have everything anybody could want, don't I? What in the world would I want with your ugly old brooch?"

Genia would have felt mortified if she weren't so convinced it was all a lie, from start to finish. She stood up. "I'm glad you're feeling better, Celeste. I'm sorry to have troubled you over the brooch. I'll let myself out."

"Better hurry, Genia, before I snatch your earrings."

With as much dignity as she could muster, Genia turned and strode back through the beautiful house by herself. She let herself out the heavy front door and quietly closed it behind her. When she got back into her car and placed her hands on the steering wheel, she saw they were shaking. That had been one of the most unpleasant scenes of her life. She feared she might have let her own pique goad her into making it worse. As she started to drive, she felt like kicking herself. But she didn't even have time for that, because she needed to get right over to Donna's to see if the Edens needed help. Suddenly, the implications of Celeste's nasty words hit her so hard that she nearly ran her car off the road. With trembling hands she straightened her wheel just in time, coming within inches of hitting a parked van.

Rumors about Jason . . .

Hennessey's body found in Kevin's boat . . .

The morning had turned ugly and dark for her; a huge fear oozed its way into Genia's heart and lodged there tightly in a space where there wasn't room for it. For a moment she felt suffocated by a terror for her nephew that was even greater than what she had felt for herself the night before. *Jason! What was happening in this town?* Quaint little Devon had become a site of grisly murders in the space of a single week. And the deepest horror of all to her was that her small family was somehow connected to each of them. It was nearly more than Genia could stand. She didn't know how Donna would bear this news.

20

COFFEE KLATCH

It seemed to Genia as if her leased car almost turned itself toward the edge of downtown Devon. Then it glided into a parking space in front of the small building that housed the Eden Art Gallery on the first floor and living quarters on the top two floors. Like its neighbors it was a red-brick Federal-style building. This one had originally been a single-family residence for a wealthy Devon sea captain. Now the little art gallery paid the mortgage, and Donna and her twins squeezed themselves into the narrow quarters up above. The guest room where Genia had stayed for two weeks was nearly a garret and had once been a servant's quarters.

Genia walked shakily into the small shop and saw that Donna was helping a customer at the antique desk where she conducted her sales business.

Donna looked up at the sound of the bell and smiled at her aunt.

"Good morning! I'll be with you in a minute, Aunt Genia."

Obviously, Donna didn't know yet about Hennessey.

"Is Jason home?" Genia asked with a glance upward. She couldn't tell her niece about the second murder now, not with a customer in the shop. But what if someone called, or came in and told Donna about it while Genia was upstairs with her son? She'd have to take that chance; it seemed even more important at the moment to talk to Jason.

"I think he's still asleep," said his busy mother as she operated a credit card device. "He got in late last night, as usual. Go on up, why don't you, and wake him up for me. If he's not going to be working at the Castle anymore, I've got plenty of jobs for him to do."

Genia went on through the shop and then up the mahogany steps to the living quarters. The three-story house had belonged to her late husband's sister—Donna's mother. It was the home Donna had been raised in, and it comprised the bulk of her inheritance from her parents, who had been Genia's brother-in-law and sister-in-law. It was quite valuable, but Donna had always been understandably loath to sell it, or even to mortgage it to raise extra money for herself and her children. Genia quite admired her niece's determination to work hard and to earn her living apart from her inheritance.

At the top of the staircase there was a small area that served as an entryway. Donna had furnished it sparsely but tastefully. A little antique table and chair were positioned below an oval mirror, and on the polished hardwood floor she'd placed a deep rose Oriental rug that had been left to her by her mother. The walls were painted white and held samples of Kevin's charming work, as well as several oil paintings of regional scenery, done by other local artists whose work Donna showed downstairs. She had explained to Genia that she'd rather hang the art here than store it back where nobody could see it; this way, if she had an art lover who might be interested, she could bring him right upstairs to see how a particular painting looked in an actual residence. The children had grown up knowing how to scoot to the third floor when the sound of footsteps on mahogany announced the imminent arrival of paying customers. One morning, Genia herself had quickly lifted her morning teacup and gotten herself, still in her bathrobe, safely upstairs to her garret before Donna walked into the kitchen with a pair of Australian tourists who had wanted to see what Kevin's work might look like in their home.

Several doors off the foyer led into the kitchen, living room, and master bedroom. As Genia walked past, she saw they were all empty this morning. She headed for the stairs leading to the children's bedrooms. The garret where she had stayed had once been Kevin's tiny art studio. Although she had not been out to see his barn/studio on Parker Island, she had heard the children say he now had "tons more space to work."

At the top of the third floor, she called, "Jason?"

"Aunt Genia?" A muffled voice returned her call. "Hold on a sec."

In only a moment the boy appeared, pulling a T-shirt down onto his chest. Below that were blue jeans and big bare feet. He grinned when he saw her. "T'sup?"

She had learned that meant, "What's up?"

"Do you have a few minutes to talk to me, dear?"

" 'Course, I always have time to talk to you. You're my favorite aunt." He planted a kiss in the air near her as he sailed past her, taking the steps two at a time. "Gotta have some coffee, though."

With a sigh, Genia followed her grandnephew back down.

She found him already measuring dry coffee in the kitchen. She watched him finish that task, set the coffee to perking, and then open the refrigerator door, pull out a carton of milk, and guzzle the rest of its contents as he stood there. If she hadn't been so sick at heart for his sake, she would have just smiled and enjoyed watching him. He grabbed an open box of donuts from a countertop, plunked them down on the small kitchen table, and gestured for her to join him. "Sorry, but I just got up, and I'm starved. Want a chocolate sprinkle? I don't recommend the plain cake donuts, they're boring."

Genia selected a chocolate donut with chocolate icing.

"Jason, there's been another murder in town."

"No shit! I mean, I'm sorry, Aunt Genia, excuse my language. No kidding?"

His surprise seemed utterly genuine to her.

"Ed Hennessey was killed down at the docks last night."

Jason raised his eyebrows in an expression of even greater surprise. But then he snorted and said, "Good. Couldn't happen to a nicer guy. Who did it?"

"I don't know."

"How'd it happen?"

"He was beaten to death."

The boy grimaced. "Ow. I guess nobody deserves that."

"Jason, they found his body in your father's boat."

He stared at her, as if he hadn't understood. "Dad's boat?"

"Yes. Jason, there are rumors. About you, about Mr. Parker's death, and now about Ed Hennessey being found in your dad's boat."

"What kind of rumors?"

She just looked at him, not knowing how to say it.

And suddenly he understood what she meant. His face darkened, and a look of helplessness seemed to come over his whole body. He leaned forward, bony elbows resting on the tabletop, his chin propped in his palms. Unkempt hair poked through his splayed fingers. He rocked slowly back and forth, his eyes focused on the distance. He mumbled into the space between his hands, "Oh, shit. This is a nightmare. I'm a dead man." When he looked at her, his eyes were rimmed in red, as if he were on the verge of crying. "They think I did it, don't they? Because of the drugs, because I worked for Mr. Parker, because everybody knew I hated Ed Hennessey, but hell, who didn't? You want to know the weirdest thing, Aunt Genia?"

"What, sweetheart?"

"The only person who could help me out right now is Mr. Parker."

"Why, Jason? Is it because of what you think you can't tell me?"

With every show of reluctance, he nodded affirmatively.

She knew that anything she said now could make a huge difference in the boy's life, so she thought carefully before she spoke. Finally, she said, "Jason, I don't know what secret the two of you had, but I think I can guess. If I do, will you tell me?"

"I can't! I promised him."

"Would he want you to go to jail to keep that promise?"

The boy looked shocked to hear her ask that. "No," he said slowly. "I guess not. No! Mr. Parker would never want that." Suddenly, a rueful smile tugged at his woebegone expression. "Aunt Genia, I think I have been an idiot."

"It happens to all of us at one time or another, dear."

"I probably should have told you. Go ahead and guess, okay?"

"All right. Here's what I think. My dear friend Stanley Parker was in a lot of discomfort this summer, and lately it seemed to be getting quite a bit worse. He would never admit any such thing to me, but I felt that he was ill. I think the illness—possibly cancer?—caused him increasing pain. Marijuana eases the pain of cancer patients. Is that why you were growing it for him, Jason?"

His eyes had widened in a look of admiration.

"Yes! That's amazing. You're good, Aunt Genia."

She smiled sadly at him. "Elementary, my dear Jason. And that's why your sister and your father were so mad at him, right? And that's why I feel like killing him myself. How could he ask you to do that, knowing you were already in trouble over marijuana?"

"He didn't know who else to ask, Aunt Genia."

"That's no excuse."

"Well, hold on, give me a chance to explain. He already had a prescription for marijuana that a doctor had given him, but it wasn't strong enough. He was really in a lot of pain a lot of the time, Aunt Genia. I think he was kind of desperate. And he had all these things he wanted to do before he died, and he wanted to feel well enough to do them. And there was that greenhouse, just the perfect place to grow his own private crop of medicine. And he figured I would know how to roll a joint...which I do...and I could teach him just enough so that he could do it for himself."

"But the risk to you, Jason!"

"He said he was a powerful guy," the boy answered her, with a naiveté that would have made her smile if she hadn't felt so exasperated at her dear, late friend Stanley. "He said he could get us out of any trouble we got into."

"Oh, Stanley!" she exclaimed, raising her palms skyward and rolling her eyes heavenward. "Of all the egotistical..."

"I didn't do much, Aunt Genia, I just got the seeds for him to plant, and some papers to roll the joints in, and I may have rolled a few for him. But he found out he didn't like to smoke it, he'd rather eat it in—"

"Jason? What's wrong?"

"Oh, my God, Aunt Genia. Cookies. I ate three big cookies the last time I was at the greenhouse, the day after he died. I didn't even think that there might be pot in them. I'll bet that's how it got in my system. Damn it! Mr. Parker usually put it in brownies, but I'll bet he made marijuana cookies the last time. Shit! Excuse me. But who's going to believe that?"

"I do," she said.

"And I do, too," said a voice from the kitchen doorway.

Genia and her nephew both looked up, startled.

"Mom! What did you hear?"

"Enough." Donna looked at her aunt. "I know about Ed Hennessey, I just heard from Kevin, and they want Jason down at the police station in fifteen minutes. They've found some of his things in the boat—"

"Mom! I always have stuff in the boat—"

His mother's face was ashen, anguished. "Of course you do, honey, so does your sister, so does your dad. We'll just tell them that, they've got to see that's only reasonable."

"Mom, are you mad at me?"

"About the pot? No," his mother said, and an expression of surprise came over Jason's face. "It may not have been the wisest thing you ever did, but how were you supposed to say no to a sick old man? If I'm mad at anybody, I'm mad at Stanley. But in a strange way I think I'm proud of you for trying to help him. Jason, I know you think I've been really hard on you this summer, but I've been so worried about what will happen to you." In the doorway, his mother began to cry. Quickly, the boy got up from his chair and ran over to her and took her in his arms in a bear hug. From the kitchen table, Genia heard her muffled voice say, "I love you so much, and I'm so worried."

"I'm sorry, Mom."

Genia stood up at the kitchen table and said in a firm, decisive voice, "Where's the phone number for your lawyer,

Donna? We're not going to that police station without her.
Jason, you are not to say a single word to the police unless
your lawyer tells you it's all right. Donna, the same goes for
you and Kevin, and for Janie, if they want to talk to her. We
know the truth, which is that Jason is as innocent as the rest
of us, and we're not going to let anybody bully him into taking the blame for crimes he did not commit. You two get
ready to go. Give me the lawyer's number, and I'll arrange
for her to meet us there." At the look on Donna's face, Genia
added, "And don't you worry about money, Donna. Your
uncle Lew would want me to help you, and that's what I'm
going to do, all the way to the end when people start apol-
ogizing to Jason for thinking such awful things about him.
Comb your hair, Jason. Dry your eyes, Donna. We may be
an innocent family, but we are not to be trifled with, not if
I have anything to say about it. Now, what's that phone
number?"

Three hours later, Jason was back home again with his
mother and sister. His father was with them. When Genia
returned to her own cottage, she felt only slightly more
hopeful. Kevin and Jason's attorneys had protected them
both fiercely, allowing them to say virtually nothing, and
there had been no arrest warrant for either of them. There
wasn't any actual evidence. "Not yet..." they were warned
by the police. "If we find out that either of you was down at
the docks last night, if we find witnesses who saw you with
Eddie, if we find your fingerprints on—"

"They'll be all over that boat!"

"Shut up, Kevin," his lawyer snapped at him.

"We'll have you back in here on a warrant next time," the
police had continued, looking annoyed at the attorney. "And
you will answer our questions then."

"Is he free to go?" the attorney asked. "What about my client?" Jason's attorney added.

Yes, they were, but only for now was the implication.

As Genia drove away from the gallery, she thought, *If the police find out how angry Kevin was at Stanley, and if they get the idea that Eddie may have known that, then Kevin will be in even more danger than his son.* Then she had a traitorous thought: *How well did she actually know her former nephew-in-law? Was she really as convinced of his innocence as she was of his son's?* It was a terrible thought, and she silently apologized to all the Edens for allowing it to slip into her mind. The problem was that once it had sneaked in, she couldn't seem to get rid of it. For that reason alone, she turned the car around and returned to Donna's home, walking in and surprising Kevin and Donna, who were both downstairs in front of one of his pieces of artwork.

"Aunt Genia! Did you forget something?"

"Yes, Donna, I forgot to ask both of you something."

They gazed quizzically at her, and her heart went out to both worried parents.

"Donna, why did Stanley have you out to lunch two weeks ago?"

With a glance at her ex-husband, Donna said, "I thought I already told you. He wanted to tell me not to send Jason to military school—"

"Good," Kevin interrupted. "I hate that idea."

Donna cast him an exasperated glance.

"But," Genia persisted, "what made Stanley think you would do as he wanted you to do? Did he threaten you in some way?"

That earned her a startled look from both of them.

"He did, didn't he? What was it, Donna?"

"Aunt Genia, you are the most amazing person," Donna

said, half laughing. "How'd you know that? Okay, I give up. There's no reason not to tell you, except..." She wouldn't meet her aunt's eyes, for some reason, and seemed to be avoiding Kevin's gaze, too. "The thing is, I have applied to the bank for a mortgage on this place—"

"Donna!" her ex-husband exclaimed, looking shocked.

"Well, we have to get the money for the kids' colleges somewhere, Kevin! And I didn't want to pressure you, because I know it's hard to be an artist and have such big financial obligations, too. I've always tried to protect you from that; I'm the businessperson, you're the artist. So I was just going to get a loan from the bank, and Stanley said that if I didn't change my mind about the military school, he'd make sure I didn't get the loan. I couldn't believe it! Who did he think he was?"

But Kevin was smiling at her rather tenderly. "I think he was your friend. Donna, you can't mortgage this house. It means so much to you to keep it in the family, we just can't take the risk of losing it. We'll find the money."

"Where?" she demanded. "I don't have it!"

"Well, I do," her aunt announced.

Donna looked crestfallen rather than pleased. "Oh, Aunt Genia, that's just what I wanted to avoid. You've always done so much for us. I just can't let you—"

Genia put up a hand to forestall the argument.

"The children will go to college," she said firmly. "And if your uncle Lew were alive, he would be so happy to help you. Why don't we talk about this later, but in the meantime, Kevin's right. You must not risk this house." She smiled at her niece. "Lew wouldn't like it."

Donna shook her head. "Oh, you two!" she exclaimed. But she was smiling.

"Kevin?" Genia turned to him. "It's your turn to answer

my question, please. Why did Stanley invite you to lunch at the Castle?"

"He invited *you* to lunch, too?" Donna asked, turning toward Kevin.

A disgusted expression crossed his face. "Oh, yeah. You want to know what he wanted from me? One guess. He wanted me cooperate with the plans for the art festival. He wanted me to be a good boy and vacate the island nicely when they needed me to, so they could let thousands of tourists tromp through my yard."

"And if you didn't do that?" Genia asked.

"He'd kick me off the island."

"Good for Stanley," Donna said, crossing her arms over her chest.

"Well, now he's dead, and I can oppose it if I want to."

"That's just selfish," his ex-wife proclaimed. "After he's been so generous to you? That's just plain selfish, Kevin Eden!"

"I thought you were sympathetic to artists," he said wryly. "How about the pressure of having to leave my work behind while they set up that festival? And how about having to do it every year? How's that for pressure, Donna?"

"Oh, Kevin. You can use your old studio here."

That seemed to flummox him; he had no reply.

"Thank you, dears," Genia said, smiling encouragingly at them.

This time, when she left for home, she felt confident of her family, even its ex-members. *If only I felt as optimistic about their fate*, she thought, fighting down a feeling of panic for all of their sakes.

21

A Recipe for Trouble

What do you think of your quiet little Devon now, Stanley?"

Genia spoke the wry question aloud as she unlocked her back door and entered her house once again. In less than twenty-four hours she had experienced a drunken scene, a fantasy of terror in the night, a scene of accusation and acrimony, a reconciliation between a mother and her son, and interviews in a police station. And on top of that there had been a murder.

When Genia went to lay her wedding rings on the shelf above the kitchen sink in preparation for washing a few dishes, she got another shock to add to the ones already layered on this day. She realized with a growing sense of apprehension that the cookbooks she kept there had been moved from the position she had left them in yesterday.

That's what has been feeling "off" to me!

Someone has been going through my cookbooks.

It wasn't blatant. It was only a subtle shift, a lean of one book into another, a space where previously there hadn't been one. There were a couple of books out of order, and she knew that was so because she had kept them in order for a purpose: general cookbooks to the left, followed by historical cookbooks, then specialty cookbooks—appetizers, desserts, seafood, pasta. She hadn't brought any with her from the ranch, not knowing she would end up needing any of her favorites. Instead, she had purchased good used ones at "tag" sales in the countryside, and she had even bought one or two new ones. She had intended to give them all to Stanley when she left Devon or contribute them to a local church sale if he didn't want them. Genia knew exactly how she had lined them up. It was clear to her, as it would have been to no one else, that somebody had moved them.

But why? Were they looking for cash among the pages?

She knew some people did hide money in books, though she never did. Somebody could ransack her entire library and never find a single dollar bill, because she was afraid she'd forget which book she'd put the money in.

She thought back to the noises which had scared her.

Maybe I'm not crazy after all, Stanley.

She could have sworn these cookbooks had all been in order when she turned out the lights in the kitchen the night before. Could there really have been an intruder in this house?

The possibility gave her such a bad case of the willies that she wanted to run outside that instant and scream for help. *Don't be silly. They're long gone.* But still, she felt as if invisible eyes were staring at her from outside her windows, as if invisible hands might reach out to grab her.

"I'll call the police," she said aloud.

But a sense of caution stayed her hand when it reached for the phone. What would she tell them, that her cookbooks were out of order? She doubted they would take that seriously, even if she told them of noises in the night. But it was more than that that kept her from dialing. It was a premonition that the police's first suspect would be her own nephew,

Jason. *They'll accuse him of wanting money for drugs. They'll say he was in and out of here all the time, and he and Janie had keys of their own.*

It wasn't Jason, she felt sure it wasn't.

But the police were not his great-aunt who loved him, and they were actively looking for justification to accuse him of things much more terrible than this.

She didn't want to give them any excuse to think worse of him.

Genia gave up the idea of calling the police for now and made up her mind to do a little detective work of her own.

Genia pulled out from under a pile of books on her bedstand a long yellow legal pad. "Thinking on paper" was her favorite way to sort things out when she was confused and upset. In other times and places, she had written down imagined scenarios about crimes. The process had helped her then; maybe it would help her now.

Leaving the first page blank, she turned it over. Out of sheer exasperation with the lady in question, she started scribbling on the second page....

Celeste Hutchinson is a born and bred Rhode Islander. She's a Swamp Yankee, just as Stanley was. Practically everybody in Devon knows her or recognizes her name from her Realtor signs if nothing else. The problem is, Celeste is an alcoholic, and her drinking seems completely out of control. Almost by definition, that suggests that her life's out of control, too. So, what used to work for Celeste in the past doesn't now.

Perhaps the successes that came easily due to her drive, intelligence, and reputation are harder to achieve these days. She's not a woman who is accustomed to failure, but she's

*drinking all day long now. Maybe missing sales appointments.
Fluffing important details in contracts. Showing up inebriated
to meet buyers and to show homes. It could be that the re-
ceptionist at the real estate office no longer directs "cold calls"
to Celeste's extension.*

"This is sheer fantasy," Genia reminded herself sternly.

*As a consequence, Celeste's income has dropped dramati-
cally.*

*She has an expensive old house to maintain and no hus-
band to support her when she falls on hard times. She has
pride in her name and her place in the community, and that
pride feels terribly threatened now because she's facing bank-
ruptcy.*

*And on top of all that Celeste is lonely and frustrated be-
cause the man she wants doesn't want her.*

I've made it sound like a pop song, Genia thought wryly, *and
yet unrequited love . . . or unrequited desire . . . can seriously tear
a person apart, especially if it's combined with financial insecurity
or other problems. It might sound like a country-western lyric, but
this may be a profoundly anxious time for Celeste.*

*Celeste's old friend, Stanley Parker, knows of her finan-
cial straits because of his position at the bank. When he sees
David courting Celeste, he pulls the man aside and says, "A
word to the wise, David. Celeste needs a fresh jolt of cash,
and a lot of it. She's bouncing checks and kiting them from
one account to another."*

*David regards Stanley suspiciously. "Why are you telling
me this?"*

"Not for your sake," Stanley retorts, "but for my daughter's

sake, and for my future grandchildren. If you marry Celeste, she'll run through the money like a fox through the woods. That would hurt my family and the philanthropic causes that Lillian wants you to continue to support, like my arts council."

"Well, thanks," David says grudgingly.

"As I said, I'm not doing this for you."

When David stops calling Celeste, she can think of only one possible reason why: Stanley blabbed. And then Stanley himself confirms it when he has her to lunch at the Castle to read her the riot act: Sober up, he commands her, get yourself to a treatment center, Celeste. She is hurt, furious, terrified of a future that might not hold David's wealth in it. And she is not about to admit she's an alcoholic! She just has a little drinking problem now and then, that's all.

Filled with self-righteous anger, Celeste determines to confront Stanley right before the dinner party at Genia's house. She knows his habits, how he loves to ride that motorbike of his along the path by the ocean, and so she plants herself right where he is likely to pass by. She will demand that he give her a bank loan to set her financial worries right, and that he tell David Graham there's nothing to worry about anymore.

"You're a drunk, Celeste," the old man tells her.

In a rage she picks up a heavy fallen branch and swings it at his head. . . .

Genia didn't want to continue with her narrative from there. Instead, she sat quietly and thought of facts rather than fantasy: Celeste had not appeared to be drunk or upset when she had arrived for the dinner party. Yes, there had been liquor on her breath, but she certainly had not looked like a woman who had just swung a tree limb or a baseball bat and horribly beaten an old friend to death.

Yes, but desperate people resort to desperate means, Genia reminded herself. If Celeste had stolen the brooch, that was itself a disturbing demonstration of the truth of that old saying. If Celeste was desperate enough to steal valuable things, perhaps to sell them, was she also desperate enough to kill? What if Stanley had not yet actually told David of Celeste's financial problems—assuming she had some, Genia reminded herself—but only planned to do so? What if that's what he told Celeste the day he had her over for lunch? Genia took up her pen again to put words in Stanley's mouth:

> *"I know what a mess your bankbook's in, Celeste. I want to help you figure out how to save yourself, but you're going to have to promise me that you won't try to use David Graham as your financial savior."*

> *"How dare you, Stanley," Celeste exclaimed. "And what will you do if I don't let you run my life?"*
> *"I'll inform David myself."*
> *"I'll see you dead first!"*

Genia shivered, remembering the sharp pine needle that had stuck on her white silk blouse and stabbed her hand when she had brushed at it. Now she thought that needle must have come from the woods where Stanley died. Someone who had embraced her at her own front door that night had caught that pine needle on a piece of clothing and carried it into her house from the scene of the murder.

Was it Celeste? Or was it one of her other guests that night, or someone else connected to Stanley? Genia picked up her pen again and started writing, but this time she selected a more obvious suspect, even though he was now a dead one....

When Stanley hired Ed Hennessey he only meant to help the unfortunate fellow.

When Eddie took the job, he only did it to cheat and steal from the wealthiest man in town.

For Stanley, it was charity.

For Eddie, it was larceny.

"You've been stealing from me, Eddie."

"Yeah? What are you going to do about it, old man?"

"Turn you in."

"Over your dead body."

It could be true, Genia mused over her playlet, but that would mean there had been two killers. Eddie, who killed Stanley, and a second, who murdered him. It wasn't impossible, but wasn't it improbable? Considering the type of man he was, Eddie's death could easily have been completely unrelated to Stanley's murder. Surely Eddie had known dozens of disreputable people, any of whom might have slain him. In the name of mercy, Genia tried to find within her heart a twinge of pity for the late Ed Hennessey; what she did find there was abstract at best, an understanding that some lives grow so crooked they may never straighten out. Perhaps Eddie's ill-fated life had been one of those.

She took up her pen again and forced herself to imagine one of the worst of all possible scenarios. . . .

"Dad, you could try to like Randy!"

"Why should I? Look at the divorce rate, Nikki. In a few years he'll be gone, and I'd have wasted all that effort on your ex-husband."

"Oh, Dad!"

Sometimes she hated her own father, though she held her rage inside of her just as she had done all of her life with her

*overpowering father. She hated him for treating her mother as
if nothing Mom wanted was important, and she hated him for
how he treated her own husband, and she hated him for controlling her all of her life.*

And then came the final blow.

*"I'm changing my will, Nikki. For as long as you're mar-
ried to that good-for-nothing I'm putting all of your inheritance into an irrevocable trust."*

"Which means—?"

*"Which means a bank trustee will manage it for you and
distribute money to you when he decides you need it."*

"I'll have to ask?"

*"For every penny. This is for your own good, Nikki, to
protect you from spending it all on that so-called man you
married."*

"And if I divorce him?"

*"It will remain in effect for ten years after that, to allow
you time to mature and grow wiser in your selection of mates.
And also to allow enough time to get rid of Randy. I want
him to have all the time he needs to latch on to some other
naive heiress. After ten years, you may have control of your
own money."*

*She was so inarticulate with rage at the way her father was
attempting to run her life that only physical expression was
left to her. With hatred in her heart, Nikki grabbed a branch
at her feet and swung it at him. She watched his body tum-
ble down the hillside. "You will never control me again, not
on this side of the grave, or beyond it."*

Genia made a grimace of distaste and begged Nikki and
Stanley to forgive her for even considering it. Seen on paper
like this, it looked impossible and the logistics were ridiculous, for why would father and daughter have an argument—

any argument—in the middle of the forest on a rainy night? Anyway, Genia assumed the police would thoroughly investigate Nikki Parker Dixon because she was the main beneficiary of Stanley's estate. If there was motive in his last will and testament, surely they'd find it.

She felt only slightly less guilty when she turned the page and began to imagine the person whom Stanley would have suspected first. "Oh, all right, Stanley!" she exclaimed out loud. "I'll put him first in line." She turned back to the empty first page, and wrote in block letters: *RANDY DIXON.*

When Randy heard from his resentful wife about the change in Stanley's will, he knew push had finally come to shove.

Neither of the Dixons was invited to Genia Potter's dinner party—yet another exclusion with Stanley behind it. But that gave Randy exactly the opportunity he needed to act on his motive. If he knew his father-in-law's habits as well as he thought he did, he knew where to find the old man alone and vulnerable.

Surprise would help.

There would be no time for Stanley to yell, to raise an alarm, or to fight back, as feeble as his effort would be.

It was as easy as falling off a log. . . .

Only it wasn't Randy Dixon who fell.

"Enough," Genia rebuked herself, laying down her pen and paper. It was almost time for the Devon Arts Council meeting. Personally, she didn't care if they voted for their art festival or not, but she wanted to attend so that she might squelch rumors about her family. Quickly, she dressed, grabbed a bite to eat, and ran out to her car.

22

THE PROOF IS IN THE PUDDING

It appeared that half of South County was already there, crowding into the quaint little Devon Town Hall that was used for various subcommittees and civic entities like the arts council. As Genia joined the throng, she overheard one matron say to another, "I didn't realize the art festival meant this much to you, Heather." To which Heather retorted, "It doesn't, Marge. I couldn't tell a van Gogh from a Dodge van. But two murders have been committed, and I'm not planning on staying home alone!" Local residents seemed to be expressing a communitywide urge to come together in a show of civic solidarity that made them feel a little safer. Genia suspected that the meeting of the arts council was just a timely means for them to do it.

"Aunt Genia, over here!"

She followed the sound of her niece's voice until it led her to an empty metal chair between Donna and Kevin. As she sat down in it, both of them leaned over to talk to her at once.

"Thank you so much—"

"—appreciate your help, Genia—"

"Don't know what we'd do without—"

"I haven't got a sou, and I don't want Donna to have to sell the house to pay for Jason's legal bills." Kevin's deeper voice won the competition for her attention, and she heard him add, "I'll find a way to pay my own bills, but we've got to have the best for Jason. I feel embarrassed that I can't handle it all myself, but I'm so grateful to you, Genia."

She felt embarrassed by then, too.

"How's our boy?" she asked them.

"He's all right," Donna said, looking a little amazed. "I think he was more afraid of my reaction than he was of the police. Kevin and I have decided that Jason ought to go stay with him out on the island for a while; what do you think of that idea?"

"I like it," Genia said approvingly.

She caught glimpses of people sneaking peeks at them and then quickly turning away when they got caught staring. Obviously the word was out that Jason was suspect number one, with his father running a close second. Genia thought it courageous of both Kevin and Donna to show up at all, and she was proud of them for sticking together for Jason's sake. Every now and then someone in the audience looked their way and gave the Edens a thumbs-up sign of support that made Genia's own heart glow. Several women reached out their hands to grasp Donna's and to squeeze it. And there were men who clasped Kevin's shoulder as they walked by, murmuring variations of "Hang in there, Kev." But there were plenty of suspicious-looking glances, too, and glares and frowns, the sour ingredients in this stew of humanity. Genia heard one man say angrily, "What are *they* doing here?" She even heard somebody whisper, "Who's *she*?" pointing directly at her.

The council chamber was packed in no time.

Up in front, the president of the arts council, Lindsay

Wright, looked both beautiful and nervous, Genia thought. Clearly, she had prepared her attire carefully for this event, but she seemed in no way prepared for a crowd of this size. She tapped the microphone in front of her place, in the position where the mayor usually presided over town council meetings, and said in a voice hardly anybody could hear, "... come to order." When that had no effect, she tried again. Finally, after her third try, Lawrence Averill himself stood up in the front row and boomed out, "Everybody sit down and shut up now! Lindsay's trying to get your attention! If you please!"

Lindsay smiled gratefully at him as the group began to settle down.

She was all alone up there, and Genia felt sorry for her. She was an awfully young woman to have to deal unexpectedly with a restless crowd like this one.

"Welcome to the monthly meeting," Lindsay said in a high, formal little voice, "of the Devon Arts Council." She faltered for a moment, her blue eyes seeming to search the room for something, and then she found what she was looking for: Harrison Wright, her husband, standing in a corner, with his arms folded across his chest, smiling encouragingly at his wife. Lindsay visibly calmed down, and so, it felt to Genia, did most everybody else who had swiveled their heads to see where Lindsay was looking. Harrison seemed to have that happy knack of just making people feel better, certainly a fortunate ability for a weatherman who occasionally had to forecast hurricanes or blizzards.

Lindsay continued with more confidence.

"We are meeting tonight principally to decide whether or not to sponsor and fund the proposed art festival, but before we go any further, there is something I want to say." She paused, and the audience became very quiet, sensing what was to come next. "One man was responsible for founding this arts council, one man kept it running through the years, and one man was the driving force and patron behind the idea of the festival. As president of the council, I would ask you to join me in a moment of silence to honor the late, great Stanley Parker."

Instead of silence, there was a single loud gasp.

Along with everybody else, Genia craned her neck to see who had released that shocked sound, and her gaze settled on a tall, slim woman with radiant red hair, seated toward the rear of the chamber. She looked about fifty years old, and she was elegantly turned out in a bright green silk suit with a soft white scoop-neck blouse. Her face now looked nearly as red as her hair as she registered the reaction she had elicited from the crowd. Genia had never seen her before. "Who's that?" Kevin whispered over her, to Donna. His ex-wife shrugged back at him. Behind them, the mortified stranger lowered her gaze to the floor, and finally people mercifully turned away from staring at her.

Whoever she was, Genia thought sympathetically, she had just found out the hard way that Stanley was dead and the news had startled her, just as it would have shocked any of the rest of them if they had heard it for the first time tonight.

As she settled in to listen to democracy in action, Genia surreptitiously pulled out of her large handbag a yellow legal pad and a pen. Nobody needed her opinion on this issue, which was none of her business anyway, and she intended to make use of the time by continuing the deductive guesswork she had earlier commenced.

"Taking notes?" her niece whispered. "You must be really interested in the festival. Why don't you move here, Aunt Genia? We'd love to have you here all the time."

Genia smiled at her, and then carefully shielded her notes

from the view of anyone who might be reading over her shoulder.

>All of his life Larry Averill has only really wanted two things—to be elected to the Rhode Island State Legislature and to marry Celeste Hutchinson. But he's sixty years old now and both of those desires have been denied him.

>Now, however, with the art festival about to put his town on the map—and his own name in the newspapers—Larry believes he is on the verge of making the first dream come true at last.

>Stanley is no threat to that.

>But Stanley has threatened Larry's dream girl, Celeste. In a drunken, weepy confession one night, she tells Larry everything—about her business failures, her love and need for David, and her suspicion that Stanley came between them.

>The next day, Celeste has no memory of the conversation.

>But Larry remembers every word of it. And he hates Stanley for hurting Celeste. So great is his self-sacrificing love for her that he would even see her married to another man if that would save her and give her peace of mind and happiness at last.

>How dare Stanley Parker interfere in other people's lives, their hearts, their hopes?

>Full of unrequited love for Celeste, feeling like her knight in shining armor, Larry charges off before the dinner party to do battle with the patriarch of Devon.

>"You've got no right to do things like this to people, Stanley. This is Celeste's last chance for happiness!"

>"You mean she's not willing to be a poor politician's wife?"

>It's too much for Larry to bear. Stanley's mockery, his self-righteousness, is too much. The town would be better off without the controlling old man. No more Stanley to hurt

*Celeste. With him out of the way, Larry can go to David
Graham, tell him it was a lie, that Celeste is fine, all she
needs is a stay at a treatment center, and love.*

"I hate you for hurting her, Stanley!"

He proves it by killing Celeste's enemy.

Genia flipped pages over that one to cover it and looked
up just in time to see Celeste Hutchinson standing at the microphone in the center aisle.

"...be wonderful for business in general," Celeste was
saying. Genia wondered how long she had been talking and
how many other people had gone before her. "And it would
be grand for real estate in particular." That drew a chuckle
from everyone who knew her vested interest in that subject.

Genia found that her attention peaked and waned based
on whether or not she knew the speaker. Even then her
mind drifted to other things, so that she only heard dibs and
dabs of what her acquaintances had to say.

"...just think it would be the greatest thing for Devon,"
boomed the mayor. "Put us on the map..."

"...disagree that they'll only buy art out on the island,"
Donna argued forcefully in the face of a few hostile glares.
Genia tried to pay close attention to what her niece had to
say. "A lot of tourists will wander through town, and I'm sure
that galleries like mine will do a lot of extra business...."

"...sorry to differ with my ex-wife," Kevin said next,
after bumping past Genia's knees to reach the aisle. But he
said it in a way that was so charming people had to laugh, especially when they saw that Donna was smiling, too. "But
that's a pristine island, and I don't think Stanley really
thought it through, what it will be like with thousands of
people tromping on the wildlife...."

The next time Genia paid attention, it was because David

Graham was standing at the microphone, looking handsome and a little embarrassed, as if he weren't sure he was enough of a Devonite yet to qualify to speak to these issues. "... great for business," he was saying, "even if it will cost a lot in terms of extra police protection and garbage pickup and signage, and so on. I think my late wife would have said it was worth it anyway. Yes, we'll get a little litter in our front yards, but surely we can cope with that. Yes, it may overburden our town's budget, but maybe we can raise our taxes a little to compensate." Boos and hisses broke out from scattered spots in the chamber, and David smiled to acknowledge them. "Or maybe not." There was laughter when he so quickly backtracked from the touchy subject of taxes. "Yes, the traffic may be impossible for a few days, but can't we live with a little inconvenience for just a little while?"

"More than a little!" somebody shouted out.

"Excuse me?" Lindsay breathed into her microphone. "One person at a time, please? Go ahead, Mr. Graham."

"That's all I was going to say." He smiled supportively at her. "I agree there will be problems with litter, increased traffic, extra expense every year, and as Kevin says, there may be damage to the ecosystem of Parker Island. But I don't think that's too much sacrifice to make for an event of this magnitude. I urge the council to approve the motion."

Grumblings in the audience suggested not all were so sanguine as he about the "little sacrifices" this wealthy man seemed to think the rest of them wouldn't mind making. Genia thought that in his effort to be honest about the advantages and disadvantages, David might have done more harm than good to the cause he meant to support. Up front, the mayor had a rueful look on his face, as if privately thinking that some people were natural politicians and some people were not.

In the end, the council took their vote, and it was a tie.

"It's up to me to break the tie," Lindsay said, looking scared.

Shouts broke out from the opposing factions, urging her to vote one way or the other. They could actually see her swallow hard, before she started to speak. "I vote . . ."

Everyone knew it would be "no," which would scuttle the motion. Lindsay's opinion of "art" versus "craft" was well-known, if not very popular.

"Excuse me? Lindsay? May I speak first?"

Heads turned as an attractive young woman in glasses walked down the center aisle toward the microphone.

"Nikki?" Lindsay looked nonplussed. "Of course."

Nikki Parker Dixon's soft voice was magnified for all to hear. "This may not be in *Robert's Rules of Order* for me to interrupt a vote like this, and I'm sorry to be late. But I have to tell you that I think you've forgotten something kind of important. My dad is not in charge of the island anymore. I am, because I inherited it. It will be up to me to decide whether or not I want any public events held out there, and to tell you the truth, I just haven't made up my mind. I'm really sorry, but I think you're going to have to delay your vote."

"Oh." Lindsay looked pouty, like a child who hadn't gotten her way. "Well, as you say, it's your island," she said less than graciously. "So I guess we'll have to." Murmurings ranging from outraged to relieved to amused ricocheted around the chamber. Behind her, Genia heard a woman mutter, "You'd think they would have thought of this before they asked us all to come over here." That sentiment rather neatly avoided the fact that the arts council had not, in fact, invited the whole community, Genia reflected; the whole community had just shown up.

"Is there a motion to adjourn?" Lindsay asked.

"I move—" someone said, but got no further, because up in front an elderly white-haired man stood up and interrupted the motion.

"Lindsay?" he began.

"Yes, Mr. Brooks?"

It was Genia's turn to whisper to her niece, "Who's that?"

"Willard Brooks," Donna whispered back. "President of the bank, and a member of the arts council, and a friend of Stanley's."

"Lindsay," the old man said in a kind but firm voice, which did not project very well without a microphone, "there is one more item of old business I feel it is incumbent upon me to raise. Stanley raised it last time, if you will remember, and we still have not settled it to anyone's satisfaction."

Now that the art festival discussion was over, many in the crowd were getting up to leave and the room was rapidly emptying. Genia, Donna, and Kevin stayed where they were, trying to hear what was being said up front.

"...audit" was practically the only word Genia made out, although she did hear a phrase with two large monetary figures in it, and a familiar name that made her sit up straighter in her chair. "...a memo from Stanley saying there should be thirty-two thousand dollars instead of..."

"...take that up later" was the only part of the answer she heard from Lindsay, although she thought she also heard "... easy to explain." Whatever it was, the bank president seemed satisfied with what the president of the arts council said to him, and he sat back down while the motion for adjournment carried the day. Or evening, as it were, since it was dark outside by the time Genia, her niece, and former nephew-in-law made their way down the stairs to the sidewalk. Genia heard a voice calling her name. Searching for the source, she was surprised to discover it was the mayor of Devon who was trying to get her attention. She made her way toward him, followed by Donna and Kevin, who were stopped along the way by other acquaintances.

She, too, was halted before she reached her destination.

"Hello, Genia," she heard a pleasant voice say, and she looked up to find Harrison Wright smiling down at her. "I thought Lindsay was going to have a real storm on her hands in there, but it was only a little cloudy weather. Didn't she handle herself well?"

"Very well, Harrison." Genia smiled back at him. Then she glanced at the clear night skies. "Speaking of storms, when is the big one going to arrive?"

"I'm forecasting it for Saturday."

"Two days from now? Goodness, thanks for the warning. What about tomorrow?"

"Rainy and cool."

"Thank you, Harrison. It's so handy to know you!"

He laughed and waved good-bye when she left his side.

She reached the mayor just as he was handing a small white card to the red-haired stranger, the same woman who had gasped at the news of Stanley's demise.

"Mrs. Eugenia Potter," the mayor said with good-natured formality, "I'd like you to meet Ms. Sylvia Stewart."

"Mrs.," the other woman corrected him. "But please, call me Sylvia. How do you do, Mrs. Potter?"

"I'm Genia, Mrs. Stew—Sylvia."

And then it hit her: This woman had the intials S.S., and tomorrow, if she wasn't mistaken, was 8/19. She started to say something, but the mayor was already talking.

"We have a mystery here, Genia," he told her in his genial way. "Mrs. Stewart—Sylvia—has come down from Providence at the invitation of Stanley Parker—"

Genia turned to look at the woman. *Aha,* she thought.

"—and, unfortunately, she didn't get the word that he was . . . about his passing."

"I'm so sorry," Genia said to her.

"Thank you," Sylvia Stewart replied, but she looked embarrassed again. "I didn't actually know him. I never met him. I don't even know why he wanted to meet me."

Genia blinked. "You don't?"

"No, Mayor Averill tells me you were a good friend of his, and I was hoping maybe you might know something about it. You see, Mr. Parker contacted me and said he had something very important to ask me. I think he wanted to show me something, too. And he practically begged me to come down here to join him at this council meeting. I asked him if he couldn't come to Providence to see me, but he said, no, I had to come here. He intimated it was a matter of life or death, though I'm afraid I didn't take that seriously. He seemed a rather dramatic old man, if you'll forgive my saying so. You may wonder why I would go to all this trouble for someone who called out of the blue and made a request like that, but everybody in Rhode Island has heard of Stanley Parker. When I told my friends, they all thought I should come, just to see what he was up to. My husband said there was nobody more creditable than Mr. Parker, so if he wanted to see me, I should do it." The woman raised her hands in a display of bafflement. "So here I am, and I don't know why!"

"How very odd," Genia agreed. "I wish I knew."

"We were going to have lunch tomorrow," Sylvia Stewart added, looking a little disappointed, "at that house of his that everybody calls the Castle. I was so looking forward to getting a chance to see it. I know that sounds petty, but his house is nearly as famous as he was. I'm a photographer of sorts and I was even hoping to take pictures of it."

"You can still do that," Genia assured her, feeling eager to get to the bottom of this mystery. "I am renting a cottage right down the street from the Castle, and if you will do me the honor of coming to lunch tomorrow, I will be glad to drive you over there so that you may take some photos of it. I'm sure that his daughter would like to meet you, too."

"Oh, I don't want to be such a bother!"

"Not at all, it would be my pleasure, truly." Genia had already taken note of the trim little travel case the woman grasped by a handle. "I'm assuming that you're staying overnight, since you were lunching with Stanley tomorrow. Where are you staying?"

"Mr. Parker made a reservation for me at the Devon Bed and Breakfast." Doubt clouded her face. "Or, he was going to. I don't know if he actually—"

"I would bet that he did, wouldn't you, Mayor?" Genia said.

"Yes," Larry Averill assured their guest, "and if he didn't, we'll get you in someplace else that's just as nice, I promise you. Did you drive down?"

"Yes."

"Then why don't I go with you over to the Devon B and B. . . . "

"That's so nice of you!"

"And," Genia said, "just leave your car there. I'll send my nephew Jason to pick you up around eleven-thirty tomorrow morning, if that's convenient."

"Thank you so much, um . . ."

"Genia."

"Genia."

But the mayor was frowning a bit. "You're going to send Jason? Are you sure that's—"

"Yes," she replied a bit sharply. "I'm sure."

When she glanced back at Sylvia Stewart's face, she realized the woman probably hadn't even heard that little exchange. In fact, she was staring off into the crowd behind Genia, and her face was white as chalk.

"Are you all right?" Genia asked her quietly.

"What? Yes, I thought I saw a ghost."

Genia looked back over her own shoulder, but all she saw were the good people of Devon heading off toward their cars or beginning to walk to their homes. Her own niece and Kevin were talking to Harrison and Lindsay Wright. She saw David Graham and lifted her hand to wave, but he disappeared in the throng without seeing her. Celeste Hutchinson was standing on the Town Hall steps looking in the direction in which he had gone, and when Genia turned around again she saw that Larry Averill was staring at Celeste.

"If you're sure you'll be all right... ?"

"Oh, yes. I just saw someone who..." She hesitated, To Genia, she looked like someone who is about to say one thing, but changed her mind and says another. "...who reminds me of somebody else."

"Then I'll see you tomorrow around noon."

They exchanged cordial farewells, and then the mayor escorted the stranger in town down the sidewalk to the nearby hostelry. Genia's last impression was of a graceful, elegant woman striding along beside a portly, disheveled man. She stared after them for a few moments, until they turned a corner and disappeared from view.

And then she noticed that the woman had dropped the small white card that Larry had handed to her. Genia stooped to pick it up and saw that it was one of Celeste Hutchinson's real estate business cards.

23

ON THE MENU

When she got home, Genia brought her yellow pad down from upstairs and began to write while the arts council meeting was fresh in her mind. Regretfully, she made a little amendment to the scenario she had written about Lawrence Averill, based on the white business card that had dropped from Sylvia Stewart's hand.

> "Larry, I know what you're doing," Stanley scolded the mayor.
>
> "Well, good!" the portly man said in his jovial way. "I'm glad somebody does!"
>
> "I think you'd better be serious for once, Mr. Mayor. What I know is that you are using the influence of your office to funnel business to one particular Realtor in town. Do I need to name her?"
>
> For once, the loquacious mayor had nothing to say.
>
> "I've seen you do it," Stanley continued, "so don't deny it. I've seen you pass out her business cards to visiting businesspeople and newcomers. You keep a stack of them with you, don't you, just like you keep those keys to the city, and you hand out her cards just about as often as you hand out

keys? That is a completely improper use of your office, and you know it—"

"Stanley, she needs help—"

"That may be, but as mayor you can't show that kind of favoritism. I want you to stop it immediately. If you don't, I will be forced to report this to the board of Realtors and to the town council. Do I have your promise on this?"

At her kitchen table Genia thought sadly, *Larry might have uttered the words to such a promise, but I doubt he could keep it.* She herself had seen Larry hand out one of Celeste's business cards this very evening. He must be aware that he was doing something a mayor shouldn't do. And how many other visitors had received that small engraved card from the hand of Devon's mayor?

If Stanley knew... ?

If Stanley had confronted the mayor, that would threaten Larry at the very root of the two things he held most dear in life: Celeste and his own political ambitions, modest though they might be by other people's standards.

Was it enough to motivate him to kill Stanley?

Sweet, practical, generous Larry? Genia tried to make herself believe her own scenario was possible, but there was no way to convince herself it was probable. The mayor who has given his whole life over to the welfare of the town? Could Dr. Jekyll and Mr. Hyde exist under those shabby old suits, or in that same heart that handed out brass keys with such unabashed pride and joy?

Genia didn't think so. She didn't want to think so.

I may be an old fool, Genia decided, *but I simply cannot believe that Larry Averill ever willingly harmed a person in his life, not even for the sake of Celeste Hutchinson.*

"Such a nice man," Genia couldn't help but say to herself.

He was, wasn't he?

She had one more scenario to write before bed, and this one, too, was based on what she had seen and heard at the arts council meeting. She hoped she was wrong about how she was interpreting certain nuances, but if she was right...

Lindsay Wright appears to have it all—a handsome, nice husband who is devoted to her, local standing in her own right through the arts council and as the spouse of a local celebrity, plus natural beauty and gorgeous clothes to show it off.

But Lindsay didn't come from money. Lindsay doesn't have a job, at least not one that pays, because the presidency of the arts council is a volunteer position. And how much money can a regional TV weatherman actually make? Not enough to support a clothes habit like the one his wife has.

Genia stopped writing to think: Stanley had told her that Lillian always complained that she couldn't buy a decent wardrobe in Devon; for true fashion, she had to travel to bigger, more sophisticated cities. Genia picked up her pen again.

"So how do you manage it, Lindsay?" he inquired over lunch.

"I do my shopping in Providence, Stanley," she replied easily. "At secondhand stores, but don't tell anybody, okay? I even hit the flea markets and garage sales, if you must know."

"Really? Celeste told me she spotted you buying a lot of fancy designer things at Lord & Taylor's recently."

"Oh, that couldn't have been me."

"I think it was, Lindsay."

"Well, so what, Stanley? What are you saying? What do

you care where I shop? I don't get this, what are you getting at?"

"What I'm getting at is a certain imbalance in the books of the arts council. . . . "

Again Genia paused, pen over yellow paper: Maybe Lindsay Wright wasn't stealing money from the arts council, and Celeste wasn't stealing other people's jewelry. But how did either woman manage to pay for her lifestyle without going heavily into debt?

This was all imaginary, of course, but what if. . .

"I'll make it up!" Lindsay swore to the old man. "But please, please, Stanley, don't let Harrison know what I've done! Please don't let anybody know, or you'll ruin both of us. You'll ruin our marriage, you'll ruin Harrison's future—"

"I'm not the embezzler here, Lindsay."

"Embezzler! Stanley, I'm just borrowing—"

"This is criminal behavior," was his stern response. After all, the Devon Arts Council was his special baby, and he even referred to it as "his" arts council. "How do you think you can ever repay it, Lindsay? You don't even have a job."

"I'll get one! Please, Stanley!"

He reluctantly agreed not to act on his knowledge immediately, but to give Lindsay a chance to confess to the council and to try to devise a method of repayment, if they are willing to let her do it.

But Lindsay had no intention of confessing anything.

This was a lot to base on the word "audit," and a couple of different, large dollar amounts, Genia chided herself, but she completed her writing anyway. . . .

*Terrified of the consequences of her own greed—she could
go to prison!—she decided to sneak onto Stanley's property
before the dinner party and to kill him.*

Now no one will ever know, she thinks. . . .

*Until she gets a call from Eddie Hennessey, who listened
in on her luncheon with Stanley and who saw her in the
woods that night.*

Genia was startled by her own fantasy: "Good grief, it
could have happened that way. That could, indeed, be why
Hennessey was killed, because he knew something incriminating, or he actually saw the murder and attempted to
blackmail the killer." Hadn't Celeste hinted at that very thing
last night and again this morning? She had claimed it was
Eddie who told her that Jason was growing pot in the greenhouse. What else had Ed Hennessey learned while he was
peeping and eavesdropping on his employer and Stanley's
guests?

She turned back the pages of the yellow pad and then got
up and laid it next to the coffeepot on the kitchen counter.
Her scenario about Stanley's hated son-in-law, Randy
Dixon, was on top, on the first page. Seeing it there, Genia
turned the pad upside down so only the bland gray back of
it was displayed to view. *I wouldn't want anybody reading this*,
was her final thought before she went upstairs to bed.

In a moment of inspiration before she actually crawled between the sheets, Genia turned to Stanley's old cookbook,
which she kept just under the bed within easy reach of her
hands. She felt sure that Stanley had already chosen a recipe
he planned to use for lunch with Sylvia Stewart.

She found it where the white slip marked the page:

Tuna in phyllo.

"*S.S., 8/19.*"

Genia relaxed, feeling good about having found it. Now she could prepare and serve his guest what he himself had planned. After marking the page she closed the book and put it away in its hiding place again, wondering what he had been going to discuss with her over tuna in phyllo.

And then a thought struck her: The intruder in this house had been going through her cookbooks. Looking for something? Or looking for a particular *cookbook*? Genia picked up Stanley's old one again, and this time she looked at it very differently. Was it possible they were searching for this cookbook? And that's why nothing seemed to be missing in the house? Because they hadn't found this one thing they wanted?

"But why?" she asked aloud.

It seemed a ridiculous idea. What could there be about this greasy, tattered old cookbook that anybody would want? As far as she knew, the book itself was perfectly ordinary in its own special way; that is to say, while it was a superb cookbook, it wasn't a rare one, it wasn't even a true antique, and there must have been thousands printed just like it. She checked the copyright page. Yes, it was a first edition, but even a first was worthless in this kind of condition. She paged through it, trying to see it through new eyes which might spot something of value in it. But there were only Stanley's scribbles, many nearly illegible, and bits of paper, grocery receipts and such, stuck in every which way.

"I'm so tired," she finally admitted, "I probably wouldn't recognize something valuable if it bit me." She didn't really believe the book had value to anyone but her, but just to be on the safe side, she got out of bed with it, took it into the bathroom, and placed it at the very bottom of her dirty clothes hamper. The hamper was quite full, as she hadn't had time in the past week to keep up with her housekeeping chores. She thought that a thief would have to want a cookbook very badly to look for it there.

After getting into bed again, Genia lay for a time staring at the ceiling and trying to decide how much of this she was imagining, and how much was real. She had *thought* someone was in the house last night. Then again, she might have imagined it. The cookbooks on the kitchen shelf had *looked* disarranged, but she could be wrong about that, too. She didn't think so, but she had to consider it. As for whether somebody wanted a messy old cookbook bad enough to try to steal it . . .

It seemed absurd on the face of it.

She turned off the bedside light, feeling confused and nervous. Should she accept Donna's invitation—and David's urging—and move back into the garret above the gallery? *No*, she finally decided just before she closed her eyes. *If there really was somebody in this house, and even if they did want that cookbook, they didn't do anything to hurt me or this property.*

She thought her feeling of safety was real.

Or am I imagining that, too?

24

BOILING OVER

Nothing woke her until dawn, and she arose feeling reassured.

She dug down toward the bottom of the dirty clothes hamper, found the cookbook there, and carried it downstairs. She was going to need it in order to prepare the tuna in phyllo.

Once in the kitchen, Genia turned to the recipe Stanley had chosen and read through it several times to make sure she had the complete picture of it in her mind. It wasn't a recipe for beginners. It was a rather sophisticated one that required experience, time, care in preparation. It seemed to her this was the kind of entrée to prepare when you wanted some solitary time first, time to think things through, to let your mind wander; or, it was a recipe that could be completed while your guest sat nearby drinking a glass of wine while butter sizzled in the skillet. This recipe spoke to Genia of the possibility that Stanley either wanted to spend a good deal of time with his guest, or that he wanted her to know that he appreciated the time and effort she had taken in order to come to Devon solely on the basis of his mysterious invitation.

"You're making a lot out of a mere recipe, old girl!"

She set to work, putting a pot of basmati rice on to cook.

Next, she prepared to poach the tuna. She filled an oval brass poacher with water and chicken broth, added a splash of wine, lemon juice, bay leaves, peppercorns, and parsley, and brought it all to a boil. As she worked, she imagined Stanley doing the same over his enormous cast-iron stove. How many times had the two of them stood right there, debating the merits of copper kettles over stainless steel, or comparing flavors of olive oil, while steam curled up around them, dampening their hair and skin and wrinkling the cotton chef's apron that Stanley wore while cooking.

Snippets of old kitchen conversation spun around Genia now as she placed the tuna fillets in the fragrant broth and covered it. She chopped a white onion into small pieces and tossed it into the butter melting in a small skillet. At the right moment, she removed the poached fish from the burner, and then set the fillets aside to cool in the liquid. Then she removed the cooked rice and stirred in the onions, capers, cream, and seasonings, and set that mixture aside to cool, too.

"There," she said. "Now for the phyllo."

After wiping clean a large space on the center island, she peeled off one sheet of the thin pastry and set it on the surface. She brushed it lightly with melted butter, added a second sheet, and repeated the process. *Stanley would have enjoyed making this,* she thought as she folded the pastry in half. He was as careful and creative about his cooking as he was about his other ventures. Lillian, he had once told Genia, had not liked to cook, and so during their marriage he had cooked any meals their various hired chefs had not prepared for them. His favorite chef had been a superb cook whom

Stanley had stolen from one of the finest restaurants on the East Bay.

"Do you ever not get your way, Stanley Parker?" Genia remembered teasing him.

And she recalled his answer that day. It had been somber, not in keeping with the light mood in which she had asked it.

"Yes," he had said. "When Lil refused to come back to me. She had her reasons—I wasn't much of a husband—but I thought I could make it up to her. I never convinced her. Or maybe David was more convincing than I."

It must have been terribly hard for Stanley when Lillian brought David Graham to Devon, Genia thought. David stood in such stark contrast to Stanley—younger than Stanley by almost twenty years, Genia guessed, as well as being courtly, debonair—yes, and handsomer, too. And he shared Lillian's passion for all things artistic, as demonstrated by the fact that they had actually met at an art auction in New York, David had said.

Genia scooped half of the rice mixture onto the buttered pastry, then set the sliced tuna on top. She seasoned the fish carefully, then covered it with the remaining rice and folded the pastry over to form a package. She then repeated the process three times. On the heels of that activity, Janie arrived, and Genia immediately set her to work chopping carrots and leeks into slender strips. She instructed Janie how to heat a cup of chardonnay, boiling it down for the sauce. The wine would be added to plain yogurt, enriched with an egg yolk and seasoned with bits of parsley, fresh basil, and the sautéed carrots and leeks. Just before serving, they would spoon the creamy sauce over the baked tuna. Under Genia's watchful eye, her grandniece placed the pastry-wrapped fish in the preheated oven and then they started on the dessert.

"Janie, let's freeze the rest of these berries."

Suddenly, Genia couldn't face any more cooking. Since Janie had arrived, there hadn't even been time for a cup of tea or any real conversation. They'd been too busy. The table was set, the water glasses were filled, and Janie had already started to tidy the small messes they'd strewn about on the counter-top, island, table, and stove. Genia had found a moment to run upstairs, change into a dress, put on makeup, and freshen her hairdo. They were almost ready for Sylvia Stewart, who should be arriving shortly. The tuna in its phyllo wrapping was nearing a perfect golden, crispy brown, and as soon as they removed it from the oven, they could take a brief break before Jason arrived with the guest in tow. His job this morning was to pick up his great-aunt's mystery guest in Genia's clean car and escort her to the house.

Glancing over at her grandniece, Genia thought she saw distress in the teenager's face and posture. Janie's henna-red hair stuck out in more clumps than usual this morning, and a bright blue plastic clamp provided the only color on her black-clad person. Her aunt felt sure that the child's black jeans and T-shirt were reflective of mood instead of fashion.

"Janie, are you sleeping all right these days?"

"Sleep? What's sleep? If I go to sleep, then I just wake up and find out that something else awful has happened that makes Jason look as guilty as O. J. Simpson. It gets worse and worse every day. What are we going to do?"

The last word was a drawn-out wail.

Genia pulled a chair from the kitchen table and let herself sag down into it. Everything felt heavy these days, including her mind and her spirit. She knew just what Janie meant.

What *were* they going to do? Now that her immediate cooking duties were complete, she felt a bit like wailing, too.

"Nobody cares," Janie proclaimed.

"That's not true," was her aunt's automatic response.

The girl wiped the back of her right hand across her cheek. She'd been sniffling back tears all morning, and now she allowed a few of them to flow. "Oh, you care, sure, and I guess Mom and Dad care, but what difference does that make? Jason is miserable and scared out of his wits, although he won't admit it to anybody but me." Her voice caught on a sob as she suddenly gave exaggerated attention to filling a plastic freezer bag with plump blueberries.

"The police will find the real killer, Janie."

"Yeah, right," was the bitter reply. "Like, they really want to find anybody but Jason."

Genia felt guilty relief when the doorbell rang, forestalling the need for her to come up with some reassuring answer to her niece's concerns. Genia didn't have any such answer at the tip of her tongue, but she didn't want Janie to know that.

Wearily, she walked to the front door and opened it, prepared to shed her exhaustion and welcome her luncheon guest.

But it wasn't Jason and Sylvia Stewart on her front porch.

Nikki Parker Dixon stood there, looking furious. Without preamble, she looked up at Genia and said, "If my father weren't already dead, I would absolutely kill him!"

"For heaven's sake, Nikki, what's wrong? Come in!"

"I'll tell you what's wrong." Nikki stomped into the foyer and whirled around so fast, Genia caught her breath and stepped back. "He's dead, and he's still trying to hurt me!"

"Go on back to the kitchen, dear," Genia said to the angry young woman. "I know your father made mistakes, but he loved you—"

"I don't want to hear anything about that anymore! Do you know what he had the nerve to do?" The words preceded them down the hall, spilling into the kitchen, where Janie looked up with a startled expression. "A private investigator called today, asking for a monthly payment on his bill to my father. And do you want to know why? Because my father hired him to investigate my husband, that's why! He was spying on Randy!"

"Oh, dear," Genia murmured, coming in behind her.

"I can't believe it, Genia! Oh, hi, Janie. I'm sorry you have to hear this, but just be glad you have a decent father, not somebody who wants to break up your marriage someday! My father hired a stranger to follow my husband around to try to catch him in something so I'd have to divorce him. How could he have done such a thing to us?"

"Is that what the man told you?" Genia asked, feeling confused and appalled. Nikki was so upset, talking so loud and fast that Genia felt as if certain crucial facts were falling through gaps in her tirade against her father. If what Nikki said was true, Genia wanted to think that Stanley must have had very good reason; if he didn't, he had stepped over a serious boundary that he probably should not have crossed. Still, she wasn't ready to give up on him yet, not without hearing more of the facts.

"He said just what I told you. That Dad hired him. I said hello, and he said, 'May I speak to Mr. Parker?' And I said, 'Mr. Parker is deceased.' And there was this long pause, and he said, 'Oh, I'm sorry, this is bad timing, but I'm calling about some money he owed me.' And I said, 'What for?' And he said he was a private investigator and Mr. Parker had hired him to investigate somebody and his bill was overdue. And I just exploded. I knew who he meant! I told him my dad was dead, and I'd pay the rest of his bill, and he was to stay out of our business from now on. And I slammed down the phone. I probably shouldn't have been nasty to him. It wasn't his fault, he was just doing what Dad hired him to do, but I don't think I have ever felt so offended in my whole life." A little steam seemed to go out of Nikki, and she dropped into the kitchen chair that Genia had recently vacated. "I went through Dad's papers on his desk, and I found the guy's card, look...."

She held it out for them to see, then dropped it onto the table.

"Norman Heist. Great name for a P.I., isn't it?"

"And you're sure he was hired to investigate Randy?"

"Well, who else, Genia?"

"Did Mr. Heist say that's who he was supposed to follow?"

"Well, it wasn't like I needed to ask," the young woman said bitterly. She pushed her glasses up on her nose. "All he had to do was say he was a private eye and my dad hired him, and I knew right then what he was hired for. I didn't let him say much else. I didn't want to listen to it! You know how my dad would have loved to get anything incriminating on Randy. Oh, I can't believe he really went this far!"

"I can't, either," Genia said slowly.

Nikki seemed suddenly to come awake to the fact that she had invaded a busy kitchen. "I've interrupted, haven't I? I'm so sorry!" She got up abruptly and pushed in the chair. "I'll get out of here so you can get back to your cooking. I just had to explode to somebody, and Randy's not around, so I came over here." Looking around her curiously, she asked, "Are you still working on Dad's cookbook?"

"Well, yes," Genia told her, "but we're also preparing lunch for a guest. Nikki, maybe you can help us solve a mystery. This is a woman your father had invited to the arts council meeting last night. I don't know if you noticed her in the crowd? Bright red hair, tall, slim, a woman in her forties, quite attractive?"

But Stanley's daughter shook her head no.

"Maybe you've heard of her?" Genia asked hopefully. "Sylvia Stewart?"

"No, I'm sorry, the name's not familiar. Why?"

"Because it was your dad who invited her to come to Devon to the arts council meeting last night, and he was going to have her out to the Castle for lunch this afternoon. You're sure he never mentioned her name to you? You've really never heard of her before now?"

"No, but what's the mystery about her?"

"She doesn't know why your dad wanted to see her, Nikki."

"Weird! Then why did she come, if she didn't know why?"

Genia smiled at Stanley's daughter. "Your father could be very persuasive when he wanted something, and evidently he very much wanted to meet her."

"And she really doesn't know why?"

"That's what she says."

Nikki made a cynical face. "Maybe he thought she had some dirt on Randy. Maybe I ought to stay and meet her, would that be all right? You don't have to feed me, but now I'm curious. When's she supposed to get here?"

Genia glanced up at the kitchen clock and frowned.

"Ten minutes ago." She hadn't realized how long Nikki's visit had taken; by now, Jason should have arrived with their guest. If they didn't get here soon, the entrée would lose much of its delicious crisp freshness.

She excused herself to go to the telephone to call the Devon Bed and Breakfast. When the owner of the B and B answered, Genia asked her, "Has my nephew been there to pick up Mrs. Stewart?"

Upon hearing the answer, Genia frowned again and then said, "I see. Would you put me through to her room, please?" But then in a few moments, she spoke to the owner, who had come back on the line again. "No one answered in her room. She hasn't checked out, has she? No? Well, I think I'd better come into town and pick her up myself. If you see her, would you let her know? Thank you so much." She hung up the phone gently, and turned to look up at Janie and Nikki. "She says that Jason has been there and left . . ."

Janie walked over to glance out the window, as if expecting him to drive up that minute.

". . . without Mrs. Stewart," Genia finished.

Her niece turned and stared at her. "Why would he do that?"

"I don't know," her great-aunt replied, frowning. "I wish your brother had a cell phone, so we could call him and ask him. And Mrs. Stewart didn't answer the phone in her room, so I couldn't ask her, either. She must have stepped out for a moment and they missed connections, somehow, although I would have thought that Jason would call me from the front desk to tell me if he had a problem."

"He would have, Aunt Genia."

It struck Genia most unpleasantly that once again a guest was late in arriving for a meal. The last time that had happened . . .

Genia refused to think about that last time.

Briskly, she told the other women, "Nikki, I gave Jason my car to drive, and I don't want to leave Janie out here alone without a car. May I ask a huge favor?"

"Want me to drive you to the B and B?"

"Yes, would you, please?"

"Of course. Let's go."

"Thank you so much, Nikki. Janie, would you take the tuna out of the oven, cover it carefully with foil, and set it aside until we get back? Thank you, dear."

Genia and Nikki left a worried-looking Janie to finish the preparations for the guest who had not arrived.

Having poured some of the melted water out of the water glasses and put in fresh ice, having checked to make sure the phyllo-wrapped tuna was snugly wrapped in foil, there was nothing for Janie to do but sit in the kitchen and wait until they got back. She was just at the point of feeling bored enough to clean the refrigerator when the telephone rang in the kitchen.

Janie hurried to answer it.

"Jason?" she asked breathlessly.

There was a silence, and then a man's voice said, "No. Is this the home of Eugenia Potter? I meant to call..."

"Oh! Yes, she's my aunt, but she's not here now."

"Are you Janie?"

"Yeah, who's this?"

"This is Jed White calling from Boston. Hello, Janie, I've heard a lot of nice things about you. I'm a friend of your great-aunt's. Would you tell her I called?"

"Sure. Hold on while I get some paper...."

Janie spotted a pen and an upside down legal pad near the coffeepot and reached for it. Turning it over, she grabbed the pen and scribbled at the top of the first page the number the caller gave her. After she hung up, her attention was drawn to a name written on the first line: *RANDY DIXON*.

Before she could read any further, the kitchen phone rang again, and again she eagerly grabbed it.

"Jason?" she demanded again.

"Janie—"

"Aunt Genia! Where are you? What's going on?"

"I'm at the bed and breakfast, dear." Her aunt's voice sounded funny, kind of hushed and upset and urgent. "Janie, I don't want to frighten you, but I have to tell you something very bad. Mrs. Stewart has been found in her room, badly beaten. It looks as if someone tried to kill her, and probably thought they had succeeded. She's still alive, but just barely. I don't know where your brother is, but"—and here her aunt lowered her voice even more—"we need to find him before the police do."

"Oh, my God," Janie said, shocked to her core. "They'll think he did it, won't they? Oh, Aunt Genia!"

"Janie, listen to me. This is terribly upsetting. And on top of everything else, it scares me to think of you alone out there on the cul-de-sac. Please lock up the house, get in your car, and drive to your mother's house. Will you do that right now, please?"

"Okay, but what about Jason?" Her voice rose to a hysterical pitch.

"We'll find him, Janie. You just leave now, please."

"I'm coming, I'm coming!"

"Good girl. I'll see you at your mother's house."

Her aunt hung up at her end, leaving Janie holding a dial tone. For a moment, she couldn't move, paralyzed by this awful new information. This was something else the police would try to blame on Jason! As she stood there, her glance fell on the yellow page with the name Randy Dixon at the top of it.

Her eyes took in the rest of the words before her mind did.

When Randy heard from his resentful wife about the change in Stanley's will, he knew push had finally come to shove.

Neither of the Dixons was invited to Genia Potter's dinner party—yet another exclusion with Stanley behind it. But that gave Randy exactly the opportunity he needed to act on his motive. If he knew his father-in-law's habits as well as he thought he did, he knew where to find the old man alone and vulnerable.

Janie's heart was pounding in her chest, and she felt suddenly short of breath. Her mouth dropped open, and her eyes widened as she read....

Surprise would help.

There would be no time for Stanley to yell, to raise an alarm, or to fight back, as feeble as his effort would be.

It was as easy as falling off a log....

Only it wasn't Randy Dixon who fell.

Janie tore off the first page where it was written. She backed toward the kitchen table, holding the accusatory page in fingers that had gone damp and shaky. *Oh, my God!* she thought, in a panic. *Nikki said her father hired a private investigator to find out bad things about her husband! And here, Aunt Genia has actually written down that Randy killed Mr. Parker! But if Aunt Genia knew, why didn't she tell Nikki? Why doesn't she tell the police?*

Janie thought she knew why: Because Nikki and the police would not believe her! But Janie believed it. Maybe Nikki was in on it! Maybe Nikki had come out here to distract Aunt Genia, while Randy was at the bed and breakfast trying to kill that poor woman! Nikki said that maybe the mystery lady knew some dirt on Randy! That must have been why Mr. Parker had wanted to meet her, and that meant Randy would have wanted to get rid of Mrs. Stewart, too!

"Oh, my God," Janie screamed, alone in the kitchen.

She was too distraught to question why Nikki Dixon would have needed to distract her aunt Genia while her husband committed a murder, but she did have the thought that Nikki was too nice to have done such a thing. It had to be all Randy's doing! Poor Nikki, married to a madman! And now all Janie could think of was that her brother had gone to pick up a woman that somebody wanted to kill. And now that woman was almost dead! What if something had happened to Jason, too? What if that's why Jason hadn't called? What if he had walked in on the attack, and Randy had taken him hostage?

Jason needs help!

She felt as desperately scared as she was determined. For all the times she had wished she could grow up fast and leave home, at that moment she felt as terrified as a little kid. "I can't do this by myself!" The police—hah!—they would never believe her. Her mom would just get hysterical. Her dad was way out on the island, and there was no way he could get here in time. Janie wanted adult help, and she wanted it right now! Aunt Genia was a nice lady, but she was too old and she wasn't strong enough to rescue Jason from Randy Dixon. Janie wanted an adult who was younger and stronger than Aunt Genia, somebody who would believe her when she explained that Jason wasn't a killer, he was a victim!

And suddenly she knew exactly the person who might help her.

It was somebody who had always been nice to her,

somebody who would believe her, too. She remembered writing an address on a dinner party invitation for Aunt Genia, but she flew to the phone book to make sure of it.

"Twenty-two Drury Lane," she wrote in a margin of the same page of yellow paper that held the accusation against Randy and the phone number of Aunt Genia's friend from Boston.

Janie ran from the house with the crumpled yellow paper, without a thought except to find her brother. Nobody but she had all the pieces of the puzzle, she thought. Nobody but she knew that her brother was in danger from a terrible man who had already killed two people and tried to kill a third. With fumbling fingers she opened the door of the car she shared with her beloved twin and threw the yellow paper down on the front seat so she could refer to the address again if she needed to.

She got behind the wheel and roared the car into life.

"Please, please, don't let us be too late."

When she was nearly there, right on Main Street, a chugging sound interrupted her desperate thoughts, and then the car began to slow. She glanced at the needle on the gas gauge. "Oh, no! Jason, how could you let it get this empty!" She maneuvered it over to the curb, grabbed her backpack from the front seat, and shoved the car keys into it. Her heart hammered in her chest as she jumped out and started running. It wasn't far now, she could run all the way to where she had to go to get help.

"Please be home," she prayed to the person she was hurrying to find.

"Oh, please be there, and please help me!"

25

MISSING INGREDIENT

Genia asked Nikki Dixon to drop her off downtown at the gallery where Donna and the twins lived. Both she and Nikki were so upset by what they had witnessed and learned at the Devon Bed and Breakfast that both women were concerned about leaving the other one alone.

"Genia, are you sure you're all right?"

Nikki leaned across the front seat to look up into the face of her passenger, who stood on the curb in front of the Eden Gallery.

"I'll be fine. But wouldn't you like to come in and be with us, Nikki? We'll make a pot of coffee and keep each other company."

"Thank you, but I just want to go home and see Randy."

"Oh, of course." Genia started to close the car door, but then she opened it and peered in again. "Nikki?"

"Yes?"

"Remember the week before your father died, when he had you over for lunch?"

The young woman looked surprised, but then her eyes misted over. "How did you know about that?"

Genia ignored Nikki's question and continued with her own.

"If you don't mind my asking, why did he do that?"

"What do you mean?"

"Why did he have you to lunch that particular week? Did he have something he wanted to tell you?"

"Oh, yes." Nikki's lips trembled. "He wanted to tell me he had lung cancer that had metastasized to his bones, Genia. I wasn't supposed to tell a soul, but I don't suppose it matters now. And he said he loved me. He said he wanted to make sure I knew. And he didn't quite apologize for being a jerk about Randy, but he came as close as my father could come, I guess." A hurt look came into her eyes, behind her glasses. "That's one reason I was so upset this morning when I found out about the private eye, Genia. Here I thought my father had made some peace in his heart with my husband, and now I learn he was still trying to sabotage us."

"Do you still have that card with you?"

"Card? Oh, the private investigator's? I think so." She squeezed a hand into the right front pocket of her jeans, twisting awkwardly to get into it from her position behind the wheel of her car. But finally she pulled out a white card and held it up to Genia's view. "Here."

"May I borrow it?"

"Sure," Nikki said, and held it out for Genia to take. "Why?"

"I want to ask him a question myself."

"Genia!"

"Oh, not about Randy, about something else."

"What?" Nikki asked, looking curious.

"I'll tell you later. I guess you know that your dad also had Randy to lunch the week before he died?"

"Sure, I know." Stanley's daughter shook her head, looking baffled and frustrated. "And that's another thing. Randy didn't want to go, and why should he? My dad had been so nasty to him for so long. But my dad actually asked politely, so I made Randy go. And when he came back, you know what he said? He said that Dad behaved pretty well. They didn't exactly hit it off like best friends, but it was . . . okay. And he said that all my dad wanted was to tell Randy to take good care of me." Again, Nikki's eyes filled with tears. "And all the time that private investigator was trying to dig up dirt on him."

Genia wanted to say that might not be the case. But until she was sure of it, she didn't want to claim something that Nikki would not be inclined to believe. Instead, she said good-bye, and hurried into the gallery. The questions for Nikki were important to have answered, but right now she regretted any time taken away from her own family.

"Donna!" Genia called, upon entering the empty gallery.

"I'm here, Aunt Genia," came her niece's voice from below the sales desk. Then she popped up from behind it, looking surprised to see her aunt. "What happened to lunch? Aren't you and Janie supposed to be eating with that woman Jason picked up?"

"Is Jason here, Donna?"

"Yes, he came running in about an hour—oh, no, didn't he pick her up like he was supposed to? I'll kill that kid." She whirled around as if to shout up the stairs, but Genia stopped her.

"Donna, wait!"

She hurried across the gallery to look out of one of the windows in the rear. There was her own rented car, parked in the alley beside Donna's old van. Genia walked back toward her niece and grabbed hold of her hands. "Donna, something else very bad has happened. The woman I sent

Jason to pick up has been found badly beaten, almost dead...."

Donna's hands pulled out of Genia's grasp and she clasped them over her mouth as if to keep herself from screaming. She sagged against the counter, and her aunt grabbed hold of her to keep her from falling.

"Let's go upstairs and talk to our boy," Genia said to her.

She assisted Donna upstairs, stroking her hand and telling her what she needed to hear, which was that everything would be all right. Genia had no idea if that was true, but Donna looked as if her knees were about to give out, and she required all the bolstering Genia could give her. At the top of the stairs, they found Jason standing there, pale as a sheet, looking straight at them.

"I didn't do it," he said through tightened lips.

He had been listening from up here, Genia guessed.

"What did you see?" she asked him.

"I didn't see anything! I went to the desk, and I asked for her, and they called her room, and nobody answered. So I waited in the lobby and they called again in a couple of minutes, and they kept ringing her room, and finally I figured she must have gotten a ride out to your house on her own. So I came home."

"Why didn't you call me?" Genia asked him.

Jason shrugged, looking like someone who didn't expect to be believed no matter what he said. "I didn't think I had to. I mean, if she got her own ride, then obviously you'd know it, and I had a bunch of other stuff to do this morning, so I didn't even think about it much, I just came on home."

To Genia, it sounded like normal teenage behavior.

"They're going to accuse me, aren't they?"

His mother began to cry and buried her face in her hands.

"I didn't do anything!" Jason shouted. "I didn't do any of

this stuff they say I did! It's not fair!" Before they could stop him, he brushed past them and started down the stairs.

"Jason!" his mom and great-aunt called after him.

But he kept running, and then they heard the sound of the back door slam. Genia hurried to a window and looked down. She thought he might get into her car and drive it away, but he didn't. He got into his mother's van, instead, and soon was backing out of the drive, straightening the vehicle in the alley, and taking off.

"Where will he go?" she asked his mom.

Donna, who could barely talk for crying, said, "I don't know. He could go anywhere. Oh, Aunt Genia, this will make him look guilty, won't it? They'll think he hurt that poor woman, and now they'll think he's running away. Or what if he drives recklessly, what if he gets in an accident?" She moaned and sank down onto the floor of the hallway above the stairs. "I can't take any more of this."

Genia wanted to embrace and comfort her.

There wasn't time to stop for that, however.

She had to settle for bending over and kissing the top of her niece's head, and patting her shoulders. Then she hurried to a telephone, pulling out of her purse the business card that Nikki Dixon had given her. Quickly, she punched in one of the office numbers printed there.

"Heist Investigations," a woman's voice answered.

"May I speak to Mr. Heist, please?"

"Who's calling?"

"My name is Eugenia Potter. I'm calling in regard to work he did for Mr. Stanley Parker, who is now deceased. It's urgent that I speak to Mr. Heist." When he came on the line, she blurted out her name, and then pleaded, "Mr. Heist, I need to know who Stanley Parker hired you to investigate."

"You willing to pay for this information? That daughter

of his hung up on me. I don't know if she'll pay his bills now."

"I'm sure she will, but if she doesn't, yes, I'll pay you."

"All right, then, not that I know if you're worth it, but what the hell, somebody needs to know this, if Mr. Parker's not alive to do anything about it now. He hired me to investigate a husband. . . . "

Genia's heart sank as she took copious notes.

One of the notes she took was a name: "Stewart." She underlined it several times. When she hung up, the only question in her mind was *Do I take this to the police, or to Jason's lawyers?*

"Donna, I'm going to the police station," she announced.

They might be convinced that Jason was their murderer, but the officers she had met had seemed like reasonable people to her. With this testimony from the private investigator in her possession, surely they would have to listen to her.

She left Donna, but only after advising her to get hold of their attorneys and to expect a visit from the Devon police at any moment. Genia couldn't stop any of them who might be on their way to get Jason, but she could insist on talking to the police chief in the meantime. Maybe if she hurried and went right to the top with her information, she could forestall an actual arrest. Genia rushed to the alley where her car was parked.

Her emergency run to the police chief didn't go as planned.

On her way to the Devon Police Station, she spotted the twins' old vehicle parked at an odd angle along the main street. Genia pulled her own car up behind it and hurried out to see what was wrong. Where was Janie? Had the child had a flat tire? Or, worse yet, an accident? Genia pulled on a door handle, discovered it wasn't locked, and opened it. What she saw inside made her blink in confusion, which rapidly turned to dismay.

On the front seat lay a crumpled piece of yellow paper from a legal pad. Recognizing her own handwriting, Genia picked it up, smoothed it out, and saw the little scenario she had written when she was trying to think how Randy Dixon might have committed Stanley's murder.

"Oh, no," Genia murmured. "What have I done?"

She had left the pad on the counter in the kitchen. Upside down. But here was the first page of it.... Then she noticed scribbles in Janie's handwriting: "Jed White called for Aunt Genia." She pictured the phone ringing, Janie looking for something on which to write a message, turning the pad over, taking down Jed's name, then noticing what else was written there....

What would Janie have thought?

"She'd have thought I was accusing Randy of murder," Genia said grimly to herself as she stood by the twins' car. "And she would have remembered that Nikki had just accused Stanley of having Randy investigated. And she would have heard Nikki suggest that maybe Stanley arranged to meet Sylvia Stewart because he thought she had incriminating information about Randy."

And then Janie had taken Genia's call from the bed and breakfast, telling her about the attempt on Mrs. Stewart's life, warning her to leave immediately and go home. But Janie hadn't made it home, not in all the time that Genia had stayed there. And Genia hadn't even thought about it. She had been so worried about Jason and so shaken by the events at the hostelry that morning that she hadn't even realized the other twin had not arrived as she should have by then.

Janie, where are you . . . why is your car left here?

And then Genia saw something else scribbled in a margin, an address in Devon, one not far from here.

"No," she said, feeling panicked. "Oh, dear God, no."

Genia rushed back to her own car, got into it, and raced off to look for her niece in the one place she would have tried to keep her from going. Of all the places Janie could have gone, why this one? If Janie had actually gone to the address on the yellow sheet . . .

Genia drove faster, hoping to attract police attention.

"Stop me," she begged the cops. "I don't have time to drive to you, but if you would only see me run this red light, we could go together."

No such luck. She broke every traffic law with impunity, as if she had suddenly been elected the mayor of Devon.

26

LAST MEAL

She pulled her car quietly under the overhanging branches of a pin oak tree where it was shady and where her car could not easily be seen from the windows of the residence in question. A line from a beloved Robert Frost poem came into her mind... "whose house this is, I think I know...." If she were recognized, no one would guess what she was doing here. She could make up all sorts of believable excuses if she had to. *"I want to invite you to a dinner party." "I'm thinking of moving here full time, and I'd like to ask your advice." "I was in the neighborhood and thought of you. I'm so glad that I caught you at home. I hope you don't mind that I have just dropped by like this."* If she were thought rude, fine; better that than to be thought suspicious. There was no earthly reason for anyone to surmise that she knew anything important about any of the murders or the attack on poor Mrs. Stewart.

Genia told herself that her own appearance of innocuous ignorance would cloak her in safety.

No one knows that I suspect anything, she thought.

But her heart was pounding fearfully, her palms were sweaty, and her face felt frozen with tension. There was such urgency! And yet she could not afford to seem hasty.

She decided to take her purse with her—to further the appearance of normalcy—but to leave her car unlocked in case she needed to get back into it in a hurry. Genia stepped out of the vehicle, her gaze on the pavement, her mind on her next course of action. With one foot on the street and one still inside the car, she heard her name called forcefully: "Genia Potter!"

Genia jerked her head up just as a man's hand pulled the car door away from her grasp and opened it wide for her.

"Harrison!" she gasped.

"I'm sorry, did I scare you?" The weather forecaster smiled sweetly at her and reached out his other hand to assist her out of her car. "What are you doing in our neighborhood today?"

"Just visiting," she said brightly, breathlessly. And then before he could ask her anything else, she added, "What about you? Why aren't you at the television station, Harrison?"

"I like to come home for lunch and then walk back."

"Oh. So Lindsay's home?"

He nodded as she closed her car door, and then they walked up onto the sidewalk together. Suddenly Genia knew she could not waste a second more in pretense; she had to do what she had to do.

"Harrison," she said, grabbing one of his arms, "I need your help."

When she told him what she wanted from him and why, he looked flabbergasted. Disbelief clouded his pleasant expression. "Genia, I just can't believe that's true," he protested.

"I don't have time to convince you, Harrison. But would you please just get the police for me? You don't have to believe me. They don't have to believe me. But they have to come here. Please. And then we'll sort it all out."

Instead of rushing to do as she pleaded, he shook his head.

"Genia, this is a terrible thing to do to a nice person."

"Not nice," she said, and shuddered. "You won't help me?"

He looked reluctant, and she realized who could blame him for that? Why should he believe what sounded like a wild accusation about a respectable citizen of Devon? He must be thinking that if she were wrong, he could get sued, the police could be charged with wrongful arrest, the publicity might ruin his career. Nor could she fault his reasoning. *I must sound like a crazy woman*, she thought. "All right, I understand, but do this much for me, Harrison. I'm going in there, if I can, to look for my niece. If I don't come out in ten minutes, then will you go for the police?"

"Yes," he said, with no hesitation. "I can do that."

She left him standing there beside her car, staring at her as she walked hurriedly on down the sidewalk to her destination.

She decided not to try a frontal assault. She couldn't just walk up to the front door and demand to see her niece. If Janie were in there, the owner of this house might not want anyone to know.

Trying to remain hidden by trees, shade, and shrubbery, Genia made her way around to the rear of the big house. Behind it a large brick patio led down to a private dock on the water. Large windows faced that view, and through them she could see the kitchen with its modern appliances built to fit into an old, old home. She edged up to the windows and, seeing no one there, peered in.

A backpack just like Janie's lay on the floor by the center island.

But what made Genia's heart stop was another object lying on a table right beside the window through which she was looking. It was a portable phone, made of expensive teakwood, with the name of a boat embossed boldly along its back: *Waterlily*.

That phone should have gone down under the ocean along with the drowned body of Lillian Parker Graham. What was it doing here, in the kitchen of her widower?

"Why, Genia."

She whirled to see him standing right behind her.

"No, turn back around please. That's good. You've seen that I have a gun, haven't you? Yes, that's what you feel pressed up against your spine. We'll go inside the house now and collect your niece. Don't move! Not unless I tell you to. All right, begin walking toward the door. When we get there, you open it and go inside. That's right. Excellent. You're doing very well, Genia. Now keep walking on through the kitchen. We're going upstairs now. Yes, one step at a time. Don't trip over that blue hair clip. I'll pick it up and put it safely in my pocket. You recognize it? It certainly doesn't look like something Lillian would wear, does it? It looks like something a much younger woman might use, a teenager, perhaps. No, don't talk. I said don't talk! It's really a shame you have done this, Genia."

"Where is—"

"I said don't speak. Oh, I'm sorry, did that hurt? I take it you want to know why I said it's a shame? I'll tell you, but first go toward that open door, the second bedroom on our left. Your niece is in there, Genia. You'll get to see her, just as you wanted to. The reason I said it's a shame that you have behaved like this is that now you will never get to be my next wife. You could have been the fifth Mrs. David Graham—"

"The fifth!"

"Stop here. We'll wait a moment before we go in there. I want to let you think about this for a bit. Will you find your niece alive? Or might she be dead? Have I harmed her? In what sort of condition will you find her when we go in there, Genia? You don't know, do you? You have no way of predicting what you will find in that room. You think you know things about me, but you don't actually know the full extent of what I am capable of doing, do you? Is it dawning on you that you will soon find out?

"I'm very close to you now, aren't I? Can you feel my breath on your face, Genia? Does the metal of the gun hurt as it presses into your spine like . . . this?

"I would not have hurt you if I had chosen you as my next bride, Genia. You would have been so delightfully happy with me as your husband. I know how to please women in so many ways. Lillian was ecstatic with me, you know. She loved every moment of our marriage. And I must say that I enjoyed it, too. But then, I always do. Why would I want to spend several years courting and then living with any woman whose company I did not enjoy? For her merely to be rich is not enough. She must also be beautiful, charming, delightful to be with, and oh, so lonely. My aim is to enjoy life to the fullest, and I know that in a marriage the very best way to do that is to make sure my wives enjoy it with me. And then they try so very, very hard to make my life happy. They are so grateful to me. So sweetly appreciative. I'm always touched by that. Really, I am. Sylvia Stewart's sister, Amelia—poor Amelia—was almost fawning in her appreciation for the pleasure I brought back into her life. Oh! You didn't know that the late Sylvia Stewart was my former sister-in-law? One of my former sisters-in-law. I have so many! I don't know how Stanley found that out, but it was certainly her unlucky day when he did, wasn't it? Because that brought her to Devon, where I could see her face in the crowd, where I could know that if the police put Lillian's death together with Amelia's...

"Unfortunately, Sylvia never liked me, never really trusted me. When Amelia died—another drowning, it's so easy to arrange—she was so distrustful, I was forced to leave the beautiful home I had inherited. I had to leave it all behind me, and change my name, and seek another wife much more quickly than usual. I was so lucky to find Lillian so soon. And wasn't she a lucky woman to find me, Genia?

"But you, poor Genia, will never know how full a life can be that is lived in my presence. You will only know the fullness of death. Go into the room!

"Ah, Jane, my dear. Look who has come to visit you! Shut up, Genia. Don't move a hair toward her. Jane, dear, I know it is difficult for you to move with your hands tied up like that, but do get out of that chair now and come over here. We are all three going to leave the house and go out into my little motorboat. And then we'll have a pleasant little journey out to the island where your father lives, Jane. Yes, isn't that nice? I knew you'd be pleased. There is a well there, you see. Did you know that, either of you? A deep old empty one. Well, not entirely empty, not with Lillian's body at the bottom of it. She's been so lonely there. I think the dear woman needs company, don't you?

"Move, Jane. If you try anything, I'll kill your aunt Genia.

"Yes, keep going... back down the hall... down the steps... you're both doing so well. Jane, my sweet, I'll take the tape off your mouth when we get to the kitchen. And then we'll wrap a shawl around your shoulders so that your bound hands will not be visible. But do remember that if you scream or do anything you shouldn't, I will shoot your dear aunt through her spinal column, see where I have placed my gun? Do you see it? Good. Now you understand the gravity of your responsibility, don't you?

"Genia, you would be so proud of your niece. The dear child came to me for help! Isn't that marvelous. She had herself convinced that my stepson-in-law committed the...er, killings...and that I was such a nice man, so fond of my stepdaughter, that I would want to do everything I could to save everybody from such a terrible killer. Isn't that clever? And so thoughtful of her to want to save Nikki as well as her own brother. She thought that Jason was in danger from Randy, you see. Amusing, isn't it? I don't have any idea where Jason is, truly I don't. I couldn't care less, although I admit I will be vastly entertained to watch his response—and his mother's and father's—when you and Jane go missing. Oh, don't cry, Jane. I insist. I want you smiling gaily as we all troop happily down to the docks. That's a girl, stop your crying now.

"Are we all set? Shawl comfy on your shoulders, Jane? No chance of screaming, is there? You go first, and then I'll follow close...so close...behind Genia. All right, here we go. Just the three of us, off for a pleasant afternoon of boating.

"Keep walking, Jane, a little faster if you please....

"We're nearly there, very good, ladies....

"Do enjoy the sunshine this one last time.

"Wait! I heard something.... No!"

Just as a gun was pressed against Genia, so did David Graham suddenly feel a hard metal object pressed against his own spine. Jammed into it, in fact, and accompanied by the no-nonsense growl, "Drop it, Graham."

He did drop it, and then turned with a supercilious smile.

"Watching too much TV, Larry?"

"Just enough, David."

Their unlikely savior was the mayor of Devon himself, Lawrence Averill, followed close on his heels by the police, whom Harrison Wright had notified, just as he had promised Genia he would. Harrison had found them surprisingly easy to convince, since they had just heard from Sylvia Stewart's own injured lips a description of the man who had attacked her so brutally. "He said 'room service,'" she whispered, "and I let him in without looking first. I let my sister's killer in."

The big storm that Harrison Wright had predicted for the end of the week had unexpectedly dissipated far offshore. It seemed incongruous to Genia now to watch a man being led away in handcuffs on such a sunny, cheerful day.

"Larry?" Genia asked him. "Do you always just happen to be walking along the beach behind David's house, right when somebody might need you to save her life?"

The mayor smiled. "I walk here every day, Genia."

"But do you always carry a pistol to poke in somebody's back?"

His smile turned a bit embarrassed. "It wasn't a gun, Genia."

"It wasn't? What was it?"

Larry held out his hand for her to see the hard metal "weapon" he had stuck in David Graham's back to force him to drop his own gun. "Trade secret," he said, and smiled at them.

It was a brass key to the city of Devon.

Then he swept both women into his arms in a bear hug of an embrace.

"I would vote for you for President," Janie wept on his chest.

"Oh, you don't have to do that," the mayor said modestly, "but now that you're eighteen, if you and your brother would vote for me for the State Legislature, I'd sure appreciate it, Janie."

27

CLAMBAKE

For all the rest of the year, Parker Island must seem a place that time forgot, Genia thought as she walked up from the island's dock to the site of the Lillian Parker Art Festival. In two hours she would be seated at a bookstore booth signing copies of the newly published cookbook, but for now she was free to wander on the island. Seen from the air, it was only a small green patch in the blue-black waters of Narragansett Bay, a scant three miles off the coast of Rhode Island. Once she set foot on it, she found it was a woodsy refuge rich in geese and other waterfowl, and without the noise and fumes of civilization. Even today, the opening day of the festival, motorized vehicles were banned. There were bicycles for rent, and horse-drawn carriages. Genia paid ten dollars for a seat in a carriage, in order to tour the island, a trip that took her around and then across it. The entire island, shaped like a pear, was less than twelve acres, but the thick woods surrounding the salt pond in the middle made it seem bigger, more private, more mysterious. She thought she understood very well why Kevin Eden loved to live here and create his art, and why he had so obstinately refused to budge until his ex-wife generously offered him his old studio.

The carriage took her through thick tangles of bayberry bushes and stands of pine, through small private meadows, and right up to the quiet pond in the middle of a grassy field. She heard songbirds, saw chokeberry and blackberry bushes. She heard the women in the seat beside her bragging about having already spotted a white ibis, a semipalmated sandpiper, and a black-backed gull. The shore around the island was scalloped like a clamshell, torn and ragged from centuries of storms, and there were tiny coves scooped out of the shoreline as if by some hungry sea monster's mouth.

It was a peaceful, lovely place, but she was glad she wasn't buried there! On a far side of the island, where a small cliff bordered the sea and a curve of sandy beach invited boats to land, there was a stone wall sheltered by a curve of spruce trees, and up from the wall there was a very old stone well where Nikki Parker Dixon said she used to drop pennies, listening, listening, listening for the tiny splash when they touched the bit of water left long after the well was closed.

It was generous of Nikki to have donated this island to the city.

And generous of her to have made that offer contingent on the city allowing Kevin to continue living and working there, except for when he voluntarily vacated the premises during the month in which the festival weekend was held. Genia had heard why Nikki had been willing to relinquish the valuable property: "I couldn't bear to own it anymore, not knowing that my mother had been murdered there, and that her body had lain there for all that time."

Genia shivered at the thought of her own body lying at the bottom of the old well and nobody ever knowing. Of

Janie . . . of Lillian . . . She thought, too, of the other three women whom David Graham had wedded, bedded, and slain. It was he whom Stanley Parker's private investigator was researching, not Randy. It was he whom Stanley had always suspected of foul play in the death of Lillian. And it was David whom Stanley had accused of murder on the day of their luncheon at the Castle.

In the old cookbook, Genia had found what David had been looking for when he slipped into her house the same night he killed Eddie Hennessey: a small white envelope containing two clippings. One was a photograph of a bride named Amelia and her debonair groom, whose name was something other than David Graham at the time. The other clipping was of her obituary one year later.

David, Genia learned, had gotten into her rented house by taking the master key from Celeste, and having a copy of it made. But he hadn't found the cookbook, so he hadn't been able to steal the clippings.

"What did you think you were going to do, Stanley?" Genia silently inquired of her late friend, as the carriage came back around toward the bustle of the festival. *"Did you think you could accuse David over dinner at my house?"*

She had a feeling that's exactly what he had intended to do: Spill the whole story, at least as much as he knew of it by then, and turn it all over to the good citizens of Devon to take into their own hands. He was dying, and he couldn't bear to think of Lillian's murderer going uncaught and unpunished. Nor would he have wanted to leave David—his real name, it turned out, was Donald Ray—at liberty to seduce and harm other women who, like Lillian, had too much money and not enough love. But time was running out for Stanley—if he'd only known how quickly!—and in his haste he made errors of judgment, mistakes born out of physical pain and mental anguish.

Why didn't you confide all this in me? she wondered now.

But she thought she knew the answer: As fond as he was of her, to Stanley, Genia was only a newcomer to Devon. He would be loyal to his Devon friends and not discuss their secrets with her. And in the end, he would take the question of crime and punishment to the people who—whatever their other problems—were well known as leaders in the town he loved. If they began to suspect and accuse David, then everyone else might, too, even if Stanley didn't live long enough to prove it unequivocally.

As she alighted from the carriage, she spotted Harrison.

He walked toward her, a warm smile in his eyes.

"Genia!" he said quietly, and offered his hand to her. In his other, he held a "coffee cabinet," which was Rhode Island lingo for milk shake. It looked cool and delicious to Genia; instantly, she craved one, too.

"It's good to see you, Harrison."

There was an awkward pause for a moment.

Thanks to the doggedness of the president of the Devon bank, it had been revealed that the president of the Devon Arts Council had transferred some of its funds into her own account. In a private agreement, it had been arranged for her to go to work to pay back the council; in addition, several hundred hours of community service and counseling were required of Lindsay Wright.

Genia came right out and asked: "How is she?"

"She's having a hard time admitting she did anything wrong," he said frankly, and Genia saw sadness in his eyes. "She thinks she was only doing it to benefit me, to give me a wife I could be proud of, as if I wasn't proud of her already."

"I know."

He took a deep breath. "I've quit weather forecasting, did you know? It didn't seem right to be on television anymore, because every time I appeared, I felt it gave people another chance to gossip about Lindsay. Brown University has invited me to be a guest lecturer, what do you think of that idea, Genia?"

"I think your students will be fortunate to have a teacher who loves his subject as much as you do. I wish you all the best, Harrison. You and your wife, too."

"And congratulations to you on your cookbook!"

They parted ways, Genia to locate the food fair—or "clamslurper"—and buy a coffee cabinet to drink.

There was a lot of talk about universities these days, Genia reflected as she slurped, later. Janie and Jason had gone off to schools of their choice, he to study horticulture, she to the College of Culinary Arts at Johnson and Wales University in Providence. Jason had been cleared of the second drug charge, mostly because the citizens on the juvenile board chose to believe his story about the marijuana cookies. Sometimes, it paid to live in a small town where everybody knew everybody else, Genia thought. She had been grateful to those citizens for their mercy.

From a short distance away Genia watched Mayor Larry Averill work the crowd. What a nice man! From Donna, Genia had learned that Larry had finally persuaded Celeste to enter a treatment center for drug and alcohol addiction, and she was there now. "Alcoholics steal" was the blunt reply Genia got when she asked an A.A. friend about her brooch. "It's common among us." In her absence, her best friend the mayor had made sure that Celeste had an ad in the festival newspaper, though he no longer handed out her business cards as freely as he used to do, especially now that he was an official candidate for the State Legislature. This time, every-one was convinced Larry would win the seat he had wanted for so long, and Genia hoped so, too.

She strolled toward the booth where her funny little fam-ily had Kevin's work displayed, and thought how proud Lew would be of them all. Although she didn't expect Donna and Kevin ever to remarry, it seemed they got along better now than they ever had. Genia was proud of them for that and pleased for the children. She suspected that Lew would also be happy that Jed White was coming to the festival. Jed had apologized for his attitude toward her nephew.

"I can be a hard man sometimes, Genia. Sometimes there's too much business in me and not enough heart. I guess you know that now. I feel bad about what I said with-out even knowing the boy. It made me think of my own boy, and the terrible mistake I made. . . . " The grief and regret of his life had been that he had encouraged his young physician son, his only child, to serve in Vietnam, from which the boy had not returned alive. "I hope you will forgive me, and give me a chance to redeem myself."

She was glad, even more for his sake than for hers.

"How do you raise teenagers?" Donna had asked her only yesterday, in mock despair. Jason's first-semester grades at the university weren't what they might be, and his mother had a feeling he was playing more than studying. Janie, meanwhile, had a new boyfriend with three rings through his nose. Genia had assured her niece that Donna already possessed the recipe, which was known to mothers all over the world. "The secret ingredient is love."

"Hi, Genia!" Kevin Eden smiled when he caught sight of her.

There was plenty of that secret ingredient to go around in this little family, Genia thought as she greeted them. Janie ran around the edge of the booth to plant a lipsticked kiss on her cheek, and Jason grinned and asked, "T'sup?" Their recipe might not be perfect—few were—but Genia had a feeling it would turn out fine.

She dug in her handbag for her special "autographing pen" that her own children had sent her, and thought happily, *Let's go sell some cookbooks, Stanley.*

THE RECIPES

Lobster Bisque

Serves 8.

¼ cup chopped onion
1 clove garlic, chopped
2 tablespoons olive oil
Butter
2 one-pound lobsters, cooked,
    meat removed and cut into
    chunks, shells reserved
Salt and freshly ground pepper
Bay leaf

⅓ cup chopped carrots
1 tablespoon chopped fresh pars-
    ley
2 tablespoons fresh tarragon
½ cup white wine or sherry
5 cups fish stock (chicken broth
    may be substituted)
2 cups heavy cream

In a soup pot, sauté onion and garlic in olive oil and 2 table-spoons butter. Add the cracked shells, salt and pepper, bay leaf, carrots, parsley, and 1 tablespoon tarragon. Cook over medium heat for 10 minutes, or until the vegetables start to soften. Add sherry or white wine and simmer for 15 to 20 minutes. Add fish stock or broth. Cook 45 minutes to 1 hour over low heat.

Remove the shells and puree the bisque in a blender or food processor. Place the mixture over low heat. Add the cream and 1 stick butter.

Make a roux of butter and flour. Stir into the strained bisque until the desired thickness is attained. In a pan, sauté the lobster meat quickly over high heat. Place in the soup pot and salt and pepper to taste.

Pour into soup bowls, sprinkle the remaining tarragon on top, and serve.

LINDSAY'S BLUE SUEDE SOUP
SERVES 4 TO 6.

Lindsay's mother told her Elvis Presley invented this soup in an effort to get the kids to eat blueberries.

3 cups fresh Rhode Island
   blueberries
1 cup water
3 tablespoons sugar
1 whole clove
1 cinnamon stick
3 cups buttermilk
Juice of 1 lemon
½ teaspoon lemon or orange zest

2 tablespoons crème de cassis
   (optional)
1 cup plain yogurt or sour cream

Garnish
Lemon or orange twist
Sour cream
Handful of fresh mint leaves

Rinse blueberries, removing any green and damaged berries and stems, and drain.

In a large pot, bring the water and sugar to a boil. Stir the sugar until it dissolves and forms a syrup. Add 2 cups blueberries, clove, and cinnamon stick, reduce the heat, and simmer until the berries are tender, about 15 minutes.

Cool to room temperature; remove the cinnamon stick.

In blender or food processor, blend the buttermilk and berry mixture. Add the lemon juice, zest, and crème de cassis (if desired). Add the yogurt or sour cream. Process until smooth.

Stir in the remaining blueberries.

Serve in glass bowls with a twist of lemon or orange, dollop of sour cream, and mint leaves.

TUNA IN PHYLLO

SERVES 4.

⅔ cup basmati rice, cooked and
    cooled
4 fresh tuna fillets, 1 to 1 ½
    inches thick, about 6 ounces
    each
1 cup chopped onions
4 tablespoons unsalted butter
1 tablespoon capers, drained
1 lemon
Salt and freshly ground pepper to
    taste
8 sheets phyllo
½ cup melted butter for basting
    phyllo

Poaching Broth
1 bay leaf
½ cup dry white wine
½ cup water

Wine Sauce
½ cup carrots and ½ cup leeks,
    cut in thin strips
¼ cup butter
1 cup chardonnay
2 egg yolks
1 tablespoon flour
Salt and freshly ground pepper
1 cup half-and-half
1 cup chicken broth
1 tablespoon lemon juice
1 tablespoon chopped fresh
    parsley
2 tablespoons minced fresh basil

Cook basmati rice. Take off the burner and cool.

In a skillet or fish poacher, bring the poaching liquid to a boil. Reduce the heat, place the tuna in the broth, and poach, covered, for 5 minutes. Take off the burner and let cool in the liquid.

In a small skillet, sauté the onions in the butter over low heat until golden. Take off the heat and add the capers, juice of half a lemon, and salt and pepper. Pour the mixture over the cooled cooked rice and mix well.

On a large, dry surface, lay out one sheet of phyllo. Brush

with butter. Lay a second sheet on top and brush with butter. Fold the sheets in half crosswise and brush again. Place ⅛ of the rice mixture on the dough and place a tuna fillet on top of the rice. Season carefully with salt and freshly ground pepper. Place another ⅛ of rice on top of the fillet and fold the ends of the phyllo over the fish to form a package. Brush with butter one more time and place, seam side down, in a buttered baking dish large enough to hold all 4 tuna packages. Repeat the process with each fillet. Brush all packages one last time and bake in a 375-degree oven for 25 minutes, or until brown.

Arrange on a platter and spoon wine sauce over the tuna. Serve extra sauce on the side.

To make the wine sauce, sauté the carrots and leeks in butter. Boil down the chardonnay until reduced by half. In a small bowl, whisk together the egg yolks, flour, salt and pepper, half-and-half, and chicken broth. Add the lemon juice, parsley, basil, and the sautéed carrots and leeks. Add the mixture to the wine and stir together over low heat until thick (about 15 minutes).

Janie's Apples in Jackets
Serves 6.

½ cup dark raisins
¼ cup small pieces of pecans
½ cup brandy (optional)
1½ cups granulated sugar
2 cups water
Butter
1 ¾ teaspoons cinnamon
1 ¾ teaspoons ground cloves
½ cup brown sugar

½ cup orange or apple juice
Unbaked pastry (2-cup flour
  recipe or prepared pastry)
6 medium-large Rhode Island
  greening apples (or any
  other tart apple)
2 egg yolks mixed with
  1 teaspoon water

Soak raisins and nuts in ½ cup brandy (if desired) for an hour or longer.

In a saucepan, bring to a boil 1 cup granulated sugar, 2 cups water, 3 tablespoons butter, and ¼ teaspoon cinnamon. Stir until the sugar dissolves and the mixture is syrupy.

Mix the cloves, remaining cinnamon, brown and granulated sugars into the raisin and nut mixture and add the apple or orange juice. Mix well.

Roll the pastry to an ⅛-inch thickness (approximately) and cut into six 7-inch squares.

Peel and core the apples.

Place 1 apple on each square of pastry. Spoon the filling into the hollow center. Dot with butter.

Bring the corners of the pastry together at the top of the apple, moisten, and press together until sealed.

If desired, with extra pastry, cut out designs and press into top of pastry-covered apples.

Carefully place apples, a couple of inches apart, into a large baking dish. Pour the hot syrup around the apples. Brush the tops of the apples with the egg yolk/water mixture.

Bake in a preheated oven (425 degrees) for 40 minutes, or until the crust is well browned and the apples are cooked through.

Serve warm with whipped cream or ice cream.

About the Authors

NANCY PICKARD, the acclaimed creator of the Jenny Cain series, is a two-time Edgar Award nominee and winner of the Agatha, Macavity, Anthony, and American Mystery awards. A great fan of Virginia Rich's books, Nancy Pickard is the co-author, with Mrs. Rich, of *The 27-Ingredient Chili con Carne Murders* and author of *The Blue Corn Murders*.

The late VIRGINIA RICH is the author of three previous Eugenia Potter mysteries and, with Nancy Pickard, of *The 27-Ingredient Chili con Carne Murders*. Like her heroine, Mrs. Rich lived on a cattle ranch in Arizona and also had a cottage off the coast of Maine.